Beyond Blue Frontiers

CECILIA RANDELL

The Adventures of Blue Faust:

In Which Our Heroine Continues The Adventure

Contents

ISBN – 978-0-9998728-2-6

First printing 2018

Editing by Heather Long and Jennifer Hinson

Front cover image by Katrina Curry, Crimson Pheonix Creations

Internal Formatting by Gina Wynn

Published by Blue Wren Publishing

author@ceciliarandell.com

This book is for a few different people. BL Brunnemer, whose words inspired me to write the story in my head. My editors, Heather and Jax, who keep me on the straight and narrow (or at least from driving off the cliff). The TAM Squad, and quite a few others, who continue to encourage me to get the story down.
Finally, to every single reader. Thank you for enjoying Blue as much as I do.

Worlds of Karran

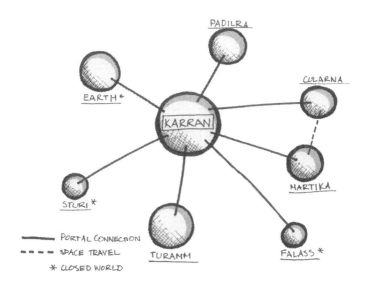

Map of Karran

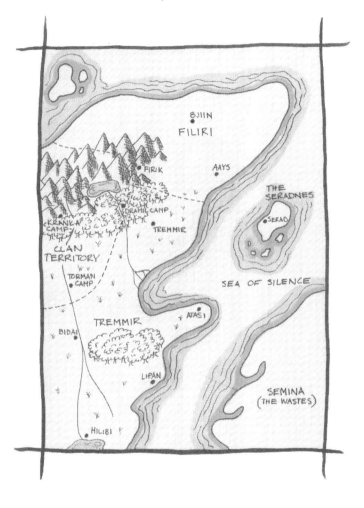

Preface

Many believe that Earth is the only world with life. Others believe that there is life out there, but it is so far away and so alien to us that we will never understand it. Both are wrong.

Somewhere amidst the universes is a world called Karran. This world has a unique trait. It has what the natives call "thin spaces," where time and space between it and other worlds become disrupted, allowing travel. One such world is Earth.

Whether human life began on Karran—traveling to Earth through the portals—or on Earth, traveling to Karran, is not known, though many suspect Karran to be the origin point.

There are other worlds as well. These worlds all contain areas where the energy corresponds to those "thin spaces." They also contain humanoid life, supporting the "Karran first" theory. Some have advanced civilizations— have even developed space travel and open trade with other worlds. They formed an alliance to advance and support the welfare of these worlds. Others are still relatively primitive and thought to be too dangerous to deal with openly. Earth falls among the latter.

While those on Karran have developed methods to control the thin spaces and portals between the worlds, these can still sometimes activate on their own, transporting accidental travelers. One such "thin space" is near Austin, Texas, and one such traveler is Blue Faust. These are her adventures through the universes.

Prologue

PHI

PHILLIP BACKED FARTHER into the doorway shielding him from sight of the workers. Etu, the Prizzoli who'd originally worked with the Zeynar Family, had promised him better pickings here in the northern region of Karran, but so far there wasn't much life to these people; the environment itself seemed to have sucked it all out already.

He watched as they rushed along the walks, heads down and covered by practical scarves and hats, their forms bundled in dull colored coats.

A pulse came from the crystal safely tucked away in his coat pocket. He patted the area with his hand, reassuring the little thing that it would have more soon. He, too, was eager for the rush.

A laugh drew his attention to a store across from where he stood. A girl stood there, smiling, teasing the young man who was helping her load her purchases into the small transport idling there. She was slight, and wisps of blond hair escaped the blue scarf wrapped around her head. It was one of the few spots of color he'd seen here in this horrible city.

Her movements were quick, lively, and they called to him and the crystal both. The boy finished loading the last of her parcels, and then she reached up to pull him down, planting a quick kiss on his cheek. The boy shuffled, ducked his head, and moved back into the shop. The girl leaned over near the front of the transport, and Phillip noticed there was a driver. She said a few words he couldn't make out and then continued along the street while the transport stayed in front of the store. She entered another shop a couple of blocks away.

Phillip abandoned the shelter of the doorway, keeping his head down and trying to blend in with the quick, purposeful pace of the rest of the pedestrians. After he'd gone three blocks, he crossed the street and made his way to the shop the girl had last entered. As he passed, he caught sight of her through the window, paying for some ribbons or some such.

He ducked into an alley she would need to pass on the way back to her transport. A bare minute later her humming, a soft and delicate sound, reached him, and the girl soon followed. The color of her scarf seemed a beacon.

He reached out, one hand grabbing her shoulder and the other quickly wrapping around her mouth and pulled her into the alley. She struggled, but there was nothing to her, and he had no issues hauling her to the darker parts of the alley where the shadows of the buildings on either side made it seem like night.

The struggle was exciting, even though it gave him no problems. It just meant he had finally gotten one that would be satisfying.

He dragged her to the ground and pinned her legs with his own, careful not to release her mouth or allow her to make a sound.

There was one close moment when he had to let her shoulders go to grab the cloth he used as a gag. She was able to wrench her head enough to shake his hand loose, just for a moment. Not long enough to cry out, but the defiance got Phillip's blood rushing even more.

He tied the gag, catching his fingers on her scarf in the process and pulling it loose from her head, revealing more of her blond hair. It wasn't the right shade, and he frowned. He'd hoped... but no. This one was for the crystal — it was better this way.

His other hand now free, he pulled the crystal from his pocket, shaking it loose from the pouch. Its light pulsed, and eagerness infused him. It had grown harder to distinguish his and the crystal's needs, but most of the time it didn't matter, they were the same.

He held the crystal before the girl's face. She gazed up at him, eyes wide and lips trembling, though she stilled now. She eyed the crystal, a frown forming, and confusion clouded her expression. She had expected him to violate her, but that was never what he was after.

He wanted the power.

Lowering the crystal to her cheek, he closed his eyes and savored the rush of life, of power, of vitality, flowing from the girl on the ground before him. She struggled again as the life left her, but it didn't last. It never did.

Finally, it was done. The crystal had taken all that she held, all that she had to give. Phillip opened his eyes and gazed at the figure lying in the dark alley.

For just a moment another face was there, smiling softly at him, dirty blond hair with streaks of blue and changeable gray-blue eyes, features he'd dreamed about for the last two months.

Blue.

The face changed back to the dead girl's, and his stomach roiled. He threw himself off the body and puked against the alley wall, heaving until there was nothing else coming up. He slumped against that same wall, heedless of the cold and partially melted ice seeping into his clothes, or the puke, or the body lying there.

I'm sorry, he thought, never noticing the tears sliding down his cheeks.

Chapter 1

BLUE

MENTALLY CHECKING OFF ITEMS, Blue lingered over the task of surveying the contents of her camping backpack. Some things she was sure she could acquire once they'd made it to Karran, but she didn't know where they would end up or how long it would take to get those things.

Extra underwear, enough for at least two weeks, socks, a few tanks, a pair of WinterSilks—she really hoped those weren't needed—two pairs of jeans, and two sweaters. A travel size sewing kit, toothbrush and toothpaste, a comb, a package of wipes, and a small first aid kit were tucked in next to those. And next to that a small journal, her List folded inside, and the pouch of coins Mo'ata had given her. Most of the remaining space was allotted to nutrition bars and water.

There were also a few items tucked down into the very bottom that she wanted to avoid thinking about, but couldn't. Cradled with the socks was a small bottle of scent... and a twelve-pack of condoms. She had started on birth control, the shots, and had just gotten the latest a few days ago, but that didn't protect against everything. Not that she didn't trust Forrest, or Mo'ata, or... Her cheeks heated, tingling. This was ridiculous; she was eighteen, almost nineteen. There was absolutely nothing wrong with her taking care of her own safety like that, and she certainly shouldn't be embarrassed about it.

Sometimes she also felt it was ridiculous to still be a virgin at her age. Other times she knew she would take that next step when she was ready. Forrest's sweet smile, quickly followed by Mo'ata's steady gaze, flashed before her. And there was the problem. She hadn't been able to break that barrier, to step over that line with Forrest. Not until she knew if she could make this crazy plan work with the two of them. And there was another part of her that she refused to acknowledge but couldn't let go of— one that kept the bottle of scent Trevon had given her. *Damn Hooligan.* She yanked the pack's zipper closed and double-checked that the water bottles in the side pouches were secure. Her heart pounded.

They really were going to do this. They were going back.

"Blue! Let's go!" Forrest yelled from where he waited in her living room. She could practically see him pacing, impatient she was taking so long to get ready. She didn't care. She was going to take her time. She didn't know when she'd be back, and this place was home.

Looking around her room, she saw not just the things, but the memories. A homecoming mum, the first she'd

6

ever made. Photos from prom with her, Forrest, Phe, and Kevin. More photos of Blue with her mom, taken at Town Lake on one of their own mini-adventures. Mom had been incredible these last several months, actively pulling herself from work to make time to go on expeditions.

There on her wall was the drawing of the tree that Forrest and Derrick had worked on that first day of school. Forrest had finally finished it, months after The Incident Where Everything Changed, and given it to her.

Sitting on her dresser was the make-up kit Phe had gotten her. It had been touch and go for a little bit on their friendship. Blue had blamed herself for the whole thing, and while Phe never had, there had been a lot of stuff to work through. Eventually, with Forrest's help, Blue had realized that even if she had originally set off the natural portal, the Zeynar Family, specifically Aterian Zeynar, was really the one responsible. His son had tried to clean things up as best he could. The deaths and Phillip's situation simply… were.

"Pixie, let's go!" Forrest said, now standing in her doorway.

Blue turned to him. "You really need to learn patience, Fo," she said, smiling.

"You know I don't have that. Come on! Everything's settled! We're going!" Like a kid, he bounced, practically coming out of his shoes. With his wide shoulders and tall frame, it was a bit incongruous.

In the year since The Incident, he had grown. Not much in height, maybe a couple inches, but he'd definitely put on more muscle and lost some of the softness of youth. He'd also gotten his tattoo. Though she couldn't see it now, covered as he was by a long-sleeved thermal, it stretched from his upper right arm and shoulder over most of his upper back. It matched the original sketch, except for a few adjustments his uncle had needed to make. Stylized trees and animals—deer, wolves, even a mountain lion—flowed over his skin. He'd also been able to incorporate Beast. Forrest had allowed her to sit in on the session when his Uncle Vic worked on that part.

It had turned out beautifully, perfectly representing Forrest's love of color and his affinity with nature. No matter what he said, there was a large part of his father in him. Though, after watching that needle move over his skin and the way he'd flinched, she had moved "get a tattoo" even further down the list.

Blue gave him a stern look. "We are going to take our time. And I'm not quite ready yet." Giving him a little grin, she teased, "Besides, it's not like you're going anywhere without me."

He stopped bouncing, but he held himself tightly, too much energy needing to be released. "True. Well, what do you still need to do?"

She studied her room again. The books on the shelves, her favorite stories. She'd written down all the tales her father had told her of the Piper Boy and others, and her mother had helped her get them printed and bound. She looked at the plants she'd managed to keep alive for the last few months and the ticket stubs taped to her mirror of all the concerts she and Phe had attended. "I need to finish saying goodbye," she finally said.

"Hey, it's not goodbye, you know that." He gave her a one-armed side hug. "You'll be back. Even if the Ministry is going to be inflexible about it, you know the Dean of the Academy and Mo'ata would figure out how you can visit. Besides, I'm pretty sure your mom and mine both would come up with a way to cross through and track us down if we don't come back for holidays."

"You're not wrong." She took a breath. "Okay, let's go." Before they even got to the door, she stopped, hurried to where the tree drawing hung, and took it down, tucking it under her arm. It was too large to fit in her pack, which was full anyway.

"You sure you want to do that?" he asked.

"Just in case," she said, not saying the rest. *Just in case we don't make it back.*

Stalling once more, she re-checked the knots in her boot laces and adjusted her wool socks. Wool in summer was insane, but they also didn't know what the weather would be on the other side. She draped her blue scarf around her neck and her puffy jacket over her arm, hooking the pack's straps over the other. Something niggled at her, something she had forgotten. Something important.

Just as she passed through the door, it hit her, and she rushed back to her dresser, scooping up a small sack of pennies. The coins he had given her were safe in her pocket, but she owed at least one of these to Mo'ata.

"All right. *Now* I'm ready."

She and Forrest made their way down to the living room. Mom, along with Sheila, Kevin, and Phe, waited for them. Everyone who knew the truth.

Setting down her pack and the picture, Blue approached her mother. She swallowed, pushing back the premature homesickness. How could she miss something before she'd even left?

"My adventuring Blue," her mom finally said. "So much like your father. Just promise to stay in touch so I don't worry *too* much."

Blue snorted. "It's not like I can just pick up the phone and give you a call."

"Maybe the Dean can help, or Jonas. I just know I'll worry. It *is* what mothers do, Blue."

"I know," she whispered and moved in for a hug.

Clutching her close, Mom whispered, "Are you sure you want to do this?"

"Yes. I've thought this through, a lot. It's not just for… Mo'ata. It's for me too. I'm not the same girl I was a year ago. And I *want* these adventures. I want to find them, instead of them finding me. I… miss the feeling, like anxiety and excitement rolled together, and the sense that anything was possible." She *had* changed in the last year. It was time to get out there, fight for what she wanted. The Year of New Things had gotten a makeover and become The Life of New Things. Or maybe it was more of an upgrade. Ultimately, The Incident hadn't made her give up her Plan, only strengthened her resolve.

Unless you're off on a wild goose chase. Why not just stay here where you know what you have? She shoved back that stupid voice, but it jumped right back. Face it, you're going to be in over your head.

"Okay then," Mom said. "Stay safe —well, as safe as you can."

Blue shoved aside the annoying voice, again, and

focused on her mother. "I love you, Mom." She gave her one last squeeze and stepped back.

"Love you too, baby."

Next, she approached Forrest's mom. This woman had been incredible. Forrest had spilled the whole tale to her almost right away, and she had believed him without question. She'd acted as an incredible pillar of support for all of them. Blue had made sure her mom and Sheila met, too. As she'd suspected, they hit it off right away.

"Take care of her, yeah?" she said low, subtly tilting her head at Mom.

Sheila smiled. "Of course. And you'll take care of mine?"

Blue knew she was talking about Forrest. "As much as he'll let me."

"Oh, he'll let you, or he'll hear about it." Sheila leaned in. "He's eighteen now, almost nineteen—he can do what he wants. But I am still his mother, and he has strict instructions not to do anything stupid."

Blue gave her a skeptical look. "You really think that will work?"

"No." Sheila pulled her in for her own hug.

Next it was Phe and Kevin. "We're not saying goodbye now. We're driving you there, so get in the car," Phe said. Blue open her mouth, and Phe interrupted. "No, no arguing."

Forrest threw his arm over Blue's shoulder, pulling her to the door. "Come on, you're not going to change her mind."

She looked back at Kevin. He shrugged. "Nope, we're

taking you there. Besides, you need someone to bring the car back."

Strangely, the spot looked exactly the same.

Phe and Kevin had hiked to the lookout point with them, unwilling to say goodbye until the last moment. Now they were there, and it looked exactly as it had a year ago. The same scrubby cedars and limestone. The same flat expanses of wavy rock below, surrounded by water and trees. The same gorgeous blue sky with fluffy clouds.

"Makes you wonder if any of it ever happened," Kevin said, pausing next to her.

This was it. She wasn't sure if, or when, she'd see him again. Sometimes she wished he'd decide to come with them, but the unspoken desire was just another way of staying in her comfort zone. She needed to do this for herself.

"Am I doing the right thing?" she asked.

"Depends. Would you be happy if you stayed here?"

"I love you, I love Phe and my mom and Forrest and Sheila. I enjoy my life. It's a good life, you know?"

"Yeah, but would you be happy? Not content, but happy? Forget about Mo'ata for a minute. If he wasn't in the picture, would you still want to go? Would you miss that place? The possible adventures? Would you always wonder if you'd missed out?" he asked patiently. He knew the answers—they'd had the same discussion plenty of times—but he asked to make a point, as he always did when Blue spoke her doubts.

She answered with no hesitation. "No, I wouldn't be happy if I stayed. It's just hard to say goodbye."

"And we want you happy, Phe and I. We'll miss you, so much. Won't lie and say I don't want you to stay. It's a selfish want. I love Phe, but you're my best friend, Blue. I talk with you about things I can't talk to her about, not yet."

He meant Jason. Phe still wasn't able, or willing, to talk about the Ministry agent. Kevin still expressed some loyalty to the guy and missed their friendship. Whenever he needed someone to talk to, Blue had done her best to be there for him.

The day they'd arrived back from Karran, and even after, everything had gone much more smoothly than Blue had anticipated. They had all stuck to the story, kept it simple, and eventually, the four missing teens became just another piece of rumor for the student body.

Though never for the four currently standing at the edge of an overlook.

Of course, kids had speculated Phillip and Derrick were somehow involved in Eric and Danny's disappearance, but nothing was ever proven. Kevin and Jason had played at growing apart at school, and with Jason's coldness, no one questioned it. Kevin and Phe had officially started going out, and he spent his lunches at the hooligan table, which slowly morphed into the hooligan-theater table after Phe joined the drama club. Blue had also stopped alternating tables. When Jason's "parents" had to move for work, he went with them, and it was over.

"Still miss him, huh?" said Blue.

"He's a good man, Blue, despite everything."

"I'm reserving judgment." And she meant it. She knew the guy had a lot of conflicting commitments pulling him in different directions. While she disliked what he'd done, she doubted she would have acted any differently. She just couldn't bring herself to forgive him or trust him, not really.

"Well, if you see him…"

"I'll tell him you said hi."

"Thanks."

They stood that way for a little longer, just looking out at the hills.

"Are you guys done? I have to get my time in too." Not waiting for an answer, Phe grabbed Blue's arm and pulled her off to the side, away from Forrest and Kevin.

"So."

"So," Blue said.

"I've been thinking. I say go for it."

"Huh?"

"Go for it. With your hunky clansman. I know you're going to be a pansy about this. Damn, Blue, it's obvious to everyone you love Forrest. And you haven't been able to forget about the big redhead." She leaned in and whispered, "Don't think I've forgotten about your kiss with that Trevon guy, who, let's face it, was the real hero of that whole fiasco, despite getting Derrick killed."

Blue grimaced. She should have kept that little detail to herself, but it had slipped out one night after one too many homemade mochas and tongue-loosening chocolate cookies. Trevon Zeynar, the wild-child son of the Zeynar family had kidnapped her, kissed her, and then let her go.

She'd later learned that Derrick had been shot and killed in the attack when Trevon's men had taken her. He was the one Blue refused to think about, yet couldn't quite seem to let go. As with Jason, she didn't know how she felt; unlike Jason, she trusted Trevon—she trusted him to be exactly what he was, a hooligan.

Phe continued. "I say go for it, make your own harem. I would, if I thought Kevin would agree. I'm pretty sure he won't though. Anyway..." She waved a hand. "My point is that Forrest knows the score. And he's the one pushing this, isn't he? So, go for it."

"God, Phe, I'll miss you."

Phe made a dismissive sound. "Just means you'll need to visit. So?"

"It's been almost a year. What if Mo'ata's changed his mind? What if it was just an 'in the moment' thing?" Blue verbalized her biggest fear. It wasn't the first time she'd thought it or spoken it. She wouldn't be surprised if Phe decided to slap her.

"Then he's an idiot, and I don't think he is."

"Yeah, that doesn't help. Didn't help the last hundred times you said it either."

"Okay, put it this way. What if all that *is* true? What if he's forgotten all about you? Would you rather not go? I mean, you keep saying you're not going just for him. So, so what? If he's moved on, then you know and can start moving on too. Or get him interested again," she said, wagging her eyebrows.

"That easy, huh?"

"That easy. Time to woman up. You're not the same Blue from a year ago. What if you get there and see him and realize for *you* it was just an 'in the moment' thing, as you put? Too many 'what ifs,' and they're pointless." Phe waved her hand again in dismissal. Blue knew she meant it; Phe really didn't believe in "what ifs." After the day when they'd found out Phillip's car had been found and she and Phe had finally talked about what had happened on Karran, Phe had moved on. There was the occasional late night discussion about the people they missed, but never an expression of regret. "Plus, you *know* you've got Forrest."

Blue looked over to where Forrest stood, surprisingly patient now that they were at the overlook. Everyone knew the reason for her hesitation in cementing any sort of relationship with him. He had surprised her. It had been his idea to return for her to see where things went with Mo'ata. If he was willing to try, could she do any less?

Doubts lingered. Plus, when she'd tried to discuss it with him, all Forrest had said was, "The guy loves you, Blue. I know how that goes." Then he'd grinned. "Quack." Blue had then laughed and let it go. Maybe it really was that simple for him.

"What if I fuck that up?" she asked.

Phe smacked her on the arm, not hard, but enough to sting. "What did I say about 'what ifs? Besides, you'd have to try pretty damn hard to fuck that up. The boy is gone on you, Blue, seriously. So, stop it."

Grinning, Blue rubbed her arm. "Yes, ma'am."

Phe snorted. "Now, Kevin and I are headed back to the car. Give us a few minutes to get out of range, will you, and try not to take some other hapless soul with you."

Phe didn't even wait for a hug, just grabbed Kevin and pulled him down the path.

Kevin called over his shoulder, "We'll wait around for a little bit, just in case. Good luck!"

After they were out of sight, Blue and Forrest moved to the edge of the lookout. "Ready?" he asked.

"You know I have no idea what I'm doing, right?"

"Yeah, but you'll figure it out." He circled his hand in front of them. "Now, get to it."

She grinned and shook her head, admonishing. Taking a deep breath, she looked out over the park, trying to recreate the feeling she'd had that first time. After a few minutes, nothing had happened. She was too anxious, too worked up, and couldn't relax.

Forrest moved behind her, circling his arms around her lightly. He leaned into her and whispered, "Close your eyes, pixie. Now, picture it. The forests, the pines. Can you smell them? Think of Beast purring for you. Think of Mo'ata. What about that night on the way to Tremmir? Or our first sight of the city. Incredible, wasn't it? All those people and the animals, so different. What about that fountain in the lobby of the Ministry? Awe-inspiring…"

His voice lulling her, she gradually closed her eyes. She thought of Beast, of the clansmen, of the different animals they'd seen, and the people hurrying all around. She thought of Trevon, too, and the small bottle of scent she still had tucked away. Finally, she thought of Mo'ata, of that night in the forest. He'd understood her longings and fears. She thought of how it felt to be wrapped in his arms, and a sense of peace and excitement came over her. She opened her eyes and looked out over the hills, and her awareness spread out, encompassing everything before her and beyond, more than only what she could see.

The ground shook, and Forrest pulled her down. When the tremors subsided, the cedars and limestone cliffs were gone, replaced by pines and a needle-covered ground.

They'd done it!

Chapter 2

BLUE

BLUE AND FORREST STOOD SLOWLY.

"It really worked," she said, wonderingly. Her chest was tight, but she felt light, like she'd float away if she wasn't held down by her pack.

"Did you ever doubt?" Forrest's words were playful, but his eyes were wide as he took in their surroundings.

"Well, yes." She shrugged. "It was the first time I've tried to do it on purpose." The terrain was slightly hillier than where they'd landed last time. The trees smaller. The air cooler. It still had that fresh pine scent—the real kind, not the stuff you sprayed on the fake tree during the holiday.

"Pretty sure we aren't where we were last time," she said, slipping on her puffy jacket. It was thinner, and she already wished she'd brought one of the ones that made you look like a marshmallow.

"Yeah, I get that. Not too worried, though. Mo'ata said all the clansmen speak English, right? We just need to make sure they don't mistake us for smugglers or something," he said.

"Aren't we though?" asked Blue, a teasing grin on her face. "Didn't we just smuggle ourselves?"

Forrest let out a snorting laugh at that. "That's us, the rebellious criminal mastermind and her chief minion." He nudged her shoulder playfully. "Come on, it looks late, and we don't know when someone will find us. Let's start looking for a good place to set up camp."

"And not get kidnapped this time."

"Yeah, yeah, take all the fun out of things."

Laughing, they set out, picking their way through the trees and brush, then following narrow game trails. It was different, being here deliberately. She took the time to really look around her, while also searching for a clear area to set up camp. As they walked, the pines cleared and larger-limbed trees appeared. The paths widened in some areas while the brush grew even denser in others. She also struggled a bit to hold on to the picture in its frame, but no way was she abandoning it.

"Here, minion, take this for a minute. My hand is cramping," she mock ordered, holding out the picture. "I really should have figured out a way to pack this."

Forrest had just reached out when they heard the sound.

Both of them froze.

It was low, a rough growl, but had a high-pitched whine to it as well. Forrest eased his arm back and slipped his hand under his jacket. There was a soft scrape of metal on metal as Forrest pulled his knife from its sheath. Blue still hadn't moved a muscle.

The sound moved closer, accompanied by the faint rustle of leaves. Something about it tickled her memory.

It came to her. Her father had talked about it in his Piper Boy stories. This was a piquet. In one story, a piquet almost killed the Piper Boy and left him with a scar on his neck. *Well, feces on a cracker.*

Scanning the area, careful to keep her movements small, she located the animal crouched in the branches of a tree about ten feet away. It had a thick ruff of fur around its throat, a bony eye ridge, and tufted ears. Its coat was a silvery beige, and faint darker spots clustered around its hunched shoulders. From this angle, she couldn't make out the size, but according to what she'd gleaned from her father's stories, it couldn't be full grown.

Not that that meant much to a piquet with razor-sharp claws.

Its gaze seemed fixed on Forrest's back, and it crouched lower, gathering itself like she'd seen cats do before they sprang.

He couldn't see it, and there was no time.

Her heart pounding, she didn't think, tackling Forrest just as it leaped. She hunched over him and squeezed her eyes shut, anticipating tearing claws and piercing teeth, even as Forrest held her close and rolled them into a patch of underbrush.

A whump, a piercing cry, and a thud.

Forrest shifted under her, and she clutched at him, refusing to let him go. Any minute now her lungs would remember how to breathe and her heart to beat. For now, her arms were the only body parts that seemed to know what to do.

"Blue?" A low voice came from above them, and she sucked in a breath. For a moment, just a moment, she thought it was Mo'ata. The accent was right.

"Forrest? Are you both really here?" Not Mo'ata. The tones weren't his, but it *was* a voice she knew, though she hadn't heard it for a year.

"Mo'ran?" Her heart and lungs were working, finally. Her arms remained on automatic and would not loosen their hold on Forrest.

He must have realized that and rolled over so that they lay on their sides. She twisted her head and spied the clansman standing over them, his face in shadow, backlit by the afternoon light that filtered through the trees.

Mo'ran looked unchanged. And it *was* him; she didn't think she'd forget anyone she'd met on Karran.

Her gaze moved beyond him, searching the trees.

"He is not here." The words pulled her attention back to the clansman. "It is just me. I needed to be away…" He trailed off and shrugged. "How…?"

The adrenaline caught up with her, and Blue laughed. Even to her own ears it verged on hysteria. Forrest shifted, sitting them both up. Mo'ran stared for a moment more then did a sort of full-body shrug. "We need to get out of this area. It is not marked as piquet territory, and this may have been a simple matter of a juvenile venturing out on its own, but we should not take the chance." He held a hand down to them. "Come."

Forrest took his hand and stood, then helped Blue to her feet. She took a few deep breaths and rolled her shoulders. Brushing off leaves and twigs that clung to her, she searched the area for where her pack, and the picture, had ended up. It took a moment, but she located them a few feet from the body of the cat-like creature. Carefully checking over the drawing, she was relieved to find it unharmed.

Mo'ran crouched over the piquet and pulled his *toka* from where it protruded just under the dense ruff. "It is the only spot, unless you can get the eye, that will kill them fast enough, and it is hard to hit. I got lucky." He eyed them then wiped the blade. "*You* got lucky."

He sheathed the weapon and, with a sharp gesture, indicated for them to follow as he set off at a fast pace through the trees.

Not the greeting I expected. Blue, taken aback by the almost cold attitude of the clansman, shrugged her pack on and set off after him, Forrest right behind her. It was probably just what he said—they needed to get away from this area.

She was also embarrassed. Her relief had been so strong when Mo'ran saved them she couldn't hold the laughter back. She'd probably looked like a fool. Of course, if he hadn't shown up, she and Forrest would be dead. From what her dad had said, piquet were extremely difficult to kill. It hadn't even occurred to her that they would run into any, though it should have; the mountains and lowlands around the clans were their territory.

I have to stop thinking of them as stories. They're the best guidebooks I've got until we learn more about this world.

They'd been following the clansman for about fifteen

minutes when another sound caught her attention, barely there. Not the growl of a piquet, more like a... cry? She stopped, trying to hear it better, and Forrest stopped with her.

"What is it?" he whispered.

"Do you hear that? Like something crying out?"

He cocked his head, straining to hear what she did. Finally, he shook his head.

She took a step to the left where, through a particularly dense grouping of trees, she could see a hillside. "It's coming from this direction. Do you think someone else is in trouble? Hey!" she called out, trying to get Mo'ran's attention. He'd moved on without them. *Yup, something was definitely up there*. "I think someone is it hurt over here!"

He returned to them. "What is it?"

"Listen. It sounds like someone's hurt."

He tilted his head, eyes distant and narrow. When the cries came again, they widened. "It is a piquet cub." He jerked a shoulder. "The pack will care for it. And all the more reason to leave this area. Come." He strode off, cutting through the trees.

Though torn, she set off after him. Forrest followed a beat behind, twisting his head toward where the cries sounded once again. According to her father's stories, Mo'ran was correct; the piquet lived in packs, and one of the adults would care for this cub. *The one that had been killed was probably its mother...* Her thoughts trailed off. There was something bothering her, a detail from the story of the Piper Boy. The cub of the one he'd killed had attacked him, and he'd subdued it, taking it home with him. *Why did he do that instead of leaving it…?*

Blue gasped, stumbling to a halt, Forrest narrowly avoiding her. She remembered now. The Piper Boy had been scouting the area, trying to learn more about the clans. He'd been tracking the piquet, learning their patterns. In this case, there hadn't been a pack in that area. The mother had moved off to start her own territory, and she had just gone through her first heat…

"Wait! Mo'ran, wait!"

Up ahead he paused, then ghosted back to them, weaving through the trees.

"Is this usually a… piquet territory?" She reached out, her fingers digging into his arm.

"Why do you ask?" His hand crept to the hilt of his blade as he scanned the trees.

"I just remembered something I heard once. What if there is no pack? What if this was a juvenile who went off to find her own territory, start her own pack? What happens to the cub?" Some instinct told her not to let this go.

Mo'ran stared at her stone-faced. Finally, he sighed, a very put-upon sigh, and they backtracked.

"He's being chatty," Forrest whispered. "What do you think is going on with him?"

"Maybe he wants to get the hell out of here before we're attacked again."

"Yeah, but why was he here in the first place? Alone, I mean. Seems weird."

Blue chuckled. "Maybe, but I'm glad he came when he did."

"We could have handled that thing."

Was he serious? She slapped his shoulder. "No, we couldn't have. That was a piquet. You read my dad's stories of the Piper Boy, right? Remember the one of the feral felines that ran in packs? The one where he got the scar on his neck? A *cub* did that to him, Forrest. The one that was after us was not a cub. We would *not* have been okay," she retorted. She softened her tone. "Please, let's not be reckless, I don't want to lose you to some wild thing that we didn't even think of encountering."

"'Let's not be reckless, she says, right after going through a space portal to a different world and then convincing a grumpy clansman to help her rescue a killer kitten. Sure, pixie, we won't be reckless." Forrest almost choked on his laughter, trying to get all that out.

"Shut up."

They continued through the trees and soon came upon a small hollow in the side of a hill, partially protected by a fallen tree. Mo'ran crouched before it and reached in, pulling out two squirming bundles. They were each about the size of a small house cat with fluffy, white-gold coats that showed a faint indication of the spots they would develop. They squirmed in his hands, sending out faint peeps. Their eyes weren't even open yet. And they were amazingly cute. Her five-year-old self had once wanted one of these with all her heart. A little bubble of delight welled in her.

One of the cubs let out that squealing cry, the sound piercing now that they were so close. She set the picture down and swung her pack off her shoulders, pulling out one of the thin sweaters she'd brought along. She held it out to Mo'ran. He grunted and took it, handing her one of the cubs in turn. While she held the wriggling bundle of cute, its fur so soft she wanted to rub her face all over it, he carefully wrapped its sibling. Forrest pulled a sweatshirt from his own bag, handing it to Blue, and she carefully wrapped the cub in it.

She gazed down at this vulnerable piece of life, entranced, and lightly stroked its little head, trying to sooth its cries. It was probably hungry. Forrest hovered beside her, a goofy grin on his face.

"Think we can name it Garfield? Or would Sylvester be more appropriate?" he asked.

FORREST

Forrest gazed at Blue and suppressed the urge to kiss her. He'd had to do that quite a bit lately.

She stood there, a few twigs still stuck in her hair, and smiled for all she was worth. Hell, his own grin was likely a mile wide. He'd never really been a cat person, but damn these things were cute. *So is Blue.*

When he'd first met her, he'd thought the same thing. He'd also worried about her. What had happened the year before had only made it worse. Then, as months had gone by, he'd realized something. Blue was Blue. She had her lists and her plans. You could reason with her, but you couldn't *stop* her. She'd once told him that her goal was to become a Cheerful Bulldozer. He'd laughed then, but that was exactly what she had done. Damn, he loved her for it.

Oh, she spoke about her uncertainties and whether returning to Karran was the right thing. Other times, she questioned her decisions and choices. She made noises of self-doubt, but they were just that: noises. It made it hard to worry when he knew that Blue was going to do what Blue was going to do.

Now they stood in a strange forest petting a killer-kitten while a surly clansman looked on, holding out another for Forrest to take. *Adventures*.

"Here," Mo'ran said. "Take this one as well. Now, we will get back to the camp. It is still a few hours travel." Then he turned and walked off again. It was getting annoying how he'd do that. *Definitely not just worried about killer-cat territory*.

Forrest thought about just letting the guy keep walking, but that would be stupid. He'd promised his mom he wouldn't do anything stupid. He intended to keep that promise, at least for a few weeks.

He nudged Blue, who continued to gaze raptly at the little thing in her arms. "He's getting away," he said, tilting his head to where the clansman was disappearing into the trees.

"Then I guess we'd better catch him," she said. They quickly shouldered their packs, and he grabbed the tree picture.

BLUE

They'd been walking for an hour or so, and their little charges were getting louder and louder. Blue had been doing her best to keep the one she held quiet, but she wasn't having any luck. Finally, desperate, she started singing a lullaby. Sure, her voice was horrible. She'd been able to cross karaoke off her list when Phe arranged an 80s night for a joint birthday celebration, and it was not an item that should ever be revisited.

This little lullaby was one her mom would sing, and it had always made Blue feel better. The little guys probably needed food, but the protein bars she and Forrest packed weren't going to work for this.

> "Baby's boat's the silver moon,
> Sailing through the sky
> Sailing o'er the sea of sleep,
> While the clouds float by"

In a way, her strategy was successful. The cub quieted, and its little body wriggled, trying to bury itself deeper into the sweater. Was it her imagination or did it look horrified? She was about to cease her own squawking noises, when another voice joined in. It was Forrest, who *could* sing. A slightly rough tenor joined in.

> "Sail baby sail,
> Out across the sea
> Only don't forget to sail,
> Back again to me

Baby's fishing for a dream,
Fishing near and far,
His line a golden moonbeam,
His bait a silver star.

Sail baby sail,
Out across the sea,
Only don't forget to sail,
Back again to me,
Back again to me."

They'd stopped walking. Blue's voice was almost a whisper, Forrest's strong. As the last notes trailed off, the cub slowly opened its eyes and looked at her. Blue felt something snap into place. A connection. It was similar to what she'd had with Beast, but more... defined. She could feel a faint distress in the back of her mind, along with a warmth. Caring? Safety?...Hunger? *What the... Was that the cub?* This wasn't in any of her father's tales.

"Forrest, I think I just had my first baby," she said, distracted. The little guy's eyes were a bright blue fading to silver at the edges. When Forrest didn't answer, she looked up, only to find him wearing a dazed expression, focused on the little bundle in his arms, mesmerized.

"Forrest?" Blue tried again.

"Hmmm?"

"Do you also have the feeling that we suddenly have kids that we don't know what to do with? I don't think we're going to be able to give these little guys back."

Forrest looked back down at his ball of cute and grinned. "Nope. They're stuck with us now."

Both of the little cubs had quieted. Blue tried to project thoughts of safety and future food, but she had no idea if she was successful.

"What did you do?" Mo'ran's whisper pulled her attention to where he stood at the edge of their barely-there path, wide-eyed.

"What do you mean? Oh, they opened their eyes. Look!"

He sighed, then shook his head. "No, it is nothing. Come. If we are to make it to camp before dark, we must hurry." He turned on his heel and started out. He also, pointedly, did not look at the piquet cubs.

"Methinks there is something fishy, Denmark..." Forrest whispered.

No kidding. Her father's tales said nothing about animals with mental abilities. Maybe the Dean had never told him that part. But why keep it a secret?

Mo'ran faded among the trees. "Damn, what is going on with him?"

"I don't know, but I agree. Let's get to the camp. We'll sort it out there."

Forrest and Blue both quickly tucked their new charges in close to the warmth of their bodies and hurried after Mo'ran. They were now doubly motivated to make it back to the camp; they had little ones to feed.

It took at least another three hours before they hit the camp. Anticipation warred with fatigue, and she had struggled to keep her thoughts calm, not wanting to upset the cubs. She was a bundle of over-sensitive nerves, though. Speculation on what had caused Mo'ran to become so surly fought her nerves on seeing Mo'ata again. She was so close...

They broke through the tree line, and the camp was laid out before them. Nothing had changed. How was that possible? The same square tents were decorated with colored streamers and sparkling glass ornaments. The healer's tent stood in its place, the white of its fabric like a beacon. The dining tent stood about thirty yards away, directly in front of them. Clan members hurried about on their various tasks, a few pausing to stare at them before continuing on. Farther out would be the corrals and Beast. Would he have gone on to another rider?

Mo'ran signaled to a clansman, who rushed off in the direction of D'rama's tent. Well, Blue thought that was where he went, if the layout really hadn't changed from last year. A breeze gusted by, bringing with it the scent of cooking meat and something roasting.

Stew? Her stomach rumbled just as Garfield and Sylvester let out yowling cries. Three clansmen mending armor nearby stiffened, and their heads shot up. Eyes wide, their gazes locked on Blue and Forrest. Mo'ran signaled with his hand, held low near his leg, and the men relaxed, though she could see them shooting side-eyed looks at the bundle she held.

"So," Blue started, then had to pause to get a more secure hold on her squirming bundle. "So, Mo'ran. Why are you so... grumpy?" She needed to focus on something. Other than her urge to scream at him to take her to her clansman—probably not something that would go over well—his mood was foremost in her mind.

Forrest rolled his eyes and leaned into her, whispering, "Think there could have been a more tactful way to ask that?"

"Maybe," she whispered back. "Give me a break. There's a lot going on. And my arms are tired. Damn, these little guys are heavy." They were. They also weren't all that little, since they were about the size of a small house cat.

Mo'ran's expression remained stony through this byplay. At the end, a hint of sorrow entered his expression, a slight tightening of his eyes, furrowing of his brow, and Blue's throat tightened.

"It's not Mo'ata, is it? He's okay, isn't he? I know you said he wasn't with you, but I kind of assumed you meant just then, like he was here at the camp—"

Mo'ran held up a hand, cutting her off. "As far as I know, Mo'ata is well. He is not here at the camp, though. He, Levi, and Felix are still searching for your friend."

Still? She'd thought that would be over by now. "So then, tell me why you're such a grumpy-face."

He raised a brow, and the corner of his mouth twitched. "Grumpy... face? I may need to remember that."

Just then, the clansmen he'd sent off ran up, halting beside Mo'ran and speaking low in the clan tongue. Giving the man a sharp nod, he dismissed him and gestured for Blue and Forrest to follow him. "The Mamanna will see you."

Straightening her shoulders, Blue prepared to meet Mo'ata's mother. Again.

Chapter 3

BLUE

THEY WERE HALTED at the tent entrance. Mo'ran and the guard spoke, and soon two men took Blue's and Forrest's packs from them. One tried to take Sylvester from Forrest, but the little guy put up such a fuss no one tried with Garfield. More words were exchanged, and someone, a woman with time, headed off to the cook tent as the men carried off the packs.

The guard held open the tent flap, allowing Blue and Forrest to enter, but she hesitated. Mo'ran didn't join them, and she looked back, only to find his gaze fixed on a woman. She sat bent over, working on something small, though Blue couldn't make out what. Then the woman sat back, and her eyes locked with Mo'ran. They widened then narrowed, and she twisted her head away. Mo'ran let out a sigh that Blue felt all the way to her toes.

So that's *it*. She definitely understood romantic-y

things making you grumpy. "Mo'ran, you coming in with us?"

"No. The Mamanna requested an audience alone with the two of you first." He gave her a small, brief smile. "I will be here when you are done and see you to your tents. Welcome back, Blue, Forrest. I—" He swallowed and shot another look at the woman. "I am glad you are here." And then under his breath, "*Someone* has to get who they want."

This was more the Mo'ran she remembered. "I am glad to be back, too. And I am very glad you were where you were earlier today. She's an idiot, by the way."

Another small smile. "It is not that straightforward." He gestured to the tent entrance. "Do not keep the Mamanna waiting."

The interior of the tent was the same. Colorful cloth rugs scattered over the floor. Hangings separated the interior into different spaces, while additional streamers and glass decorations adorned those cloth walls. A heavy wooden chair—you couldn't *quite* call it a throne—sat foremost in the entry space, imposing. The Mamanna was not seated there, though.

The older woman sat on a cushion at a low table to the side. The same table she'd used when meeting with Blue the year prior. Two more cushions had been placed opposite her. If Blue remembered correctly, the layout was reserved for more intimate audiences. A small knot of tension sitting in her stomach dissolved.

"So," D'rama began. "You are back."

Forrest shifted beside her and cleared his throat. Ignoring him, Blue answered, "Yes, ma'am."

"Why?"

A simple question. She had thought the answer simple as well, but when confronted like this, the words wouldn't come. Forrest shifted again, and she latched onto him as a distraction. "You didn't meet Forrest last time, did you? Forrest, this is D'rama the Mamanna of the clan. D'rama, this is Forrest. Oh God, was I supposed to do that the other way around?"

Forrest's shoulders shook with suppressed laughter. After a moment he spoke, his voice strained. "It is lovely to meet you. We come in peace."

Blue shot her hand out, slamming it into Forrest's stomach. "I apologize for him. And for me. I... came back because I..." She took a breath then plunged onward. "I came back because I wouldn't have been happy where I was unless I took a chance and found out what this world held for me."

"Including my son?"

"Including your son."

Her gaze shifted to Forrest. "And this one?"

Blue hung her head. "Yeah, and that one." Then she looked up with a grin and shrugged. "He's got his good points."

The corner of her mouth turning up, the older woman gestured for them to sit. "You will want to be stern with that one. He will be trouble." As they settled she continued. "Mo'ran was supposed to send for food. We will... catch up, is the phrase, yes? We will catch up and enjoy a meal together."

"I would like that." She eased Garfield to her other

side, giving her right arm a rest. "Have you heard from him? Mo'ran said he was still looking for Phillip?"

"Is that the boy's name?" She sighed and sat back. "My son has never been very good at informing me of his actions and whereabouts. I last heard from him just after you left, nearly two months ago."

"So, you don't know if— What do you mean, two months ago?" Her body went slack, and she fumbled the cub, who released a loud yowl.

D'rama gave her a concerned look. "It has been... sixty-seven days since you left. This is two of your months, yes?" She twisted to the pitcher and cups sitting beside her on a low side table and filled one, passing it to Blue.

She gulped the water down. "It's a little longer, but yeah, basically," she said, dazed and clutching the cup in her free hand. It had been a year for her and Forrest, now D'rama was saying they'd only been gone for a little over two months? *How was that possible?* When the Ministry had sent them home, they'd manipulated the time factor, but it was supposed to be an advanced technique. She definitely hadn't anticipated something like this.

"Wow. So. Huh." Forrest wasn't any more articulate than Blue's thoughts.

Just then, two women entered, carrying trays. One held small bladders of some liquid, the other held three bowls of stew and fresh bread.

Mmmm... stew. Well aware she was avoiding thoughts of time, space, and science, Blue tore off a chunk of bread and stuffed it in her mouth. Niggling thoughts of hunger drove her to take another bite before she realized it was not her own hunger, but the cubs'. Garfield let out another cry, punctuating his distress.

"Are those for the little guys?" she asked, her gaze sliding to the bladders. D'rama nodded, and Blue reached for one. On one end was a small nipple. It looked like rubber but softer—some sort of washable leather?

She held it before Garfield's mouth, and he latched on, suckling. Forrest did the same for Sylvester, and the tent fell into silence, broken by the occasional mewl from a cub or the clink of a spoon against a stone bowl as D'rama ate her own dinner.

Eventually the cubs were satisfied, and Blue was able to eat her own food. It had cooled off some but was still wonderful, just as she remembered it. The meat was fall-apart tender, and the vegetables not too mushy. Why did the stew on Karran taste so much better than on Earth?

She looked down at the sleeping cub and stroked a gentle finger over the soft fur of his nose. She remembered Pats, her old cat. This little guy would be nothing like her, and already he was filling a hole she didn't know she had in her.

Who knew?

"It is curious that they are so well behaved for you two. Most cubs found are not able to bond with another. We usually have to leave them where they are. It is surprising Mo'ran even allowed you to try." D'rama took a sip of her water, her gaze on the small piquet.

Blue blushed. "We—I didn't really give him a chance."

She chuckled. "I see. And the young man here let you go after such a dangerous animal?"

39

Forrest stiffened beside her. "Blue can take care of herself. Plus, we weren't in any danger just then."

"Hmmm…" The woman took another sip of her water, then set the cup aside. "You may be able to tell by now that the piquet can be… different."

Blue dipped her head in a nod, wary at D'rama's cautious tone.

"It would be best if no one learned of this. The piquet can be dangerous in the wrong hands, as our history has proven. I would rather that *remain* in our history."

Blue sighed, torn between calling the woman out for her cryptic statements and simply letting it go… for now. As the matriarch, D'rama was probably used to her "suggestions" being followed.

Forrest took the dilemma out of her hands. "What does that even mean?" He placed Sylvester in his lap but kept one hand over him protectively.

D'rama pinned him with a glare. "It means that this world is filled with a past you do not know and do not understand, and it is too long for me to tell you, young man."

Well now, that was a little much. "Yes," Blue said. "However, could you summarize for us?" *Tact, Blue, tact.* "I can probably get the whole from Mo'ata, or even Mo'ran, later." *Or, no tact.*

She raised a brow. "Perhaps." She looked at Garfield again, just as he let out a small sneeze in his sleep. "It is not something ever shared with outsiders. Even then, few in the clans know the full truth."

A small stab of disappointment hit Blue. What did she

expect, just showing up like this? *Ta-da! I am here; tell me all your secrets.* No, not likely.

"But," D'rama continued. "You are not truly an outsider, are you? Not if you have bonded." Her eyes went distant, and her gaze seemed to lock on something over Blue's shoulder. "It was a dark time for the clans. And it was long before the Alliance or the Ministry. For the rest of Karran, it may as well have never happened. We were at war with the clans of the north. Both sides used the creatures as battle animals. But it was not an honorable practice." She met Blue's gaze. "To train them, to bond with them, hunters would kill the mothers and steal the cubs. The bond is usually only successful with a first imprint."

"Just like what we did," Blue whispered, appalled. "If I had known…"

D'rama snorted. "'If I had known' is the excuse of the young and of fools. But in this case, you were correct in your actions. If it really was a juvenile with her first litter, it is unlikely there was a pack nearby. Those young ones would have died."

Blue stroked her finger along the silky edge of Garfield's ear. "They don't seem so savage. I mean, the mother, deadly, yes—the claws on her were terrifying. But these guys' thoughts… or feelings—I don't know exactly how to describe it, but they're almost… gentle."

"And this was the problem. They can be ruthless in defense of their young, their mates, or their pack. But they did not kill indiscriminately. Then they were twisted, taught to kill for the sake of blood." The woman slid her eyes closed and took in a shaky breath.

"Eventually, only a handful remained in the wild. The rest were being bred for battle, for savageness, and it destroyed them."

"The rest of Karran doesn't know about the bond," Forrest breathed out. "You're afraid if they did, then the piquet would be used again. But are there even wars on Karran? We weren't here long, but I got the impression the Alliance worlds were at peace."

"Again, you show your youth. Is the Alliance at war? No. But struggles for dominance and power are always ongoing. Who is to say that these animals would not be a tipping point for some ambitious or unscrupulous person? There are also worlds that are not part of the Alliance."

Blue's thoughts skipped to Phillip and the crystals she'd handed over to Levi. She still didn't know exactly how they worked, but she'd pieced together some of it based on what Phe had told her and what she'd seen herself. These were also not something anyone wanted out in the world being used indiscriminately.

Was "figure out politics" too general an item to go on her list?

"What if someone finds out, though? How do you know no one will tell?" *Like someone did with the crystals*, she finished silently.

A sly smile. "The best kept secret is one which does not exist. There have always been rumors of the savage piquet and the primitive clansmen who choose to live so close to them."

Forrest gaped at her then laughed, loud and long. Sylvester let out a grumbling peep from his lap. When he recovered he stared in admiration at the matriarch. "It's why you turned your backs on technology. You, all of you, created this... illusion."

Could that be true? The still present smile on D'rama's face told Blue it was. "Talk about convoluted," she said.

"Oh, it is not all for that reason. But yes, protection of the creatures in our area is a large part of the... motivation for our chosen way of life." She looked again at Garfield. "May I?" The slightly wistful tone had Blue gently passing the cub over.

"Wait. Creatures?" Forrest asked.

This time Blue was the one to make the connection. "The quorin. They choose their riders. Mo'ata mentioned a bond once..."

"Yes."

"But the connection isn't as deep as the one with a piquet."

"No."

This was a lot to take in for one day. Blue had a feeling there would be many more days just like this one. "Okay. Next time someone says something is complicated, I'm going to roll with it. Why is the whole damn universe so complicated?"

Her frustration and weariness must have leaked through. D'rama handed the cub back over and rose. "You have traveled far today, and you must be tired. It will be at least a few days until my son can be found and informed of your presence. We will have many more opportunities to talk."

Blue and Forrest rose as well. The Mamanna called out, and a guard entered. She spoke to him, their native language like their accents, musical and harsh at the same time. Then she switched back to English. "Di'man and T'ram will host you for the next few days. He will show you now to the tent, and then you will be able to get clean and rest." Stepping closer, she placed a light kiss on Blue's cheek. Then she moved to Forrest and looked up at him expectantly until he lowered his head. She kissed his cheek as well and stepped back. "We will talk more tomorrow."

It was a clear dismissal. Blue wondered what had happened to Mo'ran, why he wasn't escorting them, but the day had caught up with her, and all she wanted was, as D'rama had said, to get clean and rest. They followed Di'man from the matriarch's tent and toward a small grouping of medium-sized tents at one end of the camp. The sun must have set while they were with the matriarch. Long shadows were broken by oil lamps and fires dotted through the camp.

A screaming cry tore through the night, followed by a crash of wood and pounding hooves. She tensed, her heart pounding, and clutched the cub to her, searching for a place to hide. What new creature was this?

Forrest grabbed her arm and pulled her between two tents when the creature came into view. It had a dark coat, allowing it to blend into the shadows. It galloped toward them and came to a crashing halt, twisting to face her.

"Beast?" she whispered, then laughed. "Beast!" She launched herself at the devil-mount and wrapped her arms around his neck, waking Garfield. The cub let out a small yowl.

Beast startled back and eyed the bundle in her arms. He slowly stretched his neck until he nudged the sweater with his nose. Garfield let out another mewl, and Beast cocked his head. Blue stared, fascinated by this meeting. Curiosity and... a sense of welcome came to her. She didn't know who it was from or who it was for.

Garfield's little paw made its way out of the folds of the sweater and waved in the air. Beast sniffed at it once then snorted and shook his head, sending his mane flying. Then he turned his attention to Blue, sniffing her all over, lipping at her hair. He moved to her, draping his neck over her shoulder and twisting, pulling her into the best beast-mount hug ever. "I missed you too," she whispered as tears gathered in her eyes.

At her words he pulled away and snorted again. She was sure she saw an eye roll in there as well. He sniffed the cub one more time and turned, flicking his tail at her as he walked away.

Clansmen and women had gathered, staring wide-mouthed at the reunion. Two men, panting hard at the edge of the path, glared at Beast as he trotted back to the corral. He, of course, ignored them.

Blue laughed, becoming aware of the wide grin stretching across what must be most of her face.

"Damn," Forrest said beside her, draping an arm over her shoulders. "I need a Beast."

"Find your own. That one's mine."

A throat cleared next to them. Di'man stood there, disapproval and a new wariness reflected in his tight expression.

Yay! Gotta love making a spectacle of myself. She sighed as they continued to follow the clansman to a tent on the outskirts of the camp. *They probably think I'm their doom*

45

made flesh or something. The thought was so ridiculous she laughed, which drew even more strange looks.

"This is pretty different from last time, huh? It feels weird—even more awkward, like we're interlopers." Forrest kept his voice low.

"Yeah, like when we were here last time, it was an accident, so it was okay. Now, when we've come deliberately…"

"Like the tourist who decides to move to the small town."

Di'man twisted around to look at them, even as he kept walking. Two women passing them on the path stared at the still mostly wrapped in cloth cubs, barely glancing at Blue and Forrest.

"Or it's the cubs," Blue said.

"Are you—" Forrest broke off when Di'man stopped in front of a tent with one flap pulled open. Colored streamers of red and orange hung to one side of the entrance along with a decorated panel, designs in green, red, and orange standing out. Looking around, Blue noted that all the tents in this section had a similar panel, some with three colors, some four, others only two. The designs were each different as well, a unique one for each tent.

A woman ducked out, a pile of clothing clutched to her chest. It was the same woman from earlier, the one who had snubbed Mo'ran. Di'man spoke to her, and she nodded, waving Forrest and Blue into the tent.

"I welcome you. I am T'ram. I do not speak well of the English. My prida know more, but Di'man go and other not here now. Please, sit." She gestured to a table where five chairs were gathered, setting aside the pile of clothes.

46

As with the Mamanna's tent, this one was separated into sections with cloth partitions.

"Thank you," Blue said. "Actually, we've... had a tiring day." Understatement Blue? "It would be great if we could clean up and then get settled for the night, if you don't mind?"

T'ram nodded and gestured for them to follow her back to another section of the tent. Their packs lay near the cot. "You stay here for night. Is Fo'tan's area, but gone for few more days. Patrol. Stay, I will bring clothes and show you baths."

Blue watched the woman walk away, speculative. She wanted to ask her about Mo'ran later. Something felt off.

An hour later, Blue, Forrest, and the two cubs were clean. It was an interesting experience, trying to get the little devils to stay in the water long enough to get washed. The clothes T'ram had brought were damp pretty much everywhere now.

They now sat before a small fire that had been lit in an area behind T'ram's tent and was shared with five others. It created a cozy courtyard and a bit of privacy. The little guys were asleep again, having worn themselves out. Blue chuckled as she watched Garfield let out little wheezing snores while Sylvester snuggled against him.

"Forrest," Blue said, drawing his attention from where he was warming his hands. "I think we need to rename Sylvester. I couldn't really tell, but I think he's a girl."

"Nothing wrong with Sylvester. It stays Sylvester." Forrest mock-pouted in her direction.

"Sylvie."

"No."

"Vivi?"

Forrest hesitated. "Maybe."

She laughed. They'd been here not even one day, but they'd already acquired two of the cutest creatures ever. Oh, and had their understanding of the clans twisted and turned upside down, but if she thought about it, that was to be expected.

The bath had refreshed her, and she wasn't sure if she would be able to get to sleep now. They were here. And she would, hopefully, get to see Mo'ata soon. She studied Forrest from the side of her eye, and that little, wiggling, *disgusting*, slug of doubt stirred. Dammit, she would make this work. *Don't borrow trouble.* She couldn't remember where she'd heard that saying, but it seemed appropriate now.

A shadow fell over where the cubs lay. She looked up, mildly surprised to see Mo'ran. He sat beside her, keeping his gaze on the piquet.

"Hey," she said.

"You okay, man?" Forrest asked, leaning forward to peer around Blue.

He pulled his shoulders back. "I must not stay long, but I thought you would want to know that we were able to reach Mo'ata. He, Levi, and Felix were on their way to the northern regions but will detour here first. They are about three days out."

Blue grabbed his arm. "Really?"

He patted her hand and met her gaze, finally. "Yes, really." A grin played on his lips. "It was an interesting conversation. When I told him a certain girl with blue hair had shown up in piquet territory—"

"You didn't!"

"— I thought at first the comm had shut off. But no, he had choked. Felix had to beat the air back into him."

Elation and anticipation filled her, and her heart pounded. He was so close.

On her other side, Forrest chuckled. "That's Blue. Making all the guys choke. On nothing. Just because," he teased, but there was a slight tension to it.

"You okay?"

"I'm okay. Don't worry, I'll cry coconut if I need to. I'm just..." He trailed off.

She suppressed a smile at the reference to their neediness-words. They hadn't been using them much for the last few months. "You're worried about how this all works?"

"Something like that."

Mo'ran, forgotten in that moment, cleared his throat then scrambled to his feet. "T'ram." His voice held a note that just about broke her heart and magnified the wiggle-slug of doubt.

"Mo—" T'ram's voice caught. "Mo'ran." The rest of her words were in the clan tongue, but there was something...

A sheen of tears in the woman's eyes, soon blinked away, reminded Blue of her sense that something was off between the two.

"Blue." Mo'ran broke into her musings. "I will see you

49

and Forrest tomorrow. I heard that your Beast... made known his opinion on your absence. So we will be sure to see him early."

She and Forrest called out good night to him as he strode away, threading between the tents. T'ram also looked after him, her expression hard.

Suddenly it was all too much. The piquet, the time warp, Phillip and the crystal's continued elusiveness, worry over her relationships with Forrest and Mo'ata. Now Mo'ran and T'ram. Blue stood. If this woman was playing with her friend, she wouldn't for much longer. Placing herself squarely in front of the other woman, she crossed her arms, tilting her head back to meet T'ram's dark eyes. "What are you playing at?"

"Pixie, don't." Forrest stood as well but didn't join them, keeping an eye on the cubs.

"No. Something's happened. Mo'ran is downright grumpy, and he wasn't like that before." A sigh was his only answer, so she addressed T'ram again. "What is going on with you two? One minute you're practically weeping at his feet and the next you're staring after him like you want to tear off his limbs." Okay, a slight exaggeration, but she wanted to get her point across.

T'ram's eyes widened, and then her expression closed again. "Is nothing."

Blue raised her brows, and the other woman looked away. *Okay, new tactic.* Laying her hand on the woman's arm, she softened her tone. "Could there be something?"

The woman remained silent, though she blinked rapidly a few times and swallowed.

"Please tell me? He's my friend. I'd like to help if I could."

That got a reaction. Letting out a sharp laugh, the woman glared at her. "You think easy? You come, already have man. Think take War Chief, maybe others is easy? Add others easy? Not. *Never* easy."

Blue swallowed. "Do you want Mo'ran?" It was a struggle, but she kept her voice low, gentle even.

"No matter I want."

"I thought the woman was able to have more than one man? That is how your family units work, right? You chose?"

She tilted her head and raised a brow. "They told that? *Family* choose. Woman choose first, yes. After, family choose. I have two priden already. They no want add Mo'ran."

The doubt-slug started up a dance in Blue's stomach. "Why not?" The words were barely a whisper.

"No matter. Mo'ran no fix. Priden no fix. Priden no *want* fix." Her accent strengthened as her words broke down.

Blue stared at her, trying to understand. "So, they don't want Mo'ran to be part of the priden? But, what about your wishes? Do you—do you love him?"

A small tired shrug. "I love family. If Mo'ran no..." she trailed off, struggling for words. "If Mo'ran no mend with Di'man and Fo'tan, can no be family, no prida. *Stubborn.*" The last word was said with such vehemence that Blue jerked back.

Forrest stepped up beside Blue, holding the cubs. They'd woken up, and Vivi was now batting at one of the laces dangling from Forrest's shirtfront. "There's some sort of rivalry with the three of them?"

"Yes. Is *stupid*. I tell. No Mo'ran fault. They no listen. Mo'ran no help. He be... grumpy."

Blue suppressed a grin at T'ram's use of her word. "I could talk to him?"

Another shrug. "No work. Can try." Her gaze wandered to the fire. "Tired. Sleep now." Then she spun and entered the tent.

Unsure if the woman referred to herself or to Blue and Forrest, Blue followed. When T'ram veered off to another, larger section in the back of the tent and did not indicate they should follow, she and Forrest slipped into their allotted room.

"So, that happened." Blue dropped down onto the cot.

Forrest sat beside her. "I don't really know what to say. I mean, wow."

"Maybe we didn't think this through so well." Her nerves jumped and her mind raced with all the scenarios of what could go wrong. What T'ram had said made sense; of course the existing family would be consulted, would have a say. She and Forest had already discussed something similar, should she ever decide she wanted another man, but this was a real situation staring her in the face and an example of exactly how it could all blow up.

Forrest pressed his shoulder into hers. "Hey, don't talk like that. Where's my Cheerful Bulldozer Pixie? Besides, ignore her. She's obviously letting those, ummm, husbands of hers boss her around. I can't see you ever letting that happen."

"I wouldn't... You know I wouldn't just—" She blew out a breath, frustrated that she couldn't even get the words out.

"I know that." He shifted Vivi to one arm and placed his hand on her knee, palm up. "And I don't have a problem with Mo'ata. Damn, at this point, I just want you any way I can have you."

And there it was, the perfect moment to break through this stupid wall she'd built up. She laced her fingers with his. "I want you too. I…"

"You still need to talk to him first." He squeezed her hand. "I know. Stop fretting." He stood and pulled her to her feet, then tugged back the covers. "At least I get cuddles since there's only one cot."

That wasn't all she'd meant, but she let it go. Blue scrounged around until she found another blanket, smaller, and made a small nest for the cubs. After they were situated, she let Forrest climb into the cot, then settled beside him. "Think D'rama did that on purpose? The one cot?"

"With a name like that, I think she did it *all* on purpose, including having us stay with a family that's having issues you would be nosy about. She's tricky."

She snuggled back into him as he wrapped an arm around her. "Yeah, she is."

Despite the warmth of the body behind her and the drowsy peacefulness of the cubs, Blue couldn't sleep. Images and scenarios flooded her mind. Some, like the one where Mo'ata refused to include Forrest in a family unit, she didn't really believe would come about. Others, like the one where Forrest tried to beat up Trevon before insisting on returning home, felt all too real. *Stop it with the "what ifs," Blue. You know what Phe would say.*

Then there was Phillip, still out there doing who knew what. Too many unfinished pieces of the story.

She could practically hear Phe's exasperated tones. She'd just have to woman up and make sure everyone got their happy ending.

Chapter 4

BLUE

BLUE TOOK a sip of tea and grimaced. She quickly placed the mug on the table before her and tore off a small chunk of bread, hoping it would get the bitter taste out of her mouth.

"Not what you are used to?" D'rama took a sip from her own mug, seemingly enjoying it.

"No. It's a bit bitter."

She shrugged. "I've always enjoyed it."

This was Blue's third audience with the Mamanna, including the one on the first night. She'd spent the last two days learning about the clans, communing with Beast, and building up her "brave" for when Mo'ata got here. If he was still tracking Phillip, finishing that would take priority, but she hoped to get some sort of... not closure exactly, but at least an indication of his feelings, of what he wanted. She and Forrest could plan from there.

One step at a time, Blue, one step at a time.

She'd skirted around the topic until now, instead concentrating on tackling language, both Common and Tormani—the clan dialect—and helping T'ram with her day-to-day tasks. It was quite eye-opening. Yes, the woman ruled her family and the Mamanna the clan, but there was less freedom than Blue had assumed. If T'ram left the camp, she had to be accompanied by one of her priden. She issued orders and ran the home, but she could be overruled. They did assign tasks based on skill, not gender, but from what Blue observed, roles still fell very much into what she thought of as "traditional."

"Can I ask you about the prida?" The question came out hesitant, not something she was proud of.

"Of course, child. I am surprised it has taken this long for you to bring it up." D'rama took another sip of her tea.

Garfield, cuddled on her lap, chose that moment to wake up and demand attention. *Helping me delay?* She scratched lightly behind his ear and tried to send soothing thoughts his way. Then she met D'rama's eyes. "I've figured some of it out, but there's so much that doesn't make sense to me. I thought the woman was in charge? But with T'ram, she defers to her... priden so much. And then there's the situation with Mo'ran. Also, how does someone even start. I mean..."

D'rama sent her an exasperated look, the one a mother sent a child who was asking silly questions. Blue bristled; she didn't think they were silly at all.

"It is the shopa's task to form her prida. It is her family. She takes care of it, guides it, leads it. She does not dictate it."

"So... yeah, I still don't know what you're trying to say." Blue felt like an idiot, but dammit, she was fairly new to all this romantical-ish stuff. It only made sense to ask questions, right?

"You want to know how to go on with my son."

It wasn't a question, but she answered, "Yes."

"I think yours will not be a traditional prida, but I will tell you how it is usually done. When a woman finds someone she feels will be a good First Priden to help her guide their ultimate family, she approaches him with a proposal. It is different for each couple, but will often include terms and a gift. After this, additional priden are first approached by the shopa. If they are agreeable, they meet with the full prida, and there is a... *bota*, a vote, among the family. It is to keep the... balance. The *ransyi*." She tapped the table with impatient fingers, frustration thinning her lips. "I have never actually had to explain this to someone."

"I... think it makes sense. That's kind of what T'ram said. I guess what I don't understand is... is there no recourse if the prida votes no? Because Mo'ran is a good man. I just don't see how they wouldn't want him as part of their family."

"Ahh, I see. A shopa may leave her prida, may choose to form a new one with a new First Priden. I have only seen this happen twice in my life, though. It is a hard thing, having to choose like that. Most, though, make it work." She glanced up, gaze roving over the tent's draped cloth ceiling, as if looking for the words. "Each prida is different, the people that make it up. It is the people who will rely on you and who you will rely on. There must be trust and some affection between the members, or your home will be in constant conflict.

"For Mo'ran and T'ram, there would be conflict. It is an old rivalry, but if Mo'ran cannot mend things with the existing priden, T'ram will not accept him, not fully. It would… break her prida. Trust is the key."

Garfield let out a small cry, echoing the part of Blue that ached for Mo'ran. It also twisted her own anxiety tighter. *Dammit.* "So, Mo'ran could fix this?"

D'rama's gaze was piercing. "The prida is formed for protection. Not just the physical protection of the members, but the spiritual protection as well. They care for each member and each person's happiness is important. So while the shopa, as the Heart of the Family, is usually catered to, she cannot ignore the needs of her priden. Mo'ran has a chance, but unfortunately, the burden of it falls on him to… clear the air? This makes sense to you?"

Blue took a sip of her tea, stalling for time. It did make sense, almost too much. "So… a prida is like a marriage on steroids."

"Steriods?"

"Ummm… like an uber-marriage."

D'rama tilted her head. "Uber, as in outstanding or supreme?"

Yeah, this wasn't going anywhere. "Basically," Blue finally said.

D'rama nodded. She took another sip of her tea and then set the mug down once more, this time her movements almost too precise. "Well, Blue, what shall you do when my son comes for you?"

58

The question hit her like a... wrecking ball. *Damn popular culture.* "I honestly don't know. I don't think I'll know until I see him again. It's been a *year* since I've seen him. I know only a couple months have passed here, but for me it's been much longer. Is my memory of the time we were together accurate? I felt sure he had feelings for me, or did I just build it all up in my mind?"

"Will you go back? If things between you are not as you remember?" D'rama asked.

Blue shook her head. "No, I'm not going back. Even if this doesn't work out, I still want to learn about these worlds and the portals. I need to learn to control them, if for no other reason than not accidentally setting any off." Blue grinned, "And, yes, the idea of exploring new worlds, discovering new things, is a big motivator."

"So like my boy, you are," the Matriarch said with a chuckle, the air lightening between them. She poured her a cup of water and handed it over.

Taking it with a smile, Blue figured it was a peace offering. They sipped their respective drinks, enjoying a companionable silence. She felt better for having gotten her concerns off her chest, even if nothing had actually been resolved.

There was a commotion outside, hooves pounding and muffled shouts coming from the edge of the camp. A moment later the entry flap was flung aside, and a large man rushed in. Mo'ata.

Blue cried out and leaped to her feet, clutching Garfield to her chest. She rushed into the arms held out for her. She'd said she didn't know what she would do, but that had been a lie. She was going to hold onto this man, and she was going to fight for him. The doubts fled the moment they touched. She had a plan, and he was part of it.

She stood there, lost in his closeness, his arms strong around her. She inhaled the scents of quorin and sweat, and below that was pine and herbs. She pushed against him harder, like she was trying to crawl inside his skin.

"Shhhh, little shopa, shhhh."

He'd called her that almost from the beginning, she realized and pulled in a shaky breath.

Mo'ata eased her back just far enough that he could wipe the tears from her cheeks. Then he gently cupped her cheek and studied her, eyes wide. "Are you really here?" he whispered. He stroked her hair, fingering the new length. "It's longer."

"It's still blue." She couldn't believe *that* was what came out of her mouth. This was the moment she'd been waiting for, and she was talking about her hair?

Mo'ata chuckled. "It is. It's perfect."

Blue shifted Garfield to one arm and wrapped the other around Mo'ata, snuggling into his chest. She didn't even care that it was covered with stiff armor. She wasn't sure how long they stayed that way, enjoying the closeness, before a loudly-cleared throat sounded behind Mo'ata. Blue pulled away and peeked around him.

They were all there. Levi and Felix, Forrest standing behind them, an expression on his face she couldn't read. It wasn't hurt or disapproving, simply… stiff.

Mo'ata pulled her back into him, stroking her hair as if not willing to share her just yet. It took a while, but she didn't mind. He was here and she was with him.

Someone, probably Forrest, took the cub from her, and she was able to use both arms to hold this man close.

It was one of those perfect moments.

Eventually he pulled away and took her face into his hands, studying her. She knew what he saw. She'd changed—not much, but her face was a little more mature, a little less rounded and childish. Her hair was longer and her body was tougher, more streamlined.

"It is really you." His voice became wondering as he stroked her hair.

She smiled. "Yes. It's really me."

"How?"

Blue gave him a big smile. "Well, Forrest and I got bored, so we decided to go on a little mini-adventure. We were hiking in this park near home when suddenly everything changed, all the trees were different, and the terrain. The air was definitely colder, too. It was a good thing we'd brought jackets with us. You know, just in case."

"Just in case," Mo'ata echoed. "Of course." He pulled Blue into him again and said low, just for her ears, "I thought I'd lost you."

"Pretty sure that's not possible," she whispered back.

Then Forrest pushed through the other men and stood beside Blue, gazing intently at Mo'ata, two little bundles cradled like footballs in either arm. The stiffness was gone from his face, and in its place was a mixture of eagerness, wariness, and a sort of stubborn affection. He nudged Blue out of the way and stood before Mo'ata. "So."

"Yes."

He took in a deep breath and then grinned, the one

that was all Forrest. "I know you said to keep an eye on her, but do you know how hard that is? That's a job for a whole team. Plus, she was totally pining for you. I mean, deep sigh with longing looks kind of pining. So... we came back," Forrest finished, shrugging. Blue relaxed. She hadn't been sure how that would go. She should never have doubted Forrest, though she had to suppress the urge to slap him for that "pining" comment.

Another set of strong arms came around her from behind and picked her up, twirling her around, and a booming laugh filled the tent. That sneaky mercenary had come around behind them all, unnoticed despite his size.

Blue slapped his forearm. Felix eased her down but didn't let go. One of his hands moved, and she felt him touch her hair, his fingers sliding over the back of her head and down, petting her. She felt something deep in her belly, irritation and... desire?

She slapped his hand again. "Stop. I am not a pet."

"It is longer."

She let out a strained laugh. *Looks like everyone is fascinated with my hair today.* "Yeah, it's longer." Her eyes widened, and she spun, making his fingers glide along her stomach. "Wait, that was English!"

Felix grinned. "I learn."

She matched his smile but didn't say anything, just looked up into his green eyes. Damn things practically sparkled.

A throat cleared, and her attention moved to Levi, who still stood silently behind the others. She stepped away from Felix. "Hi."

The corner of his mouth curled up, and he gave her a

small bow. The silence stretched out, and then she hit him with a flying tackle-hug, just as she had with Beast. Levi, her silent rescuer. She hadn't realized until now how much she'd missed him, his presence. He stiffened in her arms, but then slowly, hesitantly, his own rose and closed around her. He squeezed tight and let go.

She stepped away and looked around her. "So, catch us up."

"Okay. *Now*, catch me up. What's going on with Phillip? That other guy? The last stone?" She held a small bladder for Garfield while Forrest sat beside her feeding Vivi.

They were gathered in the dining tent at a table isolated from the others. D'rama had kicked them out of her tent with instructions to get cleaned up and eat. It had been entertaining, seeing those grown men scramble at a few words from her. New List item: Become as scary as the Mamanna.

Mo'ata, keeping one eye on the piquet cubs, was the one to answer. "Levi has been in contact with his people, but it has been... difficult tracking—" He broke off and shot a look at Levi, brow raised. The dark man nodded, and Mo'ata continued. "It has been difficult tracking the crystal and Phillip and Etu. They have been very good at letting no word leak out. If it was just Phillip, I have no doubt we would have found him by now, but with Etu helping him..." Mo'ata trailed off.

Felix rapped his knuckles on the table. "There is trail. We follow."

"Yes. A few days ago we heard of some suspicious deaths in the Filiri region, near Firik. We were on our way there when I got the message you had returned." Mo'ata smiled at this last part before sobering once more as he continued. "It is not much, but the reported condition of the bodies is too similar to what Levi says is the result of a crystal draining someone. He has only seen it once, when one of his Elders was ready to pass, but from what he says, it is distinctive. I wish we had thought to question your friend better when she was here since she saw the others after they were killed."

"I was hoping it would be over by now," Blue admitted. She was still struggling with the idea that only a couple months had passed here on Karran, rather than the year she and Forrest had lived through back on Earth. She had expected to find Mo'ata, learn from him how Phillip had been caught—not that Phillip was still out there, still causing death, still dangerous.

"You? How here?" Felix broke into her thoughts. Looked like it was her turn.

"Forrest pretty much said it, though I would have used different words." She twisted her head and shot him a squinty-eyed look, to which he stuck out his tongue like a five-year-old. She rolled her eyes and continued. "We got back to Earth and things pretty much went according to plan. We adjusted a little, but it worked. It… took some work, but we all were able to move on, mostly. Turns out, my mother totally knew all about Karran, she just hadn't realized Austin was a portal location. She and my dad *had* kept their promise to the Ministry and avoided cities with the thin spaces, just in case. Anyway, it's been a year for us. It was a shock when we got here and found out only a couple months had passed."

Garfield finished his meal and batted aside the feeding bladder. She set it on the table and rubbed the cub's belly. Soon little snores came from its small, pink mouth.

"A year?" Moa'ta asked. Then, "How are you here now? Why?"

She met his gaze. "We wanted to come back. To see what may be here for us."

"Us?" A slight strain entered his tone, and his fists clenched.

"Yes, but—" *Filiri*. They'd said the Filiri region. Wasn't that where the Piper Boy had said her dad was from? "We can help!" Blue knew they could. It was perfect. "The dean said that's where my dad was from, the Filiri region. Forrest and I could help. We can say that we are searching for any family I may have left or history on them or something like that. It's a great cover for us being there!"

Felix and Levi looked thoughtful, but Mo'ata scowled. "No."

"What? Why not?"

"I will not have you in danger." The serious, stubborn set of his face told Blue that he was going to be hard to budge on this.

"You didn't mind using me last time." Blue could be stubborn, too.

"That was different. It was unavoidable."

"It isn't different. If anything, this time it makes even *more* sense. Phillip is our responsibility too. He was our friend." Despite everything she'd learned about him, he *had* been her friend. More importantly, he had been

Forrest's friend, practically family. She knew Forrest would need to see this settled as much as she did.

She looked to him for support, and he didn't disappoint. "I'm with Blue on this one. We need to see it through to the end. I can't... I can't just abandon him. I still don't really understand what happened, but if we can help stop this, we will. It sounds like Blue has a good idea."

"There are issues. Even if I wanted her to come, which I don't, the story wouldn't hold up. It would explain you two, but not the rest of us." Mo'ata crossed his arms.

Pushing aside the hurt of his rejection, Blue persisted. She'd be able to tackle the overly-protective thing with him later. "Why wouldn't it work?"

The others had been silent through this, but now Felix spoke. "No one believe girl, boy, clansman, guild, and Prizzoli together. It not happen."

"Why? In the capital, no one questioned it. Well, not that I know of."

"No one questioned it because we did not make it obvious we were all working together. Clansmen were with you as those who had found you and needed to get you home. Levi was someone who had helped you when we became separated. Felix and his men, other than the occasional meeting, were not actually at the inn or seen with us. Even now in our searching, we do not allow others to make that connection between us."

"Okay, but I still don't understand why. Explain it to me." She looked at each of them in turn, even Levi, who had yet to say anything. "I'm here to stay, no matter what happens. We are here to stay," she gestured to Forrest. "I need to learn this world, all of them actually. I need to understand. Plus, I don't know why it would be a problem that my friends, who I met when I came here accidentally, wouldn't be able to help me out as I search for my family."

MO'ATA

Mo'ata held his silence. He didn't know what to say to make Blue understand. He had disappointed her somehow; it was there in her eyes when he'd said he didn't want her to come with them. He hadn't enjoyed hurting her, but he didn't want her to come. He didn't want her in any danger at all.

When he'd gotten the message that his mother needed to see him, he'd been impatient, frustrated. They'd finally gotten a lead on the crystal. He and Felix had put out feelers to all their guild and Order contacts. He'd even gotten a few tips from Trevon. They hadn't panned out, but he knew the Family head was also working to clean up the rest of his mess.

He'd almost ignored the summons. Then Mo'ran had contacted him. After he'd recovered from the news of her encounter with the piquet and that they'd taken the cubs, he'd decided to detour to the camp.

He almost hadn't come, afraid this exact thing would happen, but he hadn't been able to hold himself back. He'd needed to see her with his own eyes, to know she was real. To find out *why*. They'd reached the camp, and he'd seen Forrest standing outside his mother's tent. He looked older, taller and more filled out. The boy was turning into a man.

He'd rushed into the tent, and there she was, sitting at the low table with his mother. Her back had been to him. Her hair was longer, hitting her mid-back, but those blue streaks were still there. He still hadn't quite believed. Then she'd turned.

It *had been* her. His Blue was *here.*

Now she wanted to put herself in danger. Again. He couldn't allow it. He'd just gotten her back.

"It would attract too much attention, especially in the Filiri region. In the capital there are many travelers, many cultures mixing, and it is easy to blend in. In Filiri we would stand out badly. Additionally, there is some... prejudice against the clans."

"Then what were you going to do?" Her brows were furrowed, he could see she still didn't understand.

"We were going to go in separately," he admitted.

A small smile formed on her lips. Forrest had been watching her as well, and his eyes narrowed. "What are you thinking?"

"I just had the best idea." Blue's smile widened into a grin, and she bounced a little in her seat.

Forrest stiffened, alerting Mo'ata that he should tread carefully. "What?"

"You could all be undercover as my potential prida!"

Mo'ata jumped from his seat. Around him other clansmen froze, not daring to move a muscle, wary gazes trained on him. Forrest groaned and dropped his head to the table, his shoulders shaking.

"This is not something to joke about." Mo'ata's voice was a low growl. He could not believe she would say such a thing. *Did she know what she suggested?*

Her eyes grew wide, a hint of disappointment and hurt creeping in. "Who said I was joking?"

Mo'ata stilled, his heart pounding. "Do you know what it even means?"

"Yes." He waited for her to continue, needing more. "I know what it means. This isn't how I had really planned to bring this up with you, but my mouth ran away with me again."

This last part didn't make sense to him, and the confusion threw him off. Then Forrest's shaking grew, and the laughter leaked out. Blue turned to him, hitting his shoulder. "Hush." Forrest nudged her gently with his shoulder, still laughing, and Blue huffed.

It was small, this interaction, but Mo'ata saw how close they'd grown. Part of him was jealous of the time Forrest had had with her, but a larger part was glad the other man had been there for her. Had a year really passed for them? He could believe it when studying their appearances, but it didn't seem real to him.

Forrest got himself under control. "Tell him, Blue." His voice took on a stern note.

Blue took a deep breath, and a rush of words flooded from her, just like they always had when she was nervous. It had been cute the first time it'd happened. It still was. "Forrest didn't lie when he said I've been pining for you— I really have—and I wanted to see if we could make this work, but I didn't know how you would still feel after a year, well, I thought it was a year. Anyway, I decided to come back. Even if you didn't still feel the same, I could learn about portals and controlling my ability and explore the worlds and Forrest could learn more for his art, but I wanted to try—I did—only I hadn't planned to bring it up like *this*." Her shoulders slumped.

An emptiness in Mo'ata filled. She really wanted to be with him? "A prida with all of us." It wasn't a question, really, but he needed to hear it again.

BLUE

Blue was panicking. This had not been how she'd wanted to approach this. Forrest's earlier laughter hadn't helped, and now Mo'ata was looking at her like she was crazy. He was also still standing, towering over her, making her nerves run wild again.

"Sit, please. Crap, this *really* wasn't how I wanted to bring this up." She nudged Forrest again. "You are not helping."

As Mo'ata took his seat, Levi spoke. Felix laughed that booming laugh of his, then said, "Levi not know English. He want know what is going on," he got out between his chuckles.

Blue looked to where Levi sat, a small furrow between his brows and a frown on his lips. She really had made a mess of this.

"Can you guys give me a minute with Mo'ata, please?" She glanced around, seeing the gazes trained on their table like they were some sort of live-action soap opera.

"Actually, maybe we could go somewhere with fewer... observers?"

Forrest was the first to rise. He took Garfield from her, holding him and Vivi in one arm while he pulled the mercenary and Levi to their feet with the other. "Come on, you guys. Blue needs to sort this out. Felix, stop laughing and tell Levi what's going on." He shot her a brief smile on his way out of the tent.

Forrest knew her better than anyone at this point, knew she needed this time to sort things out, and she was grateful for his quiet support. That last smile told her he would be there when she was done.

Mo'ata rounded the table and held his hand out to her, calm, steady. Gathering her courage, she took that hand and allowed him to pull her up.

"Where have you been sleeping?"

"With T'ram and her prida. Your mother put us there."

"You and Forrest both, hmmm? And T'ram? Well, never let it be said my mother is subtle."

Blue chuckled. "No, I wouldn't say so. Sly, sometimes, but not subtle." He led her out of the tent, but when they exited, he turned left, away from the pridas' tents. "Where are we going?"

"I assume we need more privacy than we'll get at T'ram's. We'll go to mine." Her steps faltered, and he tightened his grip on her hand. "Hopefully it is still there. Though my mother has said nothing yet about disowning me, so we should be safe."

"Are you still the War Chief? I don't really even know what this entails if there is no war."

He shrugged. "It is more of an honorary title. But I am

in charge of defense and protection of the clan. Mo'ran is my second, my lieutenant, and he has done the job well in my absence."

Curiosity got the better of her. "What is the deal with him and T'ram? All I've been able to gather is vague comments and hints." A gust of wind set strands of glass tinkling and ribbons streaming. She brushed loose strands of hair from her face. When he didn't answer, she looked up.

He looked straight ahead. "It is not my story to tell."

"Yeah, those are the answers I've been getting." She licked her lips. "I guess I just want to know what went wrong."

They stopped before a tent slightly larger than the others, and Mo'ata pushed aside the entrance flap. A high table sat in the middle of the main chamber, chairs arranged around it. To the right was a sleeping area, a cloth partition only partially closed.

Mo'ata hesitated, then led her to the cot. They settled next to each other, and her stomach jumped. Like a pole vaulter. He was close enough that if she shifted her leg a little, she would be touching him. Her head came up to his shoulder, and heat radiated from him. She breathed in pine and herbs, and something lower than her stomach tightened. Desire. She wanted this man, wanted to be close to him. "You know how I feel about you," she said. It wasn't a question.

"I know what you told me before you left. That was a year ago for you." His voice rumbled through her, and her blood raced.

"Yes." Blue shifted until she was touching him, and

she relaxed. "I still feel the same. It's been eating at me this whole time. I missed you. I missed you, and I missed this." Blue gestured to the camp and beyond. "Did you know your mom talked to me that last time I was here?"

He stiffened, and she could have sworn she heard him growl. "My mother meddles."

"Well, yes, but we've already established that. However, what she told me was very enlightening. Want to know what it was?"

"I can guess." There was still a growl in his words. It was kind of adorable.

"She told me a little about your pridas. It was a thought that stuck with me. Even after I left. I couldn't stop thinking of you. But I also have feelings for Forrest. And maybe..." Her courage deserted her at this next part.

"And maybe others. You never told me what happened between you and Trevon Zeynar."

Blue stilled next to him, her heart pounding. "I..."

"I know something happened." His voice was gentle, just a hint of rumble remaining.

"He kissed me." Her voice was small, quiet, and she looked away.

Mo'ata shifted, pulling her from his side and into his lap. His warmth and the pine-and-herb scent of him surrounded her. She could feel the strong muscles of his thighs shifting under her as he pulled her closer to his chest, one arm around her waist, holding her close, unmoving. His other hand dove into her hair, cradling her head, his fingers flexing rhythmically. She saw his eyes briefly, their expression fierce and determined, before his lips descended on hers.

This wasn't like the kiss Trevon had given her. That had been brief, over too quickly for her to even react. It was definitely nothing like the brief pecks she'd shared with other boys after school dances. This was heat and joy, like coming home. It was something she'd been needing for too long. Her mouth opened, welcoming him in.

Her hands came up to his chest, moving over the muscles there before sliding to his shoulders, trying to pull him closer. He complied, picking her up and shifting just enough that she was now straddling him, and her legs tightened on his sides, her hands diving into his hair to hold him closer.

Finally, when she needed to breathe more than she needed to keep kissing him, Blue tore her mouth away, taking in a lungful of air. "Well, that broke the ice," she said when she had the breath to speak.

Mo'ata's chuckle vibrated through her. "That it did. I accept, little shopa."

"Wait, what?"

"Your proposal. I have decided. I accept. It would be my honor to be your First Priden. I believe I know who will be your second, and the rest we will sort out. We have time now, do we not?"

Her thoughts were admittedly scattered after that kiss, but was he saying she had proposed? She hadn't, not really. Well, she hadn't meant to. This was moving faster than she'd anticipated. She pushed off of his chest and angled back, studying him.

"I... think that's a little fast," she said, her voice cautious. She shifted to the side, trying to get off his lap, but he moved at the same time and she half-slid, half-fell to the cot where she had been sitting, one leg still caught over his. Blood rushed to her face, and she concentrated on untangling herself.

"Blue." Mo'ata reached for her, his voice now cautious as well.

"I really don't know what to say." Blue decided the truth was best. "I came back because I wanted to see what there could be between us, but I'm not ready for... I mean, I've kissed a couple other boys, but nothing like *that*. I have no idea where that came from. I haven't even kissed Forrest yet. It's just..."

"Too soon," he finished for her, his hand caressing her shoulder before moving to playing with her hair.

"Too soon," she agreed. "I want this, I do, but can we just date for a little bit? Get to know each other better? Everything that happened was such a whirlwind."

"Date?"

He didn't know what dating was? How was it possible that word hadn't made it into his vocabulary? Blue peeked at him. His lips were held in a serious line, but his eyes crinkled slightly at the corners.

"Are you messing with me?"

Mo'ata chuckled. "Just a little." He cupped her cheek. "I am happy to date you, shopa. And when you are ready to propose for real, know that I will say yes."

Some of the tension left her at that reprieve. She'd learned and experienced so much in the last year, but this romantic-emotions stuff was still way out of her comfort zone. She would tackle it, like she had the rest of her List. In fact, that was now a new item: Successfully build her own mini-harem with Mo'ata and Forrest.

"How can you be so sure?" she asked. Part of her needed the reassurance. It had not been easy putting her feelings, her hopes, out there like that.

"Because I cannot imagine my life without you somewhere in it. Do you know what I was planning to do once we had found the last crystal and Phillip? I had planned to find you. I knew I wanted you. I will do the dating with you. We will learn the little things about each other, like you have been able to do with Forrest." He twisted and cupped her face with both hands, his thumbs lightly stroking her cheeks. "I know the big things, Blue. Those don't change. I will say yes."

Blue swallowed, her throat tight. She felt tears gathering but was baffled as to why she would cry. *Emotions.* Definitely confusing. She leaned forward and rested her head on his chest. It was awkward; they were still sitting and half-turned to each other, but she didn't care. Something about this man evened her out.

After a full five minutes, she collected herself and sat back. Meeting his eyes, she dove in. "So, about going to Filiri. I really do think it would be a good idea if I went."

"No—"

"Please, just listen. It's the same as last year." She paused. "Month, whatever. It *is* the same. I'm the excuse. You can be more open in your search, use it to flush them out. If we do pretend to be a possible prida in the making, it allows you and the others to work more closely together. You use me as bait." His expression closed down, but she ignored it, pushing through. "You *know* that Phillip had some sort of fixation on me; that's why Trevon took me in the first place."

"I do not want you in danger."

Blue snorted. There was nothing else to say to that.

"It is *my* life-debt," he continued. "I am the one who has to repay it."

Well, that was new. "Life-debt?" Her side cramped, and she shifted so she could sit sideways, one leg up on the cot.

Mo'ata cleared his throat and glanced away before looking back to her, his reluctance obvious.

"What?"

"I gave the Prizzoli a promise. I will help him get all the crystals back. My debt is not discharged until then."

"But why do you owe a debt?" This didn't make sense to Blue; there was something he was leaving out. He gripped the edge of the cot, avoiding her eyes once more like a little boy caught doing something he shouldn't. Unlike a little boy, *this* was not cute.

"Mo'ata?" Blue tried for stern, but it came out a little too pleading. She didn't like him keeping something from her that was obviously important.

He tipped his head back and closed his eyes. "A life-debt is incurred when the shopa, the Heart of the prida, is threatened and someone outside of the prida protects her." When he finished, he looked right at her, his gaze once more direct, trying to tell her something.

She still wasn't getting it. Mo'ata was not part of a prida. How would he owe a life-debt to Levi? He continued to watch her, and her confusion grew. "It's you, Blue."

She recalled the incident at the Ministry, how Levi had come to her rescue in the alley. She'd barely known

Mo'ata then; why would he have taken on a debt for her? Wasn't that jumping the gun a little? Of course, she'd trusted him almost from the beginning and had practically fallen in love with him in a week, so who was she talk? Then it came to her, the memory of the first time he'd called her shopa, on a dark night in the middle of a forest, bare days after meeting her.

For a moment she felt overwhelmed, unworthy of this amazing man. And ashamed she couldn't just dive in with him. "I... have no idea what to say. Ummm, thank you?"

Mo'ata's eyes widened, and he laughed loud and long, holding his stomach and bent nearly double. When the laughter died down, and he stayed bent, Blue poked his shoulder. "You okay?"

He finally straightened, nodding at her. "I am fine. And you are *very* welcome." The serious face was back, but so were the eye crinkles.

"I still don't understand why the life-debt means I can't help."

"It is my debt."

"That you incurred because of me."

He didn't respond, but the smile left his eyes.

"I'm going with you." She poked his arm to make her point.

Still he didn't say anything.

"Mo'ata, I am going with you. You know I can help. Plus, I'm not as helpless as I was. I've been working on it. I've taken some self-defense lessons and even some 'take you out' lessons. I only got to level two in my Krav classes, but it's something. I also practiced riding when I could, and Forrest has been teaching me some of what his father taught him about camping and hunting. I can build a damn fire on my own now."

His face had taken on a stubborn cast as she spoke. "I *never* thought of you as helpless. Out of your element, yes, but never helpless." He pulled one leg up onto the cot and leaned back, matching her posture and facing her fully. "I can't let you do this. It is my debt. I do not want you in danger for me."

"There is so much wrong with that statement I don't know where to begin." He raised his brows and she matched him. "Fine. I came back for you, Mo'ata. For you, but for *me* as well. I missed you, but I missed this place and the possibilities." She gathered her courage and said the rest of what needed saying, the decisions she hadn't told him yet. *Time to woman up.* "I've been thinking about this for a while. I had a whole *year*. Did you know Forrest was actually the one to suggest we try coming back? I love him, but I couldn't forget about you. He knew that."

His mouth tightened, like he held back from saying something.

She waited, but when he didn't speak, she continued. "I had a year to sort through some things. I'm here to try this with you, you know that. I'm here to see if there is something real between us, or if it was just the circumstances."

"It—"

This time she didn't wait. She needed to get this all out. "That's not the only reason I'm here. If this doesn't work between us, I know I have Forrest. One of the main things I love about him is he has never once treated me like I'm delicate or can't take care of myself. He warns me, cautions me, then he helps me. I do the same for him. We're partners." Mo'ata's brows lowered, and his eyes narrowed, studying her. His expression was almost completely closed off now, and she looked away. "I want to have that with you as well." Her throat tightened on this last, the words strangled. She struggled to get out the last part. "That night, on the way to the capital, I thought you understood."

<hr />

MO'ATA

Mo'ata looked down at Blue. She was right. That night he'd found a kindred soul in the small, blue-haired girl. He thought it may have been then that he loved her, even if he didn't realize it at the time. It had torn him up to continue with the plan to use her as bait at the Ministry. Then she'd been chased, rescued, and finally kidnapped. When he'd gotten her back, he hadn't wanted to let her out of his sight. When she'd returned to Earth, he had taken comfort knowing she was back on her own world, safe, while he searched for the last crystal.

She wanted a *partner*. He wasn't sure what that meant. Fellow clansmen he patrolled with—they were partners. Felix, in his own way, was a partner, especially when their assignments took them in similar directions, as they did now. Levi had been his partner for the last few weeks, working with him to track down Etu, Phillip, and the remaining crystal.

The shopa was the heart of the prida. It did not exist

without her. She was not a mere partner. She was the *heart*. It was different. Once you committed to your one, she was yours to protect, and you were hers to lead and govern. It was their way, as it always had been. The Heart looked out for all the members of the *prida*, taking care of them, governing and overseeing the running of the camp and daily life. It was the warriors' job to ensure safety and provide for the clan. There was balance, yes, but was that a partner?

In a way, he did know, though, didn't he? As she'd said, that night in the forest, her adventurous side had called to his own. He struggled. The traditions of his clan were very clear. And though he had never been content with those traditions, they were still what he knew and, to a large degree, what he believed. Blue's idea of partners appealed to the side of him that had never quite felt at home in the clan.

He had never had this much trouble reconciling the two parts of himself as he had in that moment.

He studied the woman before him. The girl from a month ago *had* changed. What he could see of her body was firmer, more streamlined. Her face had thinned, just a little. It was still delicate, soft, but her strength showed through now. She showed so much courage in being honest about her emotions and wants; he could do no less.

"I understand some of it, but the idea of the shopa being a partner is not something I have really thought about. For the clans, the shopa is the heart, the key. Everything revolves around her, and protection is a priority. But I know how you feel about wanting more. I feel the same way." She looked back up at him, cautious but hopeful. "I will try, Blue. I don't know how it will work—if I can do it. But I will try."

She gave him a small smile. "That's all I want. I want you to try. I don't know how this is supposed to work either, you know? We'll have to fumble through somehow. Though, I am glad we broke the ice on the subject." Her eyes widened, and she reached into the front pocket of the pants she wore, pulling out a small coin and holding it out to him. It was a *tripi*. One he had given her. "I'll make you a deal. I'm cashing in my 'sorry.'"

Mo'ata tensed. Was she going to use it to force him to take her to Filiri? He held his tongue, letting her continue.

"In return, I want you to really look at whether or not Forrest and I being there would help. *Really* look at it. I'm pushing this partly because I want to learn more about where my father came from and this world and partly because I don't want to be apart from you now that I'm here. Mostly, though, I'm sure I could help." She sat forward and reached for his hand, placing the coin in his palm. "Think about it, okay? If you decide Forrest and I can't help, that we'd be more of a liability than anything, we'll stay behind. I can go ahead and travel to the capital. I've got to see the dean and sort out what to do about the Ministry and Academy anyway. You come find me when you're done." She closed his hand over the coin and stroked her thumb over the back of his hand. "All I want you to do is think about it, but be honest with yourself. I'll do what you decide." She placed a small kiss on his knuckles and then left him to his thoughts.

After a while he gave up. He couldn't separate his need

to protect Blue from her ideas of how she could help. He couldn't look at it objectively. Frustrated, he left his tent and searched until he found the one assigned to Felix and Levi.

He suspected Felix was interested in Blue as well, though it was hard to get a true read on the man's emotions. Despite meeting him when Mo'ata had joined the Order and teaming up with him on assignments, Mo'ata did not know much about him. He was always ready with a laugh and had an easy way about him, but when conversation headed into the personal, there was always a reserve, something holding him back from deeper connections. Mo'ata couldn't recall one time Felix had spoken of family or friends back on Cularna.

It had surprised Mo'ata when the mercenary requested to learn English. He suspected the big man would vote to have her come along just for the sake of having her around to tease.

Levi, he knew, would be the most objective. He was dedicated to his purpose and his people. The longer the crystal remained out in the world, the more anxious the Prizzoli became. The few times Mo'ata had asked about it, the other man had just claimed that it was too dangerous. An understatement if he had ever heard one.

Mo'ata threw aside the entrance flap and sat down heavily at the table across from the two men. They looked at him expectantly. Had they been waiting like this the whole time? *Probably.*

Felix was the first to speak. "So, how did it go with the little pet?"

Mo'ata growled. "Don't call her that."

The mercenary laughed. "Why not? She's little and cute and makes you want to take care of her. Loyal, too. Plus, she does not seem to mind the jest."

Mo'ata glared at him and was rewarded with a grin. "That does not help."

Levi rapped his knuckles on the table, grabbing their attention. "What happened?"

"She cashed in one of her coins."

This got another laugh out of Felix. Mo'ata had told him about the "sorry" coins once when they'd been practicing English and Mo'ata had been missing Blue more than usual. Levi just looked puzzled.

"She said that she and Forrest would stay behind, go on to Tremmir and the Academy, if I could honestly tell her that her presence in Filiri would be a liability."

"Then it looks like we have a new plan. I, for one, enjoy the idea of being part of her pretend potential prida."

Mo'ata glared at Felix. He had a feeling he'd be doing a lot of that. "It's not that simple. It puts her in danger. I cannot use her like that again."

"The cover would be useful." The Prizzoli looked thoughtful. "The Filiri region, they can be insular?"

Honesty compelled Mo'ata to answer. "Yes, they can be. They are not unfriendly, but they tend to handle their own affairs. Felix and I have contacts there, though. It will not be a problem." This last was more out of stubbornness; there would be problems gathering enough information, especially for him. The northerners did not deal well with the clans—too much bad blood, though the reasons were mostly forgotten. He sighed. "Actually, me being of the clans will be an issue. Felix would be best to take point once we enter the region."

Levi nodded in acknowledgment. "I think they would be useful." He stretched in his seat. "There is another factor to consider. What if Phillip hears she is back and heads to the capital to find her? From what we've learned, he has a fixation on her. She may be safer with us, even acting as bait. We can keep an eye on her better if she is with us."

Mo'ata stilled. None of that had occurred to him. Damn objectivity had completely flown out the window.

The two sides of him were suddenly in agreement. Blue wasn't leaving his sight. Felix, watching him carefully, was the one who said it. "Looks like the little pet is coming with us."

He sighed. "I told you. Do not call her that."

BLUE

Blue left Mo'ata where he sat, staring at the coin in his hand. Her own thoughts were in turmoil, and she had her own sorting out to do. She didn't understand what he wanted from her. And, unfortunately, they didn't have time to sort it out. He was leaving soon to finish this business with the crystal. Hopefully she and Forrest would be with him. Either way, now was not the time to get caught up and embroiled in melodrama.

She sought out Forrest. He was in their tent section feeding the cubs.

He looked up as she entered. "How'd it go?"

She took a seat on the cot, petting Garfield when he bounded over to her, abandoning his meal. The little ones were barely a couple weeks old. Already, in just the last few days, they had become more mobile, getting into all kinds of mischief. Well, when they weren't sleeping. She picked him up, cradling him against her chest, and felt waves of reassurance coming through their bond.

"This is not going to be nearly as easy as I thought," she murmured.

"You thought this would be easy?"

Her cheeks heated. "Not really. I guess I was just so concentrated on getting here and finding him again that I didn't think enough about *how* this would work. The last few days have been eye-opening, to say the least." She scratched Garfield behind one of his ears, enjoying the little wheezing purr he let out. "I told him that if he honestly thought we would be more hindrance than help, we would head on to the capital and get ourselves sorted with the Ministry and Academy and let him and the others deal with the crystal and Phi."

"You okay with that?"

Was she? "Mostly, but I'll be really disappointed if he decides we shouldn't go with them." She'd be disappointed in more than one way, but she trusted his judgment—and him. They'd made a deal. If Mo'ata really thought she and Forrest would be a liability, then she'd keep working until her skills were such that she could help.

Forrest sat beside her, reaching over to stroke Garfield's nose. Vivi cried out from where she sat at his feet, then started climbing his leg. Forrest grimaced and picked her up. "Little claws." They sat in silence, petting the cubs and enjoying their purrs.

"So," she finally said. "A lot of things were discussed. Apparently I almost accidentally proposed. He said yes."

Forrest snorted. "Told you."

"I'm… not sure I'm ready to go quite that far. Upshot, we're going to date." She needed to be clear on this, make sure everyone was on the same page.

"Is that what it's called now?"

"Please don't make me smack you." She twisted her head and studied his profile. A shaft of light from the setting sun snuck through a gap in the tent's side and slashed over his face, bringing out the golden tones in his skin and hair. They'd need to light the lamps soon, but for now, this was perfect. "That means that we're going to date too, you and me."

A corner of his mouth kicked up, but he didn't look at her. "I know what it means."

"So, we should do date type stuff."

"I need to buy you flowers now?" He finally turned his head.

Was it her imagination, or was that a sheen of sweat on his forehead? "No. Well, flowers are nice, but that's not what I meant."

She stopped thinking about it. Mo'ata had gotten his kiss. It was time to take this next step with Forrest to begin breaking down that self-imposed barrier. And she had to be the one to do it.

She looked into his blue eyes, at that beloved face, and reached up, cupping the back of his neck. His eyes widened as she pulled his head to her. She pressed her lips to his lightly, gently, and again harder.

Forrest froze, then, like a leash had been snapped, he moved. The cubs were forgotten as he pulled her toward him. He fell back, taking her with him. His body felt familiar but new, warm against her hands and chest. He lightly stroked her lips with his tongue, and she parted them, deepening the kiss. When it ended they were both breathing hard.

Forrest's gaze was fixed on her lips. "Finally."

She laughed, somehow even more nervous. "Yeah, finally. I'm sorry."

"You should be," he teased. "Do you know how long I've been wanting to do that?"

A small squeak came from between them where Garfield was being smooshed. Blue laughed and rolled away, taking the cub with her. "We really are doing this, aren't we?"

"Yes." The certainty in his voice reassured her.

"I love you, you know?"

"I know." He gave her a cocky grin, and she snorted.

"Channeling your inner space captain?"

He laughed and gave a little shrug. "Maybe."

She twisted and playfully slapped his chest. Then she placed a soft kiss on his shoulder. She'd taken the first steps. There was still quite a journey ahead of them, but for the first time, instead of hoping, she felt some certainty that she was doing the right thing. No matter how it ended, she was working for what she wanted.

Chapter 5

BLUE

BLUE DISMOUNTED AND STRETCHED, patting Beast. This was only their second day into the trek, but so far she'd been managing well and soreness was minimal. Her riding lessons and practice back on Earth were serving their purpose; she was better at handling the mount and able to go longer in the saddle.

Around her the others also dismounted. Mo'ata hurried to tie up his mount—she'd found out it had no name, a travesty—and set out to find a water source. The route they took was faster, cutting through some of the more difficult trails and into the mountains, but the water sources were scarcer. They carried enough with them for the whole trip, but he said he wanted to replenish every evening if they could.

She stretched a few more times, then led Beast to his

place and secured him to the line, checking that he had the right amount of slack. She stripped off the saddle and blanket and rubbed him down, ensuring he was free of any sweat and caked mud. A proper grooming would have to wait until they reached Firik. Beside them, Forrest tied up his mount—the same one he'd had before, now dubbed Tweety—before moving to help Levi unload the pack animals and set up tents.

Shivering in the cool wind, she moved on to the next mount, hurrying through her assigned task so she could get to the fire and thaw out her limbs. Living in Texas for even a year had ruined her for cold weather, and this terrain certainly called for more layers than she currently wore. Unfortunately, by the time she'd realized she would be traveling through popsicle territory, it was too late to turn back.

In Mo'ata's defense, he had equipped her with the same protections and clothing a clanswoman used. Blue was simply more... delicate when it came to the weather. The irony was not lost on her. *Dammit.*

Before her, the mountains rose. Sparse scrubby trees covered their sides, dying away into a permanent snow cover. The small clearing they were in was one of the few they'd come across with a portion of level ground. It was only going to get more difficult from here. She brushed harder, energized.

By the time she finished, the tents were mostly up and Felix had a fire going, a pot of stew simmering over it. Smiling, she reached for the ladle. "Here, let me." He reached over and scratched behind her ear, just like she would do with Garfield.

She slapped his hand away but laughed. It should bother her, his treating her like this, but she could tell he meant it playfully, and it eased her irritation. He flashed a grin at her and snapped his teeth. *Damn mercenary is going to wear me down.*

A small chirp came from behind him, and Blue's eyes widened. Vivi peeked out from behind the mercenary's head. Felix turned to grab some more wood for the fire. The cub clung to his back, her claws latched onto the armored vest he wore. "Careful of her, the claws get sharp," she said.

Felix twisted and tilted his head back, smiling at the cub, who rubbed her head against his cheek. "I no worry. She nice. And cute. Remind me of you."

The large man had been taking advantage of their new arrangement, saying he needed to practice being a potential priden. He would make comments like that or touch her in passing, her arm, her back. The damn petting. It made Blue nervous and put her off balance; she didn't know how to react. Was he practicing, like he said, or was he serious? She couldn't tell, but sometimes she caught him watching her, a thoughtful look on his face.

"Does Forrest know she's been hanging around you?"

"Yes, he say he need break from her demands, say my turn to take care her." He waggled his eyebrows, so obviously playing with words that Blue couldn't hold her laughter in. "Where Garfield?"

"He's with Mo'ata. I can't tell if it's a good thing or not, but the little guy has adopted him. He rode with him all day today."

"Ahhh, I wondering why Mo'ata look so… pain."

"Sharp claws." Blue had the scratches to prove it. She studied the mercenary's armor. It looked like cloth but had to be far stronger. "Maybe I should get a vest like yours."

He nodded. "It help, yes. I get for you. Good protection. Has same... metal? Same metal use for ships."

"Ships?" She gave the stew another stir.

"Yes. Cularna have ships in space, trade and travel. Only Karran trade through portals. If we not want use, have ships."

"There really are spaceships?" *Wait till I tell Forrest.* "I was starting to think the portals were all there was. I mean, it makes sense. There are ray guns and fancy armor and floating walkways..."

"Hah! No, Ministry want think that. Not true. Cularna and Martika trade very long time, no portals. Use ships." He snorted. "Take longer, yes, but no fee."

"Huh." And another piece of the puzzle that was this universe presented itself, dropping into place. What did the spaceships look like? How did they work? Was it like Star Trek and those other sci-fi shows? "So, do you have FTL?"

"What?"

"Faster Than Light Travel?"

"No faster.... I no have words." His eyes went big, and his head bobbed. "I show, yes? I take on ship when done. You see. You like." He indicated Forrest and Levi. "We take all. They like too."

"Really? Yes, oh yes. I would love that. Forrest would love that. Mo'ata could come, right?"

He nodded, his grin firmly in place. After a moment, he jerked and stepped back, the grin slipping away. "I help with tent. Stay food."

She gazed after him. That was different. He'd seemed almost... afraid. She couldn't really think of the mercenary that way, but something was definitely off.

A swift breeze blew, and she shivered. She moved closer to the fire, absorbing its warmth as she stirred their dinner. A warm weight dropped over her shoulders, and she looked up.

Levi had given her his coat, the dark, silky cloth heavy and warm around her. He nodded and squeezed her shoulder before moving back to finish setting up the tents. They'd still not spoken, not really. All their interactions were silent. Despite this, there was a connection to this man who had once saved her.

She watched as he worked, noting his smooth movements, the controlled grace. It was the same economy of movement he had shown when fighting, the same deliberate motions in everything he did. *It's beautiful.* Blood rushed to her cheeks, and she ducked her head. *Don't get carried away, girl, you're just pretending with him and Felix. Concentrate on Forrest and Mo'ata.*

Blue looked back at the stew, concentrating on stirring it. By the time it was done, Mo'ata had returned, canteens filled, and the tents were up. They gathered around the fire and ate.

"How much longer until we get there? Also, is there a plan?" She took another bite of the stew, almost reveling in the warmth as it settled in her belly.

Mo'ata eyed Levi's coat still wrapped around her. She had no idea how the other man wasn't a popsicle by now. "I think the first action is to get everyone some appropriate clothing."

"Everyone meaning me," she said.

"Maybe." He sent a small smile her way. "The north can be brutal, for anyone." Mo'ata set his bowl down. "The next thing is to get you in touch with any relatives of your father's. If we are using that as a cover story, we need to follow through on it and we need to do it properly."

That made sense. And she did want to try to find any of her father's relatives if she could. She'd been trying to remember anything the Dean had said, but all she remembered was that her grandparents were dead. "I don't know where to start with that. Dean Gravin only said he was from the Filiri region."

"There are places to search public records. Actually, Felix has a contact at the guards he says will help us. We'll do that first. If needed, we'll even visit your relatives, if we find any; keep up our cover. And we'll take advantage of the search to look around more." Mo'ata took her hand, concerned. "The people of Filiri can be closed and distant with strangers. I don't want you to be hurt if your family does not take you in."

"We might not even find anyone." With everything going on, thoughts of how she would handle meeting any family members had been pushed back. Way back. Now, she wondered. Would they find any relatives? How would they treat her? What would they be like? As Mo'ata had said, would they even want to see her? Had her father ever tried to visit them, despite his promises to the Ministry? Had he missed them? When she'd asked about them as a child, he'd just said they had died and he missed them, but that was it. "Besides," she continued, "I have a family." She squeezed his hand and shot a smile at Forrest. "It would be good to know more about where my father came from," she admitted.

"You should know, the Filiri region can be a harsh place, and not only the climate. They do not take well to outsiders. And there is a… prejudice against the clans. We are considered… brutal."

Something about that… "The clans of the North?"

Mo'ata released her hand and sat back. "The Mamanna spoke of this?" His gaze wandered to Vivi, perched on Felix's shoulder. "When the Ministry was established and trade became more regular with the other worlds, they changed. It is a harsh environment, the north. Food is hard to grow, and they always struggled. Gradually, they embraced technology and concentrated on manufacturing." He shrugged. "It was a smart move. Most goods are produced in the region, and it keeps the fertile lands of the south free to provide food."

He grimaced and shifted to pull Garfield off his back, setting the cub on the ground before him. The little guy promptly started climbing his leg, and Blue laughed. She could feel the playful mischief coming off Garfield; the cub knew exactly what he was doing. Sighing, Mo'ata picked the cub up, scratching behind his neck.

"It sounds like a good system," Forrest said. "I don't see the problem. The ones at—the ones at the Ministry didn't seem so bad."

Mo'ata opened his mouth and closed it a few times, as if struggling for the right words. "They are not bad. But they are… insular? For them, it is an honor to join the Ministry, to help their people in such a way. They recognize sacrifice as honorable. And they are not unfriendly, but once you enter their homeland, they tend to close ranks."

"Like the sibling you love to beat up, but if anyone else tries, they're going down," Forrest said.

"It is as good a comparison as any."

Blue shot him a teasing look. "So, it really is an advantage for me to be here."

Mo'ata's face colored, but he met her gaze. "Yes."

"So, I am looking for my family after I accidentally came through a portal and learned that my father was originally from Filiri. You are all my potential priden whom I met when I first came through a month ago. Will we include that I went back? About the rest of what happened?"

Mo'ata and Felix looked thoughtful. Levi said something in Common. Mo'ata nodded and translated. "He said he needs to start learning English, or we need to switch to Common. It is too hard."

Blue glanced at Forrest who shrugged. "We Common," she tried, then switched to English. "Except when I get too frustrated, and then I'm switching to English and you'll just have to translate."

"We'll stick to English for a bit more, let you learn more Common. Eventually, though, it would be best to switch to Common fully. Levi understands some of what we say, and I will fill him in when needed." Mo'ata turned to Levi and spoke for a full minute in Common, Felix interjecting every so often. Levi responded, and Blue could make out a few words, enough to realize he was agreeing that they should stick to the truth as much as possible.

Mo'ata confirmed that. "Yes, we will need to say that you returned to Earth but came back. You may even tell them of the time distortion. It will be more believable than anything else, and the authorities there will be able to check your story with the Ministry. It will alert them that you have returned," he cautioned.

Blue shrugged. "I was going to go to them eventually. I do need to learn to control this portal-space thing." She let out a short laugh. "I don't even know what you call it."

"Most just refer to it as 'ability.' I don't know of a name other than that."

"Okay. I have the 'ability' and returned to Karran to learn to use it and to find my priden, whom I had met when I accidentally came through before. All of you helped us when me and my friends were attacked. Should we mention the kidnappings?"

"They are not unknown. Just do not bring up the crystals or Phillip."

"All right. Is there anything else we need to be aware of? How the town is laid out? Patrolling? Strategies for searching for Phillip or Etu?"

Face blank, Mo'ata placed Garfield in her lap. "I agreed that you and Forrest would accompany us because it gave us a valid reason to be there. Also, so I could keep an eye on you, ensure you were safe. For you there will be no patrolling or searching. Is that clear?"

Blue swallowed and nodded. It was clear. "Baby steps, huh?"

"When you've been through years of training, speak the language, and I am assured you can survive an attack like the one in Tremmir on your own, then we will revisit allowing you on a patrol." The words were said calmly, but there was an underlying tension.

Yup, baby steps were going to be the way to go. "Guess I should put that on my List, huh?"

Blue's shivers had graduated to shudders. She burrowed deeper into her blankets, trying to gain a little more warmth. The nights really *were* bitter here in the mountains. Garfield curled against her back, and it helped, but the little cub was too small to provide much body heat.

She pulled her feet in closer to her center, and an image of Mo'ata's solid, muscled frame popped into her head.

Muscles were warm, so why was she still in her own tent? Wasn't she supposed to be working on getting to know them, getting more comfortable with the idea of a real relationship with Mo'ata and Forrest? *And wouldn't that include cuddling for warmth?* Plus, she didn't like how things had been left earlier.

Decided, she threw off her covers, shoved her feet in her boots, and grabbed Garfield before sprinting out of her tent. She rushed into Mo'ata's tent where it had been set up on the other side of the fire. The mountain of warmth lay on his padded mat, only half-covered by his blankets.

She kicked her boots off and dove down beside him, burrowing into his side.

He jerked, flipped her onto her back, and pinned her down, his hands strong on her wrists, his legs locked around hers, holding her immobile. His hair hung down like a curtain around them, brushing her ear. She stilled.

He blinked, his eyes barely focusing on her face. "Blue?"

"Hi." Her voice came out as a squeak, and she cleared her throat. An answering cry came from the piquet cub now partially squashed under her right side.

"What are you doing?" He sounded rough from sleep.

She cleared her throat. "I was cold."

"Oh."

"Do you think you could let me go?" She gave him a small smile and wriggled her fingers.

Mo'ata looked to where he held her wrists and blinked again. He gently released her and shifted off her legs, moving to her side. She turned to him and smiled. "I figured that since you were built of muscle you would be warm, and I was cold. So."

"So?" She really must have brought him out of a deep sleep; he wasn't being very quick on the uptake.

"So, I came to cuddle. It's the sort of thing couples do."

His gaze sharpened. "Is that so?"

"Yup." She grinned and moved closer, tucking her feet in against his calves. He flinched but didn't draw away. He slid one of his arms around her waist, drawing her in until she was nestled in and definitely getting warmer.

"Ouch." Mo'ata jerked, pulling his arm off her.

Garfield had worked his way to her back, and now the cub wanted his usual spot. It was right where Mo'ata's hand had been. She gave a low laugh and nudged his arm until he finally put it back around her, this time lower, around her hip.

"Now what?" This close to him his voice traveled through her whole body.

"Now we cuddle and talk about earlier. Or, if that horse is dead, we just cuddle."

"I know English, but sometimes the things you say make no sense to me." His thumb caressed her hipbone through her pajama pants.

"Yeah, English is weird, even for us native speakers. Ummm... beating a dead horse is when you keep doing something or working on something even though it's a waste of time."

His silence stretched out.

"So, if you want to talk, we can do that. But if there isn't anything to say, we skip that part and go straight for the cuddling. Actually, the cuddling can happen even when we talk; they aren't mutually exclusive." She wiggled her toes, which were getting nice and toasty.

"The horse is not dead, but it is very much asleep." His chest rose and fell beneath her cheek. "Maybe we can follow its example and then try beating it later? I am not sure it would feel the blows at this moment."

Her shoulders shaking with silent giggles, Blue nodded. *Who knew the serious clansman had such a sense of humor?* She caught her breath and answered. "Okay, we'll flog the horse later, when it can feel it." She dissolved into laughter, her whole body shaking.

Oh, she'd needed this.

FELIX

Felix stepped out of the tree line, drawn to the laughter coming from Mo'ata's tent.

Blue.

Damn, there was something about that girl. Woman, now. Not many had the guts to tease him like she had. And most of those who did would have opted for hitting him instead of playing. Their first encounter was practically burned into his memory. How could something as simple as a snap of teeth have such an impact?

She'd changed. The girl he'd met had been playful, caring and concerned for her friends, and sensible. She was all of those things still, but now she was coming into her own, pushing for what she wanted. She'd come back to this place after everything that had happened.

He wished…

He shied from the thought. He didn't wish anything. He was here on assignment. One The Order had extended when they'd learned of the crystals and their ramifications. He was just glad he wasn't the one who would have to deal with the Prizzoli after this. According to Levi, they had not been pleased by their agent's failure to secure the last crystal.

And when this assignment was done, there would be another. In another place, and most likely another world. No, he did not wish.

Part of him wanted to, he admitted. He had asked Mo'ata to teach him English on a whim. Something in the man's eye when he spoke of her woke an old ambition. It was one he had fought for many years, and he had yet to defeat. A desire for someone he could care for that would care for him in return, for himself and no other reason.

He'd thought he had that once.

Another giggle came from the tent, followed by a low rumble. The rest of the clearing was silent, and the sound carried. He wondered if Forrest lay awake listening. If he was truly satisfied with her split affections.

He scooped up a chunk of wood and pulled out a small knife. It wasn't a proper whittling knife, but it would have to do. He needed something to calm his mind. Keeping his senses open, he stationed himself as far from the tents as he could get while still keeping them in sight and let his hands do what they would.

He would simply enjoy her while he could, even if all he ever got was teasing banter and light smacks. Culan's bones, it wasn't as if he disliked it. He'd put on his smile, the one that came so easily around her, and they'd pretend. But he wouldn't let it go further than that, and he wouldn't let himself forget it was an act. Even when he'd somehow offered to take her exploring on a spaceship. *Maybe it's the eyes…*

A nightbird called out, warning other predators off of its prey. His hand jerked, nicking a finger. He looked down.

The carving was rough, but he could already see what it would become. He brushed a thumb over it, trying to remove a drop of blood from where it had fallen on a delicate cheek, but he only smeared it in.

No matter. He could always to do another. Not that he would get rid of this one. He smoothed his thumbed over her cheek again. Maybe he *would* let himself hope. Maybe he could take the pretend and make it real.

Chapter 6

BLUE

BLUE PULLED Beast to a halt and studied the city laid out before her. Partly cradled in a small crescent of mountains, it sprawled out from there over a flat plain broken only by short, scrubby trees.

Mo'ata hadn't been kidding when he'd called this area bleak. Everything about it was stark, from the abrupt transition of mountain to plain, to the city itself. Large areas spread out like dark stains. There were massive warehouses and manufacturing plants, some with smokestacks that spit out dirty residue.

Forrest pulled up beside her. "You'd think they would have better technology than this. Seems backward, spitting out crap like that into the air while others have spaceships."

She shrugged, but agreed. The only thing beautiful about this place was the curve of bright blue sky.

Mo'ata, Garfield perched on his shoulder, urged his mount down the trail leading to the city. There was no wall, unlike Tremmir, nor entrance gate and guards. Blue and the others followed after him, silent. Something about this city did not encourage levity or chatter.

As they drew closer, a new area came into view. Nestled under the shelter of a mountain were buildings that shone in the sun like a beacon. Bright, almost white, they were as intimidating as the warehouse area as they climbed partly up the mountain face. She craned her neck and could just make out areas of green. Someone had put some work and money into this area.

Other differences became apparent. Some of the dark areas were apartment blocks; some were shops. Everything closer to the mountains had a lighter, cleaner air, while farther out on the plane everything took on a rundown cast, people included. Most hurried, hunched, from one building to the next or into transports large enough to accommodate dozens at a time.

Not so different from Earth.

They hit a dip in the path, and her view was blocked. Half an hour later they hit the first rows of buildings, these some of the nicer apartments. Silently, Mo'ata passed Garfield to her, and she tucked him into his spot, a little pouch they'd set up in one of the saddlebags, where he could be out of sight and warm. She sent a little admonishing thought in his direction and hoped he listened. No need to attract trouble right away.

She gave it two hours before the cubs were causing a ruckus.

They entered the city, and she couldn't help but note

the differences between it and Tremmir. The capital had been busy and chaotic, colorful and boisterous. This place was busy, yes, but there were no shouted calls from hawking vendors, no different and colorful clothes or animals. In fact, she didn't see one other person on a mount.

Felix took the lead as they wound their way along the streets. According to Mo'ata, the inn they headed for was fairly tolerant of clansmen and had a small stable that could accommodate the quorin. The deeper into the city they got, the heavier the air became, and the more the blue sky was obscured in a gray haze. They also attracted quite a few side-eyed looks, but most people continued on their own way in deliberate inattention.

The inn itself was fairly deep into the city, at the edge of the warehouse district. Felix dismounted and entered, returning soon with a large man with graying hair and a solid build. He headed for a small alley to the side of the building, gesturing for them to follow. It led to a good-sized yard and shed that obviously used to be a smaller storehouse but had been converted to stalls.

Blue dismounted along with the others, leading Beast to his home for what would hopefully be only a week or so. He balked a bit at the door to his stall, and she turned to him. "What?" He craned his head over her, eying his new quarters, and let out a huffing breath. "Did you just sigh at me?"

Beast nudged her out of the way and entered, circled a few times, and then gave her a look that clearly said, *Well, grab a brush would you?*

Garfield, still in his little nest, let out a short chirp,

agreeing with Beast. The two of them had taken to teaming up together to give her trouble. Blue could feel the teasing impatience coming from the little cub. It seemed every day he matured—not just physically, but the emotions she got from him had become more and more complicated and intricate. She couldn't keep up. Not even two weeks ago he'd first opened his eyes, and now he acted like an impish five-year-old.

"They giving you trouble?" Forrest moved to her side, Vivi cradled in his arms.

"Yes." Blue pouted but couldn't keep up the expression. She thought her two animal babies were adorable. Well, Beast was more of a grumpy old man. She grinned at the old *quorin*. "Yes, I'll give you a good brushing," she told him. The demon mount flicked an ear at her.

Blue laughed at him. Damn, she'd missed her Beast.

Setting her pack down, she went in search of the grooming tools. The others had beat her to them, and Felix handed her a brush. They set to, giving their mounts a well-needed grooming and rub down. Just as they finished, a young man entered the makeshift stables with buckets of grain. Beast shuffled and sniffed the air, shouldering her aside to go stick his nose in his feed bucket, chuffing when he found it empty. As the young man reached him, he chuffed again, violently, causing the boy to jump and edge away. Blue sighed and walked around the stall door, taking the bucket from the boy and feeding Beast.

"Behave," she said. He ignored her.

"Come on, let's get inside and get some food in us.

And thaw. I swear, living in Texas does not prepare you for enduring cold weather." Forrest threw his arm over her shoulders and grabbed her pack, leading her to where the others were waiting at the entrance of the stable. They moved as a group to the rear door of the inn. Warmth and the low sound of voices rushed over Blue as they crossed the threshold. She breathed in the rich smell of bread, meat, and some sort of roasting vegetable.

"Stew?" She bounced a little on her feet.

Felix laughed. They'd had stew for almost every meal while on the road, and Blue had loved it each time. She didn't know what it was about the dish and how it was made here on Karran, but it was fast becoming her favorite.

Felix and Mo'ata headed to an unoccupied table in the corner, and Blue followed, Forrest and Levi bringing up the rear. They settled, Forrest to her left and the others arranged across from her. She loosened the straps on Garfield's pouch and set him under the table next to Vivi. There was a light tug on her boot, and she peeked down. The little devil was chewing on her bootlaces.

A server headed over, asking something in Common. Blue had continued practicing with Felix, and she got enough to know the woman was asking what they wanted to eat.

"Stew," she said in Common, hoping she used the correct word. The woman nodded, and Blue smiled.

Mo'ata caught her eye and shook his head. "I don't know if you'll like the stew here. It's a little different from the clans'."

"What about at the inn in the capital? That was stew, and it was just the same."

"That innkeeper used a recipe I'd traded him a few years back, one that the clans use. So of course it was similar."

"Darn."

Mo'ata smiled, and Felix laughed again. Forrest gave her a little side hug. Levi didn't react, but he was only just beginning to learn English. She caught his eye, saw that rare softness on his features, and smiled at him.

"So, do we go see the guards next? Felix's contacts? Or do we try to see if there is anything new about Phi…" At Mo'ata's quick headshake, she let her words trail off. Message received—don't talk about Phillip or the crystal in the open. She really needed to move spy school higher on the List, though that rule should've been pretty damn obvious.

"I know guard in—" Felix broke off and turned to Mo'ata, speaking quickly in Common.

Mo'ata took over. "His friend is with the Mountainside Guards. She's who we'll check with first. Hopefully she agrees to help us access records about your father."

Blue's eyes widened. "Is it not allowed? Why would she not agree?"

"No, is allowed. Easy this way, less waste time. She help us get name, find city in," Felix said.

"So, they may not be *here*."

"If there is any of your father's family left, they are probably here. It is the major city in the region. Many of its… upper families have those who choose to work in the Ministry in one fashion or another," Mo'ata said.

They were interrupted as the server returned, setting bowls of steaming… something in front of the group, along with a plate of bread and a handful of cutlery. Blue cautiously sniffed what was in the bowl and let out a sigh of relief. It didn't smell bad; it just *looked* like something her mother would have cobbled together and then called stew. She grabbed a spoon and dipped it into the bowl, taking a cautious bite.

Oooh, it was good. Heavier and earthier than the clan's, it was satisfying. She dug in. The men chuckled, and she realized they had watched, waiting for her reaction.

"It is different, but it's still good. It does look a little like something my mom would make, though," she said between bites.

Forrest laughed. "Yeah. Anything Brenda makes looks like this, even if it's scrambled eggs."

Blue just shrugged. It was true. She continued eating, using the bread to scrape up the last bit of gravy from the sides of the bowl. Done, she leaned back. Once again, all eyes were fixed on her. "I was hungry."

This earned another chuckled from Felix and a smile from Mo'ata before they turned back to their food. Blue took the time to study them again. These men were, each in their own ways, incredible.

Forrest—who had stood by her for the last year, helping her overcome her guilt and just generally being there. He'd never grown impatient with her, never pushed her; he understood that she needed to explore the possibilities awaiting on Karran and had never once made her feel bad for it. He took her for who she was. She was still apprehensive about how it would work trying to have a relationship with more than one person, but she wasn't going to let it get in her way.

She turned her attention to Mo'ata. He had made a promise to help with the crystals, and he was going to follow through with it. He'd made that promise because of her. It overwhelmed her, the fact that he'd made that promise so soon after meeting her. She didn't want to disappoint him and was a little afraid he may still change his mind after he got to know her better. He said he wouldn't, but could you really decide about a person after knowing them for a week? *And isn't that just what you did?* Yes, she saw the irony.

Then there were Felix and Levi. She still didn't know much about them, but she was beginning to learn. Felix was part of the Order, undercover as a mercenary. Though she didn't know much of the Order, she knew it was about helping people. She was also really coming to appreciate his ability and willingness to laugh and see the humor in things. She suspected he would be one of those people who laughed in the movie theater when no one else was.

Levi was even more of a mystery, but his determination to see his duty through for his people told her that when he made a commitment, he stuck to it. He was also the gentlest of the four, despite the harsh cast of his features and the deadly grace he exhibited when he fought.

It was only a few more moments until the guys were all pushing their bowls back or finishing off the last of the bread. Felix signaled the server, who came back over. They spoke for just a moment, and then the woman was off, back a few seconds later with five mugs.

"What is this?" Blue picked hers up and cautiously sniffed it. It was sour, but there was also a rich, almost buttery, scent. She took another sniff. Almost like... "Beer?"

"I do not know what beer is," Mo'ata said.

Blue shot him a look. *Really?* "It's an alcoholic drink made from grains. I don't remember the process— something about fermentation, I think. I'm too young to drink it, though."

Forrest snorted. "You just don't like it. The one time I got her to try a sip she nearly spit it out," he continued, directing the last to Mo'ata. "The face she made was priceless." He nudged her arm. "Come on, give it a try. You might like this one."

"You just want to see me drunk." Blue took another sniff. It didn't smell *that* bad, certainly better than the swill Forrest had convinced her to try once.

"Well, yes."

MO'ATA

Mo'ata watched the interaction between Blue and Forrest. There was a level of intimacy, not physical, but they knew each other so well. Something stirred in him. *Jealousy?* Maybe, but it wasn't of Forrest; it was more of the time Forrest had been able to spend with her. He was still struggling with the idea that it had been a *year* for them, while so little time had passed on Karran. Not the time jump, that was common enough. No, it was the fact he'd missed so much of her life. In a way it was reassuring. It had been a year, and she still came back. She said it wasn't just for him, but it was at least partly for him.

As he watched, Forrest teased her into taking a sip of the foka. Yes, there was some alcohol, but only enough to relax. It was not strong at all.

Blue, wearing an expression of mixed laughter and suspicion, sniffed the mug one more time before taking a cautious sip. She didn't spit it out, but as Forrest had said, her expression was something to remember. A grimace crossed her lips, and she gagged, just a little, her eyes watering.

They all laughed, even Levi. Felix, he knew, had been following the conversation. Levi had picked up some English and usually understood enough to at least grasp the situation. Sometimes he seemed to grasp more than the words. Mo'ata wondered if there was more to the Prizzoli as a people than the Order or Alliance had been told.

"Yeah, yeah, laugh it up." She grabbed a small piece of bread from the plate the server had left and quickly chewed. "Well, it was better than the other stuff I tried. I'm beginning to think I just don't like alcohol."

Everyone else picked up their own mugs, sipping. Mo'ata himself enjoyed a good foka now and then, and Firik had some of the best.

The nuts used to brew it were from trees only found high in the mountains, and when gathered in the cold of winter, they produced that hint of butter. The clans often made their own, but it never had this richness of flavor.

He took another sip and contemplated their next steps. Tomorrow Felix would arrange to take Blue to his contact, and they would go from there. It would be a good opportunity to learn about the recent deaths in the city; he just hoped that Blue, as the daughter of someone from the region, would be able to get the guards and other townspeople to open up. He admitted it was a good idea, using her to help them gather information. People tended to open up to her.

The foka started to do its work, and he relaxed, the tension running out of his shoulders. Their table settled into silence, each of them lost in their own thoughts.

"Can I get some water?" Blue's voice broke into his musings.

"Of course. I should have thought of it." Chagrined, he signaled the server. He could not believe he had neglected her care like that. If she would not drink the foka, of course she needed something else. It was a little thing, but the care of a shopa was paramount, and already he was failing.

When the server returned, Blue took the mug from her and thanked her in Common. The woman smiled back at her and nodded. Blue sipped her water, studying the people around her. It was something he'd noticed about her. Unless she got nervous, she didn't really feel the need to speak.

They took their time, sipping and relaxing, enjoying the respite before having to be back at it again in the morning. Finally, he saw Blue's eyes droop and knew they needed to get her to bed. Beside her, Forrest wasn't in much better shape. Mo'ata laughed a bit to himself. The young man was growing on him, becoming like a little brother. It was a good sign; they just may be able to pull off this prida.

"Come on, little shopa, let us get you to bed." He rose and came around the table. She smiled and nodded, stumbling just a little when she stood and the chair leg caught on the floor. She really was tired. He held her side lightly, more of a precaution than anything. Felix rose and went in search of the innkeeper. He returned shortly with the keys to their rooms. There were only three of them.

"Felix?"

The larger man shrugged. "He only have three rooms." A frustrated look crossed his face and he switched to Common. "Luckily, two of them have a connecting door. And we only got that because the previous occupants left in a rush earlier today. He didn't come right out and say it, but I think they were here on business and got wind of the recent deaths. I will see what I can get out of him later, after the rest of you get to bed."

Mo'ata nodded. "We'll put Blue in one of the connecting rooms. Forrest and I will take the other. You and Levi can share the third."

Blue nudged his side. He looked down to see her "tell me what you are talking about" expression, the one she got when she was frustrated at not yet knowing enough Common to keep up with their conversations. "We were only able to get three rooms, but two of them are connecting. You will take one and Forrest and I the other," he told her, switching to English.

"Like before. Okay." A large yawn overtook her, and she covered her mouth, shaking just a bit with the force of it.

He guided her up the stairs, following behind Felix. Forrest had her pack and came right behind them, Levi bringing up the rear. Felix stopped outside a door near the end of the upper hall and opened it using one of the keys before handing it to Blue. "This yours."

Blue nodded, took the key, and entered the room. Forrest entered behind her and placed her pack on the bed, a small, insistent squeak coming from within.

"Oh no." Blue rushed to the pack and flipped open the compartment she'd made for the little piquet. Garfield poked his head out and let out a loud yowl. "How could I have forgotten to feed them?" Her face held worry and not a little dismay.

Mo'ata moved into the room and scooped up the little pest. He didn't really think the piquet cub was a pest, but sometimes, like when Blue came to cuddle, he wished Garfield didn't want to be so involved.

"I will be sure he gets food. You rest." The cub climbed up his chest, his little claws pricking, and to Mo'ata's shoulder, perching there and surveying the room. Vivi chose then to let out her own yowl, and Forrest gathered her close, laughing.

"I take." Felix reached out for her. "You stay with Blue. No alone." He indicated the connecting door with his head, hands full with the cub, who was now wiggling, trying to get to his shoulder as well. With a huge sigh and small smile, he plopped her on his left shoulder, his armor protecting his skin from her claws.

Mo'ata started to turn away but stopped. He was forgetting something.

He turned back to Blue and leaned down, one hand steadying the cub on his shoulder, the other under her chin, tipping her head up to him. He leaned down and gave her a small, lingering kiss. There, that was better. "Sleep well, shopa. I will see you in the morning."

The slightly dazed look in her eyes was satisfying. "Knocking," she mumbled, and he smiled, remembering another morning when she had walked in on him.

"It's okay if you do not," he teased, sending her a wink and eliciting a smile.

Forrest gave a little cough from behind her and mumbled something that sounded like "in my dreams."

Yes, Mo'ata agreed. There had been dreams. After a last caress of her cheek, he left to get the cubs fed, Felix close behind him. They made a brief stop at the last room, across from Blue's, to let Levi drop off his own things, then the three of them returned to the dining area. As they entered, a hush fell, all eyes on the cubs.

The innkeeper hurried to them, careful to stop a few feet away, his eyes bouncing between Vivi and Garfield. That the man recognized them as a worse threat than the clansman or mercenary showed his good sense. He knew what these were.

"How may I help you?" the innkeeper finally got out after a couple of false starts.

Mo'ata remained silent, letting Felix take the lead. "We require food for the little ones. Milk is fine for now, but if you have some small portions of meat available, we would not turn it down."

Mo'ata almost smiled at hearing the larger man speak so eloquently. He held his stern expression, though, letting Felix play his little game.

The innkeeper almost bowed. "Of course, sir, of course. Shall I have it brought to your rooms?" His licked his lips, eyes never straying from the cubs, who had started to make their small squeaking cries, the ones that said "feed me."

"No." Felix's voice was sharp, causing the innkeeper to jump. "We will feed them here. Our shopa has had a hard journey, and we do not want to disturb her."

The poor innkeeper's eyes widened at his words—whether from the mercenary calling Blue his shopa a clan term, or from the knowledge that the cubs would be in the common room while they ate, Mo'ata wasn't sure, but it was amusing. The mercenary had a wicked sense of humor sometimes.

"Your...your shopa?"

"Yes. Her father was originally from this area. We are searching for any family she may have left. Otherwise..." he trailed off, his gaze running over the room, a slight disdain on his features. Mo'ata swallowed and pursed his lips, suppressing a laugh. "The food?" Felix continued, one brow raised.

"Of course, of course. Please sit. We will bring it out." He gestured to the table they had been at earlier, still empty. A server rushed off for the milk after a glare from the innkeeper. "Do you know her family name? Maybe I could be of assistance? I know many of the families in the area."

Mo'ata studied the man. It seemed safe enough.

"Faust." At his words the older man stilled and his eyes widened, swinging to Mo'ata. "I see. Well, I wish you luck with the search. Your food will be here shortly." He hurried away and out of sight, into the back where the kitchens were.

"Anyone else think he just ran away to avoid answering questions?" Felix sat, reaching up to remove Vivi from his shoulder and set her on the table.

"Oh yes. Although I was surprised he asked in the first place, from what you have said about the people of this region." The Prizzoli reached out to stroke Vivi's head, and she swatted at his fingers, though her claws remained sheathed.

"He's known to be a little friendlier than others. If I remember correctly, his mother was originally from the Torman clan. It was a great surprise to all when she chose to leave her clan and come to Filiri with a man she met on a trading trip to the capital." Mo'ata shifted, impatient. He wanted to question the man.

"I'll see what I can get out of him tomorrow," Felix said, and Mo'ata relaxed.

The server returned then with the milk and meat they had ordered, and the cubs fell to it. *Yes, tomorrow is going to be a busy day.*

Chapter 7

BLUE

BLUE WAS NERVOUS. She hadn't expected to be, but the idea of finding more, new family had her stomach twisting in a mixture of fear and anticipation.

A trim, dark-haired woman sat across from her, the low table between them spread with papers, cups, and other debris. A screen perched to one side with a flat pad in front of it. Maybe their version of a computer?

When they'd come to the guards' office that morning, she hadn't known what to expect. She had envisioned something similar to what the Ministry had, with the reception desk and individual interview rooms. Well, this had the reception, but the offices here were open, like in the cop shows her mom enjoyed. There were tables and desks scattered around and people calling out and rushing back and forth, the general chaos and clutter almost comforting.

Felix's friend, he'd introduced her as Sora, had met them at the entrance. Blue had been surprised to learn the woman spoke English. She'd thought only clansmen and some Ministry spoke it as part of their jobs. It made Blue wonder just who she was.

After the introductions she'd led them all back to where they now sat. Just as people had on the streets, everyone they passed openly stared, some glaring, others stepping back out of fear when the piquet cubs made themselves known. Sora had been the rare exception, simply smiling as she led them back to what passed for her desk.

"So," she said now. "Felix tells me that you are looking for your family." The woman eyed her, not unfriendly, more speculative.

"Yes." Blue knew she was supposed to tell her story, but for some reason she was reluctant to share with this stranger.

"He also tells me he has entered into a trial period with your prida."

The skepticism in her voice caused Blue to fidget, and she had to consciously still her fingers. "Yes, well, it's more like dating. Maybe that's the same thing. I don't know. We're... getting to know each other." Blue glanced at Felix where he sat beside her, his large frame barely fitting in the chair. "He helped me out a lot a ye—couple months ago. He's a good man," she said, turning back to Sora.

Blue felt a light touch on her hair. "Please stop petting me. I *will* bite you." Her voice came out as threatening as she could make it, but the mercenary just laughed.

Sora watched this interplay closely, then nodded, coming to some sort of decision. "I will do what I can to help you find your family. Now, tell me what you know."

Blue launched into her story, not stopping or letting herself think, only leaving out the parts having to do with the crystal and what had happened to Phillip. She really hadn't talked about this much; most everyone she *could* talk to had lived through it themselves. It was hard to run through it all, but Sora turned out to be a good listener and saved her questions for the end.

"You say your father's name was David Faust? I know of some Fausts, but there is no guarantee you are related. I never heard of one of their family running off to a closed world. A tale like that would definitely be gossiped about. We may not look it, but we Filiri do love our gossip." Blue wasn't sure she believed the woman. As soon as she'd mentioned her father's name, Sora's expression had become guarded. She'd recovered her air of mild interest quickly, but a hint of wariness remained.

"You can search for him, though, right? Or any connections?" She didn't have to fake the eagerness in her voice, or the nervousness.

"She search. She say would," Felix broke in, sending a frown to his friend when she hesitated.

Sora glanced at him, one of her brows raised. "You are learning English?" There was an odd note in her voice that Blue couldn't quite place.

"Yes." Felix didn't say anything else, just stared at her until Sora turned to the screen and, after pushing a few papers out of the way, tapped the pad a few times, then the screen itself. Lettering and characters Blue didn't know scrolled by, and she realized that, in addition to learning a new spoken language, she was going to need to learn a whole new written language as well. Why it hadn't occurred to her before, she didn't know, but she wasn't looking forward to it. She heard a groan, looked over to see Forrest watching the screen, and knew the same thing had occurred to him.

He looked over at her. "Think we can skip it?"

"No, Unfortunately."

Sora cleared her throat, pulling their attention back to her. She frowned, looking between Blue and the screen, where a picture of her father was displayed. "Is this your father?"

Blue stared. It really was him. Younger, with none of the smile lines he'd always had, but it was him. Her throat tightened. "Yes." The word came out garbled, and she swallowed. "Wow, that was fast." Her heart pounded, and anticipation coursed through her.

Sora's lips thinned, and a frown marred her brow.

"What is it?" Blue's enthusiasm took a dive seeing the other woman's expression.

Sora still hesitated. "Tell." Felix's voice was hard, and she flinched.

"It appears he did have some family, distant cousins of some kind, and they live in the area. Brendan and Dorani Faust." Her voice was guarded, and her eyes wouldn't meet Blue's. "I don't know that I would approach them, though."

"Why not?" Blue was frustrated. She understood that these people didn't like to share, but she had just found out that she had family she'd never known about, that she had a chance to learn more about the father she'd apparently not really known. Plus, she really hated cryptic, useless hints.

"There was a recent death. Their daughter."

Shame washed over her at Sora's words but Blue pushed it aside. Now was not the time to dwell on that. She also didn't fail to notice the new note of tension in Sora's voice.

"What happened?" Apparently Mo'ata didn't miss it either, and his voice came out sharp.

Sora crossed her arms and leaned back her chair, face completely closed. Everything about her posture said she was done helping.

Felix sat forward and spoke quickly in Common, pulling Sora's attention back to him. As he continued, her expression softened. Shooting one last glare at Mo'ata, who had kept silent through this, she sat forward again and rubbed her brow.

"Please?" Blue softened her voice. "I know I don't know them yet, but they are my family." She had a feeling that whatever the guard was reluctant to tell them was important.

"I don't like telling you this, for various reasons, but I guess you should know. None of this is something you couldn't find out by visiting the records," Sora finally relented. "There have been attacks through the city. We found the first body about four weeks ago. Most have been isolated to a particular warehouse district, workers and a few homeless. Two weeks ago, Gabriella Faust's body was found in an alley in one of the better shopping districts."

"What—" Blue swallowed. "What happened to her?" This must be the deaths tied to Phillip and the crystal. Though she was glad to find information and a connection they could follow up on so quickly, she regretted it had affected her father's family.

"I cannot discuss that with you." Sora's expression softened, but her voice was firm. "I will tell you to avoid the area around the outer warehouses. There is no reason you should need to go there, but just be safe."

"Thank you." Blue hesitated, unsure if she should push for more. "Could you tell me where I can find them? My father's family, I mean. I... don't want to intrude, but I've come so far. Maybe I can offer them some comfort?"

Sora nodded and turned back to the screen. "I have sent the location of their residence to Felix." Her tone was a clear dismissal, and Blue rose, Felix a bare second behind her. The others gathered their various packs and turned, making their way through the desks scattered through the room. They were almost to the door leading to the entrance when Sora called out.

"Blue, one moment please. Alone."

Blue turned back to where the woman now stood in front of her desk. She took a few steps back in her direction, but the others followed. "Guys, she said alone. I don't think she'll hurt me, and I'll be in clear view." Everyone in the room had quieted when Sora called out, curious expressions on their faces. She hadn't been kidding when she said the Filiri loved their gossip.

Mo'ata and Felix grumbled but relented, staying where they were as Blue made her way back to Sora. She had a curious expression on her face, a mix of speculation, curiosity, and wariness.

"Felix seems to like you."

Was that what this was about? Did she want Felix herself, or was she just being protective of her friend? Blue wasn't sure whether to laugh or growl with frustration. They did not need to be talking about this; they needed to get out there and track down Phillip. "I guess. We're still getting to know each other. Like I told you, he's helped me out a lot. He's a nice guy, too."

A small smile tipped Sora's lips. "He is. He's been my friend for a very long time." She stepped closer. "I am a bit protective. He needs someone who will be there for him, not toy with him."

"I'm not toying with him." The skepticism on the other woman's face set her off. "Tell me what your real problem is. Is it the prida? The clans? Is it that you want Felix yourself?" Blue stepped closer until only a few inches separated her from the taller woman. She tilted her head back, maintaining eye contact. She would not let this woman, or anyone else, make her feel bad for her decisions.

Abruptly Sora laughed, merriment lighting her eyes. *Okay, now I see why they're friends.*

"Maybe this will work." Sora took a step back, still grinning. "One more thing. I don't know what you are really doing here." Sora held up her hand, cutting her off. "I do not doubt that you are here to find your family. I also do not think that is the only reason you are here, or you would have just searched the records instead of coming to me." Her eyes narrowed, and the smile slid off her face.

"Tell me, Blue, what happened to the fourth friend? Three died, but you said there were four of you missing when you returned. Better work your story out better." Abruptly she smiled again, and Blue's head whirled with her quick mood changes. "Maybe we could meet up for a meal before you go, or some shopping—get to know each other better. Though we may want to avoid the lower shops. There has not been another attack there since Gabriella, but you cannot be too cautious." With that Sora turned, rounded her desk, and sat in her chair, waving her hand to dismiss Blue.

It was too much, and Blue laughed. Sora reminded her of Phe, with a little Felix thrown in. It was a weirdly charming combination.

It wasn't until they were back at the inn and planning out their next move that Blue realized what the other woman had done. Blue groaned and let her head fall back against the wall behind her bed, making a dull thud. The guard had practically handed Blue the next piece of the puzzle on a silver platter, and she'd been too dense and embroiled in angst to realize it.

The others were arranged around her room, Forrest and Levi on the floor to her right, Felix leaning against the wall to her left, and Mo'ata in the only chair. Mo'ata, Felix, and Levi were in deep discussion, using Common. Forrest was playing with the cubs, but Blue had been trying to follow what she could of the conversation.

Blue thumped her head against the wall again, and the

movement attracted Mo'ata's attention. He rose from the chair. "What is it?"

"I just realized what Sora was telling me back at the guards'. Ugh, I could kick myself." One more thump and she sat forward. All eyes were on her now. "She basically told me where we should go to try to track down the killer."

Mo'ata spoke quickly to Levi then turned back. "Where?"

"She said we should avoid the lower shops, even though there have been no more attacks there. Ugh." Blue crossed her arms and frowned, still annoyed with herself. "We need to get to wherever that is. You guys can do your questioning thing. Maybe I can rattle some cages."

Forrest nodded. "She also talked about the outer warehouses."

"Is there an area where those intersect?" Blue was getting excited. They had a place to start.

Felix pulled out his comm and tapped, talking to Levi in Common as he did, presumably filling him in. A moment later a three-dimensional picture was projected into the air. It looked like a map of the area. *I need to figure out how to get mine to do that.*

A few more taps and three areas were shaded on the map.

"Three? What's the third?"

"Location of Faust home. Sora sent."

Blue swallowed at the reminder that she had family members out there she'd never met, one of whom she never would. She pushed the feelings aside and concentrated on the matter before them. "Okay. Why that one too?"

"To see if there is any relation." Mo'ata sat beside her on the bed. Garfield stumbled away from Forrest and climbed the clansman's leg. He reached down and scooped up the cub, absently stroking his fur while he studied the map. Blue felt the contentment coming from Garfield, and she eased.

Turning back to the map, she studied it along with everyone else. It was obvious which areas were which. The outer warehouses were close to the border of the city and the barren open plains. The lower shops were close to the more affluent areas where the Fausts' home was, near the foot of the mountain.

"I can't see a connection between the warehouses and the shopping area." Blue deflated. They were back to zero.

"Not quite. Look here." Forrest pointed to a road that connected the two areas, then moved on through the lower shops and into another area. "What's that?" He pointed to where the road ended.

A few more taps and Felix spoke, Mo'ata translating. "Housing complex for some of the workers. It's a little nicer than most, which is why it connects to the shops there. It's mostly for the... middle-level employees."

They studied the map for a few more minutes, looking for any other connections, but that was it. The streets in this city were arranged oddly, not the grid pattern she was used to. There only a few larger roads running through and connecting the different areas. Within the neighborhoods there were smaller roads, but only a few connected to the larger roads, and even those larger ones didn't all connect to each other.

It was designed to keep people in their place, she realized, and that bothered her.

"I guess it's time to go shopping." *Finally.* "You did promise, and I need warmer undies if we're going to stick around here for a while. And a new coat."

Mo'ata leaned in and whispered in her ear. "Little shopa, I thought it was my job to keep you warm. With cuddles, yes?"

The blood rushed to her face, and she somehow managed to choke on air. Forrest, still seated near her on the floor, snorted. He looked back at her and winked. "I think our Blue is saying she needs more than just you." Then he grinned. "Quack."

LEVI

Levi studied the map carefully, ignoring the byplay going on around him. He understood their need for a little levity, but with a minimal understanding of English, he couldn't join in. He also wasn't sure he knew how. He concentrated on what he did know: crystals and how to track them down.

He had a slight sense of the crystals—it was why the Elders had sent him on this mission, over other, more experienced agents. Oh, he had been a guard and an agent for the Prizzoli for quite a while now—years—but he'd never been off-world before this. He'd studied the cultures and the languages, but until this mission he'd spent his life fulfilling his duties to his people on their own lands.

If they could get close enough, he could track the crystal down. He knew, already, that they were on the right track. The closer they'd gotten to this city, the stronger the presence of the crystal had become. It was frustrating that he couldn't pin it down better, but his range wasn't great.

He looked again at the road Forrest had pointed out. The young man was sharp. Even Levi had missed it until that point. He could also now see the strange arrangement of the streets in this city, as if designed to deliberately maintain a segregation of the population.

"We need to get to the shopping area. It is the only area we can take Blue that would not look suspicious." Levi's stomach tightened. Guilt gnawed at him for using her, using them, when he couldn't share the whole truth. He hadn't even told Mo'ata about being able to sense the crystals; it would open up an avenue of questioning that he was forbidden to answer.

They all looked at him, even Blue and Forrest, at hearing her name. The grins slid off their faces, though the blush lingered on Blue's cheeks. He wondered briefly what had been said to put it there.

"That is what we were just discussing." Mo'ata switched to Common but shifted closer to Blue on the bed. "We will take them shopping. We do still need to pick up clothing more appropriate to the climate, so we can take care of that at the same time."

"And put out the bait." Levi reminded them. Felix stiffened, and Mo'ata's jaw tightened further.

"She is not bait."

"I am." Blue's soft voice cut through the room, the quiet strength there putting a pause on the scene.

She continued in English, and Levi's frustration almost boiled over. He pulled it back, again, but he hated that he couldn't understand her. He should have joined Felix in the language lessons.

Felix, Moa'ta, and Blue entered into a heated discussion. Levi was about to put a stop to it—they didn't have the time for this—when Forrest beat him to it. He twisted, still sitting on the floor, and slapped his hand on the mattress between Blue and the clansman. He spoke quickly, forcefully. Levi had never heard the other man sound like that.

FORREST

Forrest was pissed.

They'd come all this way. He and Blue had made it to Karran against both their expectations. They'd found the clan again. They'd rescued cub-babies. Blue had followed through on her plan to tell Mo'ata that she wanted to really try a relationship with him and with Forrest. He'd known how much that scared her, even though she put on her brave face. They'd traveled for over a week through some god-awful weather, only for Blue to find out that she did have family here and one of them was dead.

Now, Mo'ata was trying to wrap her up in cotton, even after he'd already agreed they would have a better chance of finding Phi and the crystal using Blue. Oh, Forrest wanted her safe, but never at the expense of changing who she was. He'd learned that lesson from his mother. You didn't try to change the people you loved—you just loved them.

"Enough." Forrest twisted and slapped the bed between where Blue and Mo'ata sat. "Blue is bait. She and I *are* here to help. We will help. And the best way to do that is to go shopping, dangle Blue like a worm, and wait for Phillip to bite."

He looked straight at Mo'ata. The older man needed to understand that Forrest was there for Blue. He would back her, he would defend her, even from someone who supposedly loved her too. Forrest wasn't convinced Mo'ata did, though he was willing to give the guy the benefit of the doubt. But his first priority was always going to be Blue and what she needed, and right now she needed to help.

Mo'ata's eyes widened. Just then, Vivi launched herself at the clansman, her little claws out, the snarl coming from her chest no less scary for being squeaky. Garfield leaped from Blue's lap to intercept his sister, knocking her into the mattress on the other side of the clansman. Forrest quickly scooped up his girl, trying to quiet his feelings. She'd picked up on his resentment and wanted to hurt the source of it, defending him. She couldn't know that the resentment was not that the man was alive, just that he couldn't see what Blue really needed.

Forrest continued to pet Vivi, humming quietly to calm her. He picked the tune for that first lullaby he and Blue had sung for the cubs, and she quieted.

A heavy hand fell on his shoulder, and he looked up. Mo'ata was kneeling on the floor beside him, an expression of pleading and understanding mixed on his face. "I know. I know, Forrest. I am... having trouble adjusting." The man squeezed his shoulder a little. "You are a good protector for our Blue. Thank you."

A tightness lingered around the other man's eyes. There was also something else. Shame. Forrest held out a hand. "I'll make you a deal. You tell me when I'm being a reckless idiot, and I'll tell you when you're being an overprotective asshole. I'll even keep Vivi from killing you."

Mo'ata took it and shook. "Deal."

Blue snorted from where she still sat on the bed. "If you guys are done bonding, maybe we can get some shopping done? Also, I resent being compared to a worm. You couldn't have figured out something better?"

"What, like chum? Maybe a haunch of raw meat?" The teasing snapped Forrest out of his dark mood.

"Hush."

Felix laughed, and Mo'ata smiled. "Yes, let us be going. We need to ensure our Blue stays warm. And... dangle her like chum for bait."

Forrest slapped his back. "A bit mixed up, but basically." Who knew the clansman actually had a sense of humor? He headed for the door as the others bundled up, singing. "A hunting we will go, a hunting we will go..."

Chapter 8

BLUE

BLUE ENTERED the next shop and sighed at the clerk's double take. Yes, she'd already gathered that she looked like her distant cousin. Yes, she knew the other girl was dead. No, she hadn't been up to meet her family yet. No, she was probably going to put it off; she didn't want to interfere with their grief. Yes, these men were with her. Yes, she knew one of them was a clansman. Yes, she also knew they didn't really like to employ much technology. Yes those were piquet cubs, and yes, they were also with them.

She'd gotten the same reactions and questions at every single shop they'd entered. At first it had been amusing how the shop owners and clerks had opened up to her after they found out her last name was Faust. Now, after five rounds of this, she just wanted to get back to the inn and be done for the day. Surely if they were going to get Phillip's attention this way, they had it by now.

She was also pretty sure that if Gabriella's parents didn't know she was here, they soon would. And she had no idea how to deal with it when they showed up.

This store, one recommended by the bootmaker, had a wide assortment of coats and cold-weather gear, including, she saw as her eyes roamed, a section of what looked like long johns.

She moved farther into the store as the others crowded in behind her. Mo'ata had ended up taking charge of Garfield a few shops ago, making it easier for Blue to browse. They hadn't bought much yet, just some boots for her and Forrest at the last shop and a small dagger with a blue sheath and matching belt that Felix had insisted on getting for her. He'd said it was made of the same material the Cularnian mercenaries used and was a good find.

The clerk, a young man about Forrest's age, rounded the corner and approached, a hesitant and mournful look on his face.

She let Felix take the lead, as he had for all the other shops. The people of Filiri definitely reacted better to the giant than to Mo'ata, and neither Forrest nor Blue knew enough Common to do the job. Levi, despite his colorful clothing, faded into the background, watchful.

After a few moments, the clerk guided them to the rear of the store where Blue had spotted the long johns. It looked like they came in all kinds of colors and patterns, and she smiled as she ran her hand along the collection. The clerk pointed to some that were more her size, and she browsed, pulling out one set in a beautiful floral pattern and another of abstract swirls that reminded her of the tie-dyes Forrest's mom liked. The colors were bold, and she enjoyed the idea of wearing something so bright under her outer clothes.

She hesitated. "I'll need to try these on." It was the first time she'd need to be separated from the others, and after Mo'ata's protective display earlier, she wasn't sure they'd let her.

Expecting an argument, she was surprised when Mo'ata and Forrest exchanged a look and Mo'ata nodded, speaking to the clerk who indicated an area in the back of the shop. Turned out stores on Karran and Earth weren't so different.

She stripped down and tried on the first set as quickly as she could, even putting her own clothes back on over them. They were perfect. The material wasn't so thick or baggy that she couldn't get her own jeans and sweater back on, and she already felt warmer. Deciding not to bother trying on the other pair, she exited the changing area, intending to tell the clerk to just ring up the two sets. She didn't want to change back out of the one she had on.

Shoving aside the curtain, she looked for the others. Felix stood a few feet away, partially hidden by a rack of coats. As she scanned the store for the others, a figure across the street caught her eye. He was partially hidden in a doorway, and the glare of sun against the front door obscured his features. But something about him...

"Felix." She tilted her head to the building across the street, not wanting to take her eyes from the figure. Felix came to her side and looked where she indicated. "You see it?"

"Yes. Looks man. Phillip?"

"Maybe. Forrest might be able to tell for sure. I didn't know him that long."

"I tell, you stay." Felix's voice was calm, but she was sure that was just for her benefit.

He moved across the store, not hurrying—more like he was browsing. She knew he was trying not to give away that they'd spotted the figure, but anticipation rushed through her, and she had to suppress the urge to sprint from the store and tackle whoever was across the street.

Just as Felix reached the others and Forrest was turning, a large transport went by, obscuring their view. When it had passed, the figure was gone. Disappointment and frustration gripped her, and she clenched her fists.

"Damn." She'd been so focused across the street she hadn't noticed the others coming to her side.

"Yeah. Did you see him at all? I really couldn't tell if it was him. It could have been anyone really."

"Maybe. Maybe you're too tired or hyped up or something."

"Or maybe it was him. We can't be too careful." Mo'ata's voice was matter of fact. He reached out and gripped her hand, telling Blue he was far from feeling the outward calm he portrayed. He looked to Felix. "Can you find out if there is any... surveillance in the area?"

Felix nodded and pulled out his comm, moving away from the others. Blue suspected he was calling Sora, though what he would say, she didn't know, unless they gave up on keeping their true purpose here secret.

A few minutes later he was back. "She send."

"What did you tell her?" Blue was curious.

He shrugged. "I no tell, just ask."

"You must be good friends."

He shrugged again. "Yes. She know I not ask unless good reason."

The long johns bunched in her grip. Sora knew him that well? "You know, she offered to go get some lunch with me while we were here. Maybe I'll take her up on it." Her voice was speculative.

Felix's eyes widened, and he stiffened, shifting restlessly, like he wanted to run. What was that? "Maybe... not good idea?"

"You don't want me to get to know your friend?" Blue wasn't sure if she was amused or resentful over his reaction, maybe both, but she settled on the first. Seeing the giant mercenary in a near panic over something as simple as a lunch was worth a chuckle or two.

As he opened his mouth to reply, his comm let off a low ping. His relief was obvious. "This it. We go."

"Just have to pay for what I'm wearing. Also, we *should* get new coats. That was not just an excuse to get out." If that had been Phillip, he was already gone. No reason to freeze unnecessarily.

They hurried to pick out new coats for Blue, Forrest, and Levi, who decided he, too, needed something warmer. He picked the brightest thing in the store, though it still wasn't as bright as his own coat. They also bought the two sets of long johns for Blue.

Catching the first transport back to the inn, they rode in tense silence. It was a long route, going from the main road in the lower shopping district, over to another that connected to the warehouse district, and finally to the traveler's section. A trip that should have taken fifteen minutes took over an hour due to the convoluted layout of the streets.

When they reached the inn, Felix bolted for the entrance. Mo'ata signaled the others to hold back, and they strolled through the common room. Blue kept a tight grip on Garfield, Levi paused and ordered a meal to be sent up.

Keep it calm, keep it normal. The closer they drew to Felix's room, the more anxious she became until her skin crawled under the layers of clothes. Some sense told her that had been Phillip, and he had been watching her. The plan had worked.

But now, that feeling of being watched wouldn't go away. The crawling became a painful itch as an image of crazy, brown eyes haunted her. Garfield purred in her arms, and it helped, but she still felt... dirty.

"I'm going to take a quick shower, you guys." She cut over to her room, barely noting the concerned looks cast her way. She'd just go get cleaned up, then they'd dive into that footage.

She stripped and jumped into the cleaning unit, setting the mode to water. It had a sonic cleaning, and she'd used that last night, entranced by the novelty. But right now she needed to *feel* clean, and nothing beat the sensation of water washing away... everything.

She knew it was silly. Taking a shower just because some guy may have been watching her? It was exactly what they had been going for, the goal of the outing. By the time she switched off the water, she was ready to continue, to tackle the next step.

Whatever works, right? She pulled on her new long johns and bound her hair back in a sloppy bun. She added the clothes to the pile in the corner and pulled on her last clean set.

Garfield stretched up and waved a paw at the control for the connecting door. She rapped lightly, then pushed it open. Forrest sat on the bed, feeding Vivi little slivers of meat.

"Done?" he asked. When she nodded he continued. "Felix started on the surveillance, and he thinks he found a good shot of the guy we spotted earlier. I said I'd wait for you and get the cubs fed."

When Garfield and Vivi had had their fill and were tucked away for a nap, Blue and Forrest headed across the hall. Felix, Mo'ata, and Levi sat around a small table, plates of food and pitchers of water spread over it. Two empty chairs were pulled up to one end. It was crowded, but the significance was not lost on her. They were including her and Forrest.

One of the comms, propped up against a glass, projected an image at the wall. Despite the rough setup, it was clear. Phillip.

He looked awful. His face was pale and his hair was wild. She couldn't see his eyes very well—the shot was from too far away—but they looked sunken. He wore clothes similar to those they'd seen on the warehouse and factory workers.

"It's him." Forrest's voice was tight. Blue's heart ached for him.

Felix nodded and bent back over the comm. "I look more." His food sat untouched next to him, a small curl of steam rising from it.

She drifted closer, watching the images as they flashed by, and came to a halt near Felix. A tug on her sleeve pulled her away and over to the chairs saved at the other end of the table. "Come on, time to eat," Mo'ata said.

She sat and took a few bites. Felix continued to skim through the images, ignoring his meal.

"Felix." She waited until he looked over. "Eat." They needed all the clues they could get, but she didn't want him to neglect himself either.

He didn't say anything but wore a grin as he pulled the plate closer.

As they waited, Blue thought about everything that had happened so far. It had mostly been traveling and waiting and shopping—the shopping she didn't mind—but it wasn't what she'd expected. Before, everyone else had worked to find her friends and stop the kidnappings, and she'd tried to stay out of the way. Now, she and Forrest were helping, being kept in the loop. It was a lot less exciting than she'd thought it would be.

"Is this how all your missions go?"

"What do you mean?" Mo'ata shifted his attention to her.

"I don't know, I just expected there to be more fighting and spy stuff."

"What do you know about fighting and spy stuff?" Forrest asked, teasing.

"About as much as you," she shot back.

"Are you always like this with each other?" Mo'ata drew their attention.

Blue widened her eyes. "I don't know what you mean." Then she shot her tongue out at Forrest, startling a laugh out of Mo'ata. "Really, though, is this how they go?"

"Each is different, but if you are asking if there is usually so much sitting and... watching, then, yes. A lot of the work we do is information gathering." He tapped a finger on the table in front of the mercenary. "Felix, do you want one of us to take over? I would still like you to talk to the innkeeper, see what he knows. It may just be that he recognized the Faust name, but it may be more."

Felix grunted. "Almost done. Then go down." He didn't move his gaze from the screen.

"Anything I can do?" Forrest asked, and Blue nodded in agreement. She would love a specific task.

Mo'ata rapped his fingers against the table, his brows pulling together. "No, not yet. You have both already been a big help. I admit, I do not think we would have gotten as far as we have if you had not been with us. We would still be lurking around in shops and the guard stations, looking for any word of suspicious people."

"Yes. Sora give more than think. She like Blue." Felix tapped the screen of his comm a few more times then sat back. "Done."

A new image popped up, from the same angle as the first, of a figure leaving the doorway they'd seen Phillip in and heading down the road. Felix paused the video, then pointed to another figure, this one small with a blue scarf over her head. Dread filled Blue as Felix started the video again.

They watched Phillip follow the girl, who must be Gabriella, down the street. They moved out of range, and Felix paused it. "We no have more." He switched to Common, then, frustration in his voice.

Mo'ata translated. "The camera for the area they moved to was malfunctioning, so we can't see what happened next. As you saw, Sora sent not only the recordings from today but also the ones from the day of Gabriella's death. If we're right, Phillip used the same doorway both days. We can not tell where he went from there, but it is a place to start." He spoke again in Common, this time to Levi, who nodded and rose. Levi stopped in front of Blue, gave a small bow, then left.

Blue sent Mo'ata a questioning look. "He is going to investigate the area." He looked at the four of them and sighed. "I wish we could call in more people."

"Why can't you?" It hadn't occurred to her, but if they simply needed to search until they found Phillip or Etu, it would definitely be easier with more feet on the ground.

"It is not my decision. Felix and I are… on loan. To Levi and the Prizzoli."

"Forrest and I can help. Two more sets of eyes out on the street."

"We have talked about this." He crossed his arms and leaned back, partially blocking the projected image, its light winking off the metal fastenings of his coat. "No. I will not allow it."

She clenched her teeth at his domineering tone. *Baby steps, Blue. Baby steps.*

Forrest didn't let it go. Cough. "Asshole." Cough.

"Idiot," he shot back.

Felix's gaze darted between the three of them. "I need agree with... asshole, on this." He focused on Blue, who worked to suppress her grin. "I help. We practice knife." He tilted his head until he could look Forrest in the eyes. "We practice too."

"Dude, major brownie points for that one," Forrest said, then sent a smirk to Mo'ata.

Blue spoke up before things deteriorated further. "Mo'ata is correct. We have a lot of learning still to do. And we have time. Well, not for this, but for *future* operations." Mo'ata's eyes widened, and his arms tensed against his chest. Ha. "We'll do patrols then. You know, after we've learned the language and proven we can hold our own in a fight."

"Ass...hole..." Forrest whispered.

A corner of his mouth ticked, and he relaxed, sitting forward and propping his forearms on the table. "Agreed."

"I go down now, then out." Felix stood and moved to Blue, bending down to pet her. She didn't quite have it in her to play their game, but she did smile up at him.

"Be careful, okay?"

He patted her one more time and took off. Her eyes followed him out the door. She really did want to be out there tracking down Phillip. She looked to where Forrest sat, also looking toward the door. This must be even harder on him.

"I need to go as well." Mo'ata stood. "Please return to the room across the hall and do not leave. I am trusting you to stay there. We need to know you both remain safe."

He pulled out their comms and quickly reviewed how

147

to send and play voice messages. "I will try to check in with you, but do not worry if I do not. I will most likely be in an area where I need to remain silent."

He turned away and was almost to the door when Blue rose. "Wait." She hurried to stand before him. After only a slight hesitation, she reached up and pulled his head down, raising up on her toes to meet his lips with hers. After the first press of their lips his own parted. She matched him, allowing their tongues to touch. She tried to put everything she was feeling into that kiss. Her frustration, her fear. Her desire for this to work with them, her longing to have him near her. And her need for him to come back safe.

She pulled back, and Mo'ata rested his forehead against hers. He was breathing heavily, and Blue realized she was as well, taking in deep gulps of air. Finally, he touched his lips to hers once more and turned away, walking out the door and down the hall without a word.

"Wow." Forrest, who also hadn't made a sound, moved to her side.

She glanced at him out of the corner of her eye. She couldn't read the expression she saw there. "You okay?"

"You're asking me that?"

"Well, yeah."

"I'm gonna call 'coconut.' Maybe even 'octopus.' I need a kiss like that."

Blue laughed and grabbed his hand. "Come on, let's get back across the hall and check on the kids."

"I'm not kidding Blue. 'Coconut, coconut, coconut.' Seriously."

Forrest allowed her to pull him along. Once they were

back in their rooms, Blue collapsed on her bed, where the cubs found her, climbing up and snuggling in.

"Blue?" Forrest stood in the connection doorway.

"Yeah?"

"I really wasn't kidding."

"I know. Get over here."

Forrest, careful to shift Vivi out of his way, climbed into the bed with her. They turned onto their sides, and he pulled her in until her back was snuggled tight against his chest, his arm firmly around her waist.

She needed to be the one to start. "It's weird. We've talked about this. Well, it's more like we half talked about this. I'm so used to you being right there, right beside me. I love you. I've said it before, but I really love you, Forrest. I honestly don't know what I'd do without you." Blue stared at the wall opposite her. Beside them, the cubs stilled. Gathering her courage, she continued. "I just don't know how to... break through whatever it is that's sitting between us. I've gone a year without kissing you, without really touching you in... that way. I don't know how to start." She blinked, feeling a tear slide out of the corner of her eye. Where it came from, she didn't know.

Behind her, Forrest relaxed, further molding his body around hers. "You kissed me back at the camp."

"I know. And it was a relief to finally do it."

She felt the rumble of his laugh. "You're telling me." He moved, pulling back just enough to roll Blue onto her back. The cubs grumbled and made their way to the end of the mattress. He looked down at her, his expression soft but eager. "I think we just need to practice."

"You just want an excuse to kiss me."

"Well, yeah. That's kind of the point. But I don't want to need an excuse to kiss you, Blue. I just want to kiss you and, when you're ready, more." His voice lowered on the last word to almost a growl. Forrest's eyes, their bright blue drilling into her, held a heat that she'd not seen until now. Had he been suppressing this part of himself?

His head lowered to hers, and she trembled. He partially covered her, his lips a bare inch from her own. He held himself there, waiting, until she couldn't take it and closed the gap.

Kiss two. Not that she was counting, but this was a relief in its own way. The first kiss had been special. It was the first.

This was just as special because it showed her these feelings weren't only the anticipation and suspense. No, this was all Forrest.

She burrowed closer to him, wanting no space between them. She embraced him, alternately caressing and pulling him close. She worked one hand under his shirt, loving the feel of his warm skin against her.

Forrest was propped up on one elbow with one hand buried in her hair and the other kneading her side. She pulled back, gasping in a breath, hating the need to breathe. It must be a design flaw. As he moved his mouth down her neck, he alternated small bites and licks with kisses. A small portion of her mind wondered where this had come from, this heat, but she knew. They had both been holding back so much.

"Forrest. Oh God." She moved her hand up to clench his neck, holding his head to her.

He chuckled, then groaned. "Are there no seams on this damn thing?"

Only then did Blue realize he had been trying to get the long johns off her, and she came back to herself, just a little. She pushed on his shoulder, and he froze.

"Blue?"

"I think that's enough practice for now." She hated that her voice shook.

He took a breath and moved off her, cautious. "You okay?"

The heat from earlier was gone, replaced by concern and maybe a little regret. She reached up to cup his cheek. "Oh, I am peachy-keen fine. I'm just not sure I'm ready for the... rest. We should definitely keep practicing, though."

Forrest grinned. "Oh, I'm up for practice whenever you want."

It took her a moment, then she felt the blood rush to her cheeks and lower. She slapped his arm and pushed him off her all the way. "Hush."

They lay there together, Forrest playing with her hair. It was a comfortable silence.

"Why don't you go get ready for bed. Then... maybe you can come back? I've gotten used to my cuddles at night."

Forrest tugged her hair. "Oh, I noticed."

"Jealous?" Blue's tone was light, playful. A little teasing would be good at this point.

"Oh, terribly. And I'm not above taking advantage of that clansman's absence to get my own cuddles in."

She gave him a nudge. "Then go get ready and get back here."

He eyed her long johns-turned-pajamas. "Are you going to change?"

"It's this or nothing. I have to figure out how to do some laundry." She frowned. "Damn, I forgot to ask about that."

"Nothing?" The heat returned to Forrest's eyes.

The blood rushed to her face, and she swallowed. "I'm thinking clothes are a good idea right now."

Forrest laughed, but the heat was still there. He gave her a quick kiss, then bounded out of the bed. A bare minute later he was back, wearing a T-shirt and sweatpants that didn't smell too bad, and climbed in next to her. She snuggled back, ignoring the firm length she could feel against her back, and closed her eyes. The small weights of their cub-babies nestled close, and Blue let the comfort of having Forrest beside her sweep away the weariness and stress, sliding into sleep.

Chapter 9

ETU

ETU SLAMMED his hand down on the table, catching that idiot Phillip's attention. If the crystal hadn't managed to connect to this fool, he would have left the kid behind long ago. Unfortunately, he needed him now. He couldn't even kill him; things had gotten to the point that the crystal wouldn't let him.

He'd tried *once* to use the traitorous thing since they'd found this boy, and it was not an experience to repeat. The crystal had rebelled, reversing the flow of energy so that it was draining Etu, and he'd had to hand the task off to Phillip.

Phillip jumped, and his eyes shot to Etu. The shadowed room they were staying in was filled with the scent of unwashed bodies and stale food. He'd been trying to remain undetected in this city, far from the prying eyes of the Order and the agent he knew the Elders must have sent. Now, Phillip had ruined that.

"Do you know what you've done?" Etu's teeth were clenched so hard he could barely get the words out.

Phillip shrugged and looked away again, drawn into whatever visions kept him going. It was too much. Etu stood and rounded the table, slapping the boy across the face. "I said, do you know what you've done? They have found us."

"They already in city." Phillip's Common was rough but understandable.

"But they did not know for sure that we were here. Not until you just had to go back to that shop. Why were you even there?" The fool looked away, refusing to answer. His lips set in a stubborn pout, and he crossed his arms. "Phillip. You knew we just needed to stay undetected for a little longer, just until I can finish getting a new arrangement worked out with a patron. Now we have to leave, start over again."

Etu knew exactly what the boy's problem was. He had found him huddled against an alley wall, the body of a young girl growing cold and stiff only a few feet away. He'd seen the resemblance to the one from the boy's world. Since then, only a few weeks ago, Phillip had deteriorated. He'd already been showing signs of crystal sickness, which came to those who were not trained properly in their use—the wandering mind, short attention, and obsessive need for more energy. Now he only ever came out of his daze to feed the crystal. He practically haunted the streets and shopping district, obsessed with the shop where he had seen the girl.

Something new had happened today. Phillip had rushed in the door, excited, alive again. He'd gone on and on about seeing "her." It had taken a while, but Etu had finally gotten it out of him. He'd seen that girl he was obsessed with, the one from his world. Blue.

Etu hadn't believed it until he'd checked with a source at the guards. A group of strangers had been in earlier that day. One was a small woman sporting blond hair streaked with blue.

"You not know saw me. I hid." Phillip's tone was morphing from sulky to angry.

"I know they did because after they left the shop, there was another call to the guards and someone sent over surveillance of the area. Of course they saw you. Why else would they ask for the camera feeds for the area?"

"You not *know* saw me."

Etu was too far gone in this own thoughts and frustrations to hear the warning note in Phillip's voice. The boy loomed before him, a slight purple glint in his eyes masking the natural brown.

The same color as the crystal. Etu froze and swallowed.

"We not leave." Phillip's voice deepened, an echo of another sounding through it.

Etu shivered with dawning horror. This was more than just crystal sickness; this was something else. Etu scrambled for some way to regain control. An idea formed.

"What if we get that girl for you? You can drain her, keep her, whatever. We will need to kill her companions, but I doubt you'd have an issue with that, would you?" His voice was sly, coaxing.

He swallowed as Phillip reached out. A small arc of pale purple shot from the tip of Phillip's finger to Etu's nose, and he closed his eyes, exhausted from the small drain of life.

He knew what this was. It was a Bonding. And it was very well developed if Phillip could drain without the crystal to use as a medium. If things progressed further... Etu swallowed.

"The girl is not to be harmed," Phillip said. Echoes of power still sounded in that deep voice.

Etu nodded quickly, and sweat beaded on his forehead. He'd heard the legends of Bondings gone wrong, and feared he was getting a first-hand view of the birth of a monster.

"Find her." The light left the other man's eyes until they were once again a dull brown. "Please, find her." This last was the whispered plea of a scared little boy. "I can't…"

Phillip's eyes gained that purple light again, and his face twisted. Etu inched away, trying to put some distance between them without drawing attention.

"Find her. Or you are no use to me." Phillip turned away, leaving Etu to gather the remains of his composure and set out on his newest mission: finding the girl.

LEVI

Levi stilled himself. One by one he blocked out his senses. He closed his eyes, shutting out the darkness and shifting shadows of the alleyway he had chosen. It stood along the main corridor they had identified as the one Phillip was most likely to use. He ignored the shuffling steps of the late-shift workers heading to their factories and warehouses and the slice of cold wind that bit through his jacket.

Then he calmed his thoughts. This was the hardest. They teemed with images of his companions. Mo'ata, Felix, Blue, even Forrest. In the short time he'd known them, they had all come to mean much to him, touching a place in him and bringing forth emotions he hadn't known he had.

His whole life had been about his duty. The protection of the Crystals of Shardon and of the Elders and his people. He'd been chosen at a young age because of his ability to sense the crystals, and since then, that had been his life. His friends were his fellow guards. His family was the Elders and the priests of the crystals. They had his devotion and loyalty.

Since this assignment—no, since saving Blue and then meeting Mo'ata, he had been struggling. His loyalties divided, his thoughts focused on their welfare more than on getting the crystal back. Back at the Dramil camp, when Blue had suggested coming with them to act as bait, and again at the inn, he'd had to suppress his own protests and remind himself his priority had to be getting the crystal back. The consequences of having it out in the worlds unchecked were beyond horrible.

With this knowledge, he finally brought his mind under control. He shoved out any concerns or feelings other than duty and—holding onto that—opened his mind, searching out the tendrils of energy the crystal emitted.

He was about to give up when he felt it. It was faint, barely there, but that one little wisp of energy told him the direction he needed to go.

He headed farther into the warehouse district, careful to keep his senses open. He drew looks from the workers but ignored them, intent on getting to the crystal. He was drawing closer when a figure caught his eye.

A slight man dressed in the rough garb of the Firiki workers walked toward him. There was nothing there to gain his attention, nothing overtly out of the ordinary, but something was off. Levi studied him closely, but the man kept his head down and continued on down the walk, never pausing or looking up.

Levi watched him for a few moments, then pushed the man to the back of his mind, deciding to examine the almost-encounter later. He focused back on the crystal's trail, but it was gone. Either his distraction had caused him to lose it, or it had moved out of his range. He tensed, stopping himself from kicking the grimy building next to him in frustration.

He moved to a doorway partly hidden in a small alcove, similar to the one near the shop they'd been in earlier today. *Is this city designed to let people lurk in dark alleyways and doorways?* There was no lack of dark areas, it seemed.

He concentrated again, but the crystal's trail eluded him.

His comm pinged, breaking his concentration. Again.

"Yes?" His voice was curt.

"You missed your check-in time." Felix's deep voice was just as brusque. This, too, was a man who knew duty. He also knew how to step out of it, though. It was something Levi admired.

Levi glanced at the time displayed on the screen of his comm. He had missed the set check-in. He'd let the time get away from him, too absorbed in tracking the crystal. He debated again whether he should share his ability with the group, but the need to keep his people's secrets was so ingrained he couldn't do it.

"I thought I had a track on something." He kept it simple.

The silence on the other end was telling. The others weren't stupid; they knew there were things he wasn't telling them. So far it hadn't been an issue, so they'd allowed him his secrets for the time being.

"Anything we need to know?" Felix's voice sounded just a little strained.

"No."

"Don't miss another check-in." The small beep indicated Felix had cut the line.

Levi made note of where he was and the direction he'd been heading. There was no use continuing now—the crystal wasn't there anymore—but he could start here at another time. Now was the time to keep his eyes and ears open for what he could learn—whispers from workers of unusual things, strangers in the area.

He continued farther into the warehouse district. Gradually, the other people on the street stopped meeting his eyes, stopped even glancing in his direction. Most moved out of his way on the walk, avoiding all contact. The complete and deliberate avoidance of any interaction was eerie, and it got worse the deeper he got into the worker's territory. It was telling of the culture of this people, how closed off they were. Though at the guard station and later at the inn, the people had been a little standoffish, but not skittish like this. Could they have had run-ins with Etu? Or Phillip? Surely Etu would have been smart enough to change his clothing, though.

Frustrated, Levi turned around to head back to the inn. There wasn't anything more he would be able to do tonight in this area. He needed more to go on, and he needed to see what Mo'ata and Felix may have found.

As he rounded a corner and headed to the main corridor, once again his gaze caught on a small figure. It looked like the same one as before, this time heading away from him. Either a small man or a large woman, it was hard to tell with the bulky coat and scarf.

Acting on his instincts, Levi followed. That was twice this person had distracted him.

They headed in the direction of the shopping district. No other workers were headed this way, and Levi's suspicions grew. The ones who held the higher positions and lived in the nicer districts were all home for the day, and anyone shopping in this area would have been dressed more nicely. Levi drew closer to the figure, no longer trying to stay unseen. *It is pointless anyway, unless I change my clothing.*

As if sensing the presence behind him, the figure started turning down smaller streets and alleys. Levi lengthened his stride and closed the gap, not wanting to lose this person.

Almost running, he turned one last corner and immediately realized his mistake. It was dark, a dead end alley, buildings rising high on either side. The figure faced him, and it was a man. A man with the dark skin of the Prizzoli, until now obscured by clothing and a bowed head. A man with a familiar face.

"Etu." The diverted gazes of the workers made sense now. If they had seen this man and connected him to the deaths and disappearances in the area, his own skin would have been a warning to them. He didn't know Etu well, but enough to recognize his face and to not have been surprised when he received the message from Zeynar naming him as the traitor.

Now Levi faced his people's betrayer.

There was a small scuff behind him, the sound of a leather sole on stone, and Levi twisted his head. Another man stood behind him now. The same man who had been on the cameras. Phillip.

Levi turned fully to face this new presence. *This* was the danger. He opened his senses again, seeking the crystal, and was overwhelmed. He staggered back against an alley wall, his mind assaulted by the poison pouring off the former man. Because he wasn't a man anymore, he was more.

Horror and disgust twisted inside Levi. His mind writhed under the feelings of obsession, greed, and hate that rolled off of Phillip—or what Phillip had become.

"Tell where she is," Phillip said in rough Common. The young man's voice echoed with deeper tones.

Phillip crept closer, the movements slow and dangerous. Levi moved down the alley wall, keeping distance between himself and Phillip. He saw the young man's eyes light with a faint purple glow, and his suspicions were confirmed. This was a true Bonding, and they were in more trouble than he'd ever imagined. He'd suspected from the descriptions Phe and Blue had given of their experiences, but now he had confirmation.

Levi cut off his sense of the crystal and braced himself. His mind scrambled for a way out of the situation. Their idea of bait had worked all too well.

"What do you want with her?" He bent his knees and tightened his core. "Will you drain her?"

A wicked grin grew on Phillip's face. "No. But it should not matter to you. She is mine to do with as I please."

"And what if we give her to you? What will you do with us? With the people here in this city, on this world?"

A shocked breath from behind reminded him of the other man's presence, which had been overshadowed and forgotten. "Never thought a perfect Shardon Guard would even utter words like that. Doesn't it go against your honor, Levi?"

Levi ignored the distraction. "Well?"

"They are mine as well. I will do with *them* what I please."

"What about Forrest?"

Phillip's eyes pinched, and a flicker of regret, of remembered friendship, passed quickly. It was enough to tell Levi that the boy Phillip had been was not fully gone, that there was still hope.

He gentled his voice. "Phillip. I can help you. Please let me help you."

"You can't." The glow faded, replaced by despair.

"I can. We can." He moved out from the alley wall, reaching a hand to the young man now slumped in defeat. "We just need the crystal. We can fix this, but not while you have it, not while you're connected to it." Another step forward. "Please."

Phillip, his shoulders slumped, bowed his head and moved closer. He paused and lifted his hand as if to take the one Levi still offered. Just before contact, his head came up, the glow and grin firmly in place.

"No."

Phillip closed the distance between their outstretched hands, small arcs of purple light tying them together. Levi struggled to break the contact, but his limbs were heavy, the life leaving him. His knees buckled, and the weight of his own body pulled him down to the alley floor. As his sight dimmed, using the last of his strength, he reached to his comm and pushed the emergency beacon, the one Mo'ata had installed on all of their comms, and the same one Levi had secretly scoffed at.

MO'ATA

An alert sounded on Mo'ata's comm, and his heart skipped. Blue and Forrest should be safe at the inn. If they had left and gotten into trouble, he did not know what he would do, but it would probably involve tying them up so they couldn't move. He didn't need this distraction now; he needed them safe.

He was frustrated. On any other area of Karran or of any other world, he would be respected as a clansman and, to those who knew, as a member of the Order. Here, he was a second-rate citizen. All he was good for was muscle or back up. It was ironic because that was exactly how the Filiri thought of the clans, and it was their own attitude that forced him into the role.

The beacon indicated an area fairly close to the inn. From now on he was just going to stick with them. He couldn't believe they'd gone against his orders like that, especially Blue. He thought she was smarter than that.

It was a testament to his distraction and frustration that he was already on a transport before he looked harder at the alert. He had assumed. But it wasn't from Blue or Forrest, it was from Levi.

In a way that was worse. What could have happened that the Prizzoli couldn't handle himself? He'd seen that man fight, the way he moved. There was not much that would bring him down. He and Felix had once gone up against him together, and even then it had been a struggle to get any hits in.

Mo'ata silently urged the transport to go faster and jumped off as soon as he could. Keeping an eye on the map, he followed it to the mouth of a dead-end alley and skidded to a stop. The Prizzoli was slumped against a wall, his skin ashy, lips colorless.

Mo'ata scanned the area, making sure they were alone before hurrying to check for a pulse. It was faint but there, and he breathed a sigh of relief. He didn't know what had happened, but whatever it was, Levi had survived it.

The sound of running steps reached him, and Mo'ata tensed, pulling his toka. He moved protectively in front of his incapacitated friend. And, yes, this man was his friend. Felix rounded the corner, and Mo'ata eased back. He sheathed his blade and gestured to Levi.

"He is alive. Help me get him up."

Felix knelt on the other side of Levi and propped up his back while Mo'ata got one arm under his legs and a shoulder to his chest. It was awkward, but they managed to maneuver the man into an over-the-shoulder hold.

"What happened?" Felix moved to the mouth of the alley, watching for movement as Mo'ata shifted his burden until the weight was as well distributed as he could get it.

"I don't know. I got here just before you. He was as you see him." Mo'ata's mouth tightened. "I thought for a moment he was gone."

"I talked to him after he missed his first check-in. He said he thought he may have something but did not say anything else." Felix gestured that they were clear, and Mo'ata moved out of the alley.

"He has been holding back information. I respected it and his people's secrets, but it has gone too far."

"Yes. He will need to explain, fully."

"If he lives."

"If he lives," Felix sighed.

Chapter 10

BLUE

BLUE CAME AWAKE SLOWLY, her face buried in Forrest's chest, her arms wrapped around him, one of his legs thrown over hers. They lay entwined, and peace moved through her. Whatever else happened, she had this man, and he had her.

She breathed in, loving their combined scents. She drifted off again, but muffled voices intruded. Thuds came from across the hall, and a small crash brought her awake. She moved away from Forrest, or tried to. His arms tightened around her, and he shifted, tucking her into him so she was half-buried. His hips moved into her, and he groaned.

She froze, completely awake now and completely distracted from whatever was going on across the hall. She knew what *that* was. Not that she'd seen one before. She'd felt one, well, at night snuggling with Forrest and

Mo'ata. But it had never been quite this obvious, and she suspected they'd been careful. This was pressing into her hip, and it was obvious and right there. The firm length of… she couldn't even think the word. This was ridiculous. She needed to get over her shyness about… intimacies. *Ugh. You are a dork, Blue. It's not that hard. Penis. It's just a word.* She snorted to herself. *Hard.*

Forrest moved again, and his hand moved down her back to her butt. Her lower stomach clenched, the feeling pleasurable. She moved back into him and placed a small kiss on his chest. She liked that and did it again. She wiggled up until she could reach his lips with hers and kissed him softly. His eyes were still closed, and she kissed him once more, harder this time. She wanted him awake, and she wanted to keep kissing him, touching him. She stroked his back, loving the feel of bare skin, and wished she had had something other than her new long johns to wear to bed. The barrier was frustrating.

"Forrest." One more kiss, this time on his chin.

His only reply was a small grumble.

"Forrest. Wake up." She reached down and grabbed his butt, matching his gesture. It was a stretch; her arms weren't long enough to reach his butt and keep kissing his lips at the same time. She also couldn't quite believe she had just grabbed his butt. Ass. *Tush?* She squeezed.

Voices and another crash came from across the hall, reminding her why she had woken up in the first place. She snatched her hands back from where they'd seemed to have taken on a life of their own and pushed at Forrest's chest.

"Wake up. Something's going on." She pinched. "Come on, wake up!"

"What?" Forrest blinked down at her. "Ow. Why did you pinch me?"

Blue pinched him again. "Because you needed to wake up. Something's going on, and you have a death grip on my ass." She grinned, pleased with herself for actually using the word out loud. She mentally added to her list: Get more comfortable thinking of and using the words for body parts and sex.

His hands tightened before releasing her so quickly you'd think her butt was on fire and burning him. His face filled with color, and he moved his hips away as well. Blue was a little sorry for it, but she also wanted to get across the hall and find out what was going on.

The voices rose, and she pushed away again, harder this time. Forrest let her go, and she rolled out of the bed, hitting the floor with a soft thud. The voices stopped, and her door flew open.

Mo'ata filled the opening, his eyes wide and expression stiff. "What happened? Are you okay?"

Blue couldn't suppress her snort. Weren't those the questions she was supposed to be asking? "I'm fine. I just fell out of the bed." She picked herself up and moved next to him. "What's going on?"

The covers rustled behind her, and Forrest stood. "Is everything okay?"

Mo'ata, face hard, turned and gestured for them to follow.

Blue stopped just inside the door to Felix and Levi's

room. Horror swept through her at the state of the man lying on the bed, still as death. Levi's chest wasn't moving, and the ashy color of his skin brought a small cry from her. "Is he...?" She couldn't finish the sentence, let alone the thought. He was her silent savior. He couldn't be—

"He is alive. We do not know what happened. He must have remained awake long enough to push his emergency alert, but he was as you see him when we found him."

Forrest cleared his throat. "Was it Phillip?"

"Not know. Getting image from Sora." Felix stood across the room, comm to his ear. His expression was cold, almost blank. Blue saw the true mercenary, not her playful bear. This was the man she'd first seen back at the capital when he and his team approached their table at the inn. She hadn't seen this side of him since, but here it was. This was bad.

She moved to the bed and took Levi's limp hand. "Have you called anyone? A healer?" She couldn't look away from that lifeless face. She hadn't realized how alive his face was, how many of his thoughts and emotions usually showed, until she saw him like this.

When she got no answer, she pulled her gaze away and looked to Mo'ata. He glared at Felix, whose stony expression never wavered. This was what they had been arguing about.

"I don't read minds. Talk to me." Her voice was harsh, but she was worried and frustrated and didn't want to deal with whatever manly dramatics they had going on. She just wanted Levi to be okay.

It was Mo'ata who spoke. "As Felix pointed out, we can't let anyone know what's going on. If word got out that there was some sort of crystal out there draining life, there would be a panic in the city and we would lose any leads we have. We're close." His voice lowered, the anger clear. "But he needs to get checked out by someone, if for no other reason than to be sure nothing vital was damaged."

"Word is already out. Sora knows something is up. She may not know it's a crystal, but she knows we're here for more than my family. The shopkeepers know something is going on, and I bet, with how much everyone seems to love to gossip around here, that all the workers know something too. Hell, the innkeeper could probably tell you exactly where all of the deaths have occurred and all of their names. We should just go talk to him, and we could solve the whole thing." She hated how shrill her voice sounded, but she was so angry and so worried she didn't care to rein it in.

The stunned looks on the men's faces, Forrest's included, almost pushed her over the edge again, but a small groaning sound came from the man on the bed, and she recalled herself.

Levi groaned again as his hand tightened briefly on hers, but he didn't open his eyes and he didn't wake up. She sat beside him on the bed, keeping a tight hold of his hand. "Get a doctor or someone who can at least check his vital organs or something." No one moved. "Now."

That pushed them into motion. Mo'ata hurried to the door, and Forrest followed, returning shortly with the cubs and an extra blanket. He set the fur-babies next to Levi on the bed, and they snuggled next to him. The purring soon started. *Did his eyes flicker?* She couldn't be sure if he was coming to or if it was her hopeful imagination.

She looked to where Felix still stood, arms crossed and silent. She wasn't sure what his problem was. He hadn't said anything since telling them Sora was sending the surveillance footage.

"Is there anything on the footage?" It was a peace offering, the closest she could get right now.

Felix looked at her but didn't answer. She let it go and put all of her attention back onto Levi. Forrest joined her, sitting at her feet on the floor beside the bed.

An hour must have passed before Mo'ata returned with a doctor or healer or whatever they called them. Blue moved aside, reluctant to let go of Levi but knowing she needed to give the healer some room.

The doctor set a large case on a chair and pulled a small device from it, holding it over Levi's chest until it beeped rapidly. He and Mo'ata spoke for a few minutes, the doctor frowning and Mo'ata shaking his head. Their voices raised, and the doctor gestured wildly. Blue looked at Felix, who just stood there watching. *Why was he doing nothing?*

"Excuse me." She tried in Common, keeping her voice at a normal level. When neither the doctor nor Mo'ata looked to her, she spoke again, louder. "Excuse me."

The doctor spun to her. "Yes?"

She continued with her small vocabulary. "Levi well?"

The doctor raised a brow, looking her over. He wasn't bad looking, with dark hair and green eyes, but she didn't like the way he eyed her and he wasn't answering. She frowned and looked to Mo'ata.

His own frown grew. "He says Levi will heal. He needs rest and nutrients. His body is depleted but otherwise fine," he said in English.

"So why are you arguing?"

"He wants to take him to a healing center and would not listen when I told him we could manage."

"Is he going to be a problem?"

Mo'ata's gaze shot to Felix then back to Blue. "No. But I am having trouble getting him to listen to me. It is a matter of me being a clansman, and the same reason we have been having Felix take the lead here."

Blue also looked at Felix, who still did nothing. "Maybe I should talk to the doctor. The shopkeepers at least seemed to show some respect for the Faust name."

The doctor jerked when she spoke. His eyes darted back and forth between her and Mo'ata and Levi. He didn't even seem to see Felix and Forrest in the room. "Faust?"

Blue stepped closer to the doctor, prepared to make herself understood somehow and get the doctor to leave. Suddenly there was a body in front of her blocking out everything except the broad back of Felix. He'd done the silent, sneaky-fast movement thing again.

Felix spoke quickly, harshly, and this close to him, Blue could almost feel the anger radiating off him. She wanted to put a hand on his back to soothe him, but she didn't know what to do with an angry Felix.

A moment later the door opened and closed, and silence descended on the room once more. Felix didn't move, so Blue stepped back and around him. The doctor was gone.

Blue looked up at Felix. "Thank you."

He nodded once jerkily and went back to the corner of the room. Blue sighed and moved back to the bed, taking Levi's hand once more. She squeezed it tight. "We're here, Levi. Come on back to us, okay? Who knows what will happen if you're not here to save me."

This time she knew she hadn't imagined the return squeeze, and a tightness in her chest eased. "He's going to be okay."

Mo'ata moved behind her, and his arms wrapped tightly around her middle, hugging her to him. "Yes, he will be okay."

Forrest came up from the side and hugged them both, squeezing in a big bear hug. "Hugs are good. Let's all do hugs." He rocked a little back and forth. "See, Blue, we're one big happy family. This'll work out great."

She smiled and gave Forrest a quick kiss on the chin, the only place she could reach, wrapped up in arms as she was. "Yes, hugs are good." She enjoyed their closeness for a little longer. "Do you think we can all stay in here tonight? I don't want to split us up, not tonight."

"Is good idea." Blue looked to where Felix still stood outside of them all. He didn't look angry anymore. He looked… lost. She freed the hand that wasn't attached to Levi and held it out. This time he took the peace offering.

───────

It took some arranging, but eventually everyone was settled. They left the cubs with Levi, and Blue snuggled into his other side. Felix was in his own bed, while Mo'ata and Forrest had dragged in mattresses from the other room.

Everyone laid down, but Blue didn't think anyone slept. She certainly didn't. Every time her eyes closed, she found herself listening for Levi's breaths, scared that at any moment they would stop.

"You awake?"

Blue didn't know who Forrest was talking to. "Yeah," she answered, just as Mo'ata said, "Yes," and Felix grunted.

Forrest gave a little choking sound. "Okay then."

Silence.

"Blue, do you think he did this?"

She didn't need to ask who he was talking about. Phillip. "I don't know. I didn't really get a chance to know him."

"Kevin told you about what he tried to do to Jason."

It wasn't a question, but she answered anyway. "Yeah."

"I don't want to believe he could do this." Forrest's voice was small, quiet, like a boy asking for reassurance after a bad dream.

"I know." Her voice was as gentle as she could make it. She needed to say something, anything. "Let's just wait till Levi wakes up, see what he has to say. Maybe it was that other guy."

"Yeah, maybe."

She heard the doubt in his voice—the same doubt she had. She didn't think it had been anyone but Phillip. The last time she'd seen him, he'd already changed, his mood swings scary and out of control. And they all knew he was obsessed with her for some reason. Hell, she was the bait.

It was about time she started pulling her weight. She had the beginnings of an idea, but she needed more information. She needed Levi to wake up. And she would need to convince the others. *That* was going to be the hard part, but this needed to end.

"Forrest?"

"Yeah?"

"You know, I've been done with this particular adventure for a year now." She tried to inject some lightness into her voice, but her throat was too tight, and she just came off as a manic squirrel.

"It's like the never-ending epilogue, isn't it?" His words were strangled.

Had she made it worse? "Is this a coconut moment? Do I need to come over there?"

That got a laugh. It was short and soft, but it was real. "No. No, the coconut moment has passed. Levi needs you right now. You stay where you are."

Blue smiled. Forrest was okay, at least at the moment. She concentrated on listening to Levi breath.

The cubs' purring picked up. It permeated the entire room and soothed her into sleep. Just as she was drifting off, a whispered question reached her. "What is a coconut?"

Chapter 11

BLUE

IT HAD BEEN TWO DAYS, and Blue was about to insist that the healer be sent for once more. Levi still hadn't woken.

"This has to end."

"You've said that before," Forrest teased, but he had barely left her or Levi these last couple of days.

"When are Felix and Mo'ata back? Have they checked in?" That was something good to come out of the attack on Levi. Mo'ata and Felix had started to really include Blue and Forrest in the actual hunt for Phillip. They'd been mostly helping with check-ins and coordination on the searches, but it was better than the waiting.

Sora had sent over all the surveillance recordings, not only from the area and time of the attack, but from all the other deaths as well. There were seven, including Blue's cousin Gabriella. It had taken another visit from her and Felix to convince the guards to share their information, and more than Sora had gotten involved. Blue had even thrown around her family name. She had a feeling *that* would come back to bite her, but she was beyond caring at this point.

The guards had already combed through the footage, but Blue and the others had an advantage. They knew who they were looking for. It hadn't sat right with her that they were withholding information from Sora. After what had happened to Levi, who knew more about what they were dealing with than anyone, she had agreed that keeping quiet was the best course of action.

She also had a better appreciation for how Jason must have felt. He'd had actual orders to keep quiet. There was no way he could have known that the Zeynars were going to attack that night. He'd probably saved Kevin's life by drugging him.

"Felix just checked in. He's at the site of the third murder. Apparently the workers there are just as close-mouthed."

That was another change. After the night of the attack, Forrest had... hardened, just a bit. He wasn't avoiding the truth of Phillip anymore. They didn't have confirmation, and wouldn't until Levi woke up, but sometime that night Forrest had acknowledged what she already knew. It was Phillip causing the deaths, and Forrest called them what they were—murders. She still couldn't bring herself to do that.

Her comm pinged, and she grabbed it up from where she'd set it next to Levi's bed. Every time she used it, there was a moment of unreality. It was so similar to a cell phone that she expected it to *be* a cell phone. She just stopped herself from bringing the device up to her ear, and hit the part of the screen that would accept the transmission.

Mo'ata's voice sounded in her ear. "I am checking in." They'd tried to explain how it was done without some sort of secondary receiver, but she finally just accepted there would be things she didn't get about all the new technology she was sure to encounter.

"Where are you now?" She brought up the map they had generated of all the known sightings and deaths. The ones Felix and Mo'ata had already checked out were marked in blue, the ones still to be investigated in orange.

"I am heading to the fifth site."

She double checked the map. He had been at the second, but the fifth was only a couple of streets down. Made sense.

"Were you able to find out anything at the last site?"

Silence.

"Mo'ata?"

"No."

She sighed. "Felix came up empty as well. I'm beginning to wonder if we'll find anyone who will talk to us."

"They talk. They just do not answer what we need answered."

"Do you think Sora would let us tap into the live feed of the surveillance?"

"Live feed?"

"Watch it as it is happening? Maybe we can see something new."

A pause. "Maybe. We will have Felix check with her."

"Okay."

"I need to go."

"Okay." She was speaking to an empty line. Her stomach twisted. Every time he checked in, she felt like she could breathe again, and every time he had to go, the fear returned. This hadn't happened before the attack. Just one more change.

"Anything?"

Blue pushed down the fear and turned to Forrest. "Nothing new. He's at the fifth site."

He nodded. "Okay, I'll let Felix know to head to the fourth."

Blue averted her gaze. Forrest had been dealing with Felix while Blue liaised with Mo'ata. Not because they each needed their own handler, but because Blue still wasn't sure how to act around Felix. Their easy playfulness had been replaced by something else, and there hadn't been time to sort it out.

A knock sounded at the door, and they exchanged glances. Her stomach flipped. At this rate, she'd never be able to eat again.

Silently, Forrest moved to the door and brought up the view screen, another thing Mo'ata had finally shown them how to use.

An older man stood on the other side, his sandy-blond hair just starting to turn to gray, his face lined and weary. He wore the same coat and scarf most everyone else in this area sported, but his were finer, the colors just a little... more.

Forrest pushed the intercom button. "Yes?"

"I'm looking for Miss Faust." He spoke in Common,

but she understood well enough. "My name is Brendan. Faust." The man grimaced slightly as he said the last name.

Blue froze. Brendan Faust. That was the name Sora had given her earlier. Her family was here. Now. She hadn't prepared; she didn't know what to say.

Forrest looked back at her. He must have seen the panic on her face because he quickly turned back to the door. "Moment, please." He left the view screen up, and Blue saw Brendan's face twist into a frown. This was not a man people usually kept waiting.

"Do you want me to tell him to go away?"

"No, but... I'm not ready. And I want Mo'ata here. And someone needs to stay with Levi. God, Forrest, what do I say?" Her voice rose until the end came out as a faint squeak.

A throat cleared, and they looked back to the view screen. "I can still hear you." This time he spoke in heavily accented English.

Blue covered her face, embarrassment mixing in with anticipation and dread. What would she say to him? She needed to get this under control. She reached over to the screen by the door and turned off the sound.

"We can't let him in here." Forrest glanced at where Levi lay.

"No, but I can't just tell him to go away. Maybe he knows something, and... he's family." Blue looked at the screen to see Brendan still standing there. The frowns were gone, and all she could see was the exhaustion. If this man—a cousin, if Sora was correct—was now feeling anything other than tired, it didn't show. "I'll talk with him in the hall, see what he wants and if he can come back later when the others are here. Can you...?"

"Yeah, I'll let them know he's here and we may need them to come in." Forrest studied Brendan, frowning. "I don't like it. Why is he here now?"

Blue shook her head. "This isn't like you. Since when are you the suspicious type? The man's a relative, and he just lost his daughter. He probably heard I was here and asking around. The way gossip seems to travel around here, that's not strange."

Forrest's eyes hardened, but he never looked away from the screen. "That's exactly the problem. He just lost his daughter. Why just show up like this? Why not send a message?" He crossed his arms. "I'll say it again; I don't like it." Forrest edged closer to the door in front of Blue.

Vivi let out a small growl from where she was snuggled into Levi's side. The cubs had remained with him, sensing the general worry and anxiety everyone was feeling toward him. She could feel their own in the back of her mind.

"I'll take one of the cubs out there with me. Leave the view screen on, leave the sound on." She stroked his arm. "I need to talk to him. He's family. And... his daughter is dead."

He placed his hand over hers, stilling it on his forearm. "Not your fault, pixie." He squeezed her fingers and let go. "Don't make me say it again."

Blue smiled and turned to pick up Vivi. She was probably not the best choice, but Garfield was sound asleep and tucked under Levi's arm. He looked too comfortable to disturb.

Forrest opened the door for her, and she stepped through, pushing the older man back from the doorway. They studied each other in silence.

He wasn't overly tall, maybe a few inches taller than her, and this close, the lines around his eyes and mouth were prominent. His eyes… were the same as her father's, and Blue's throat tightened. She saw an answering echo of sorrow in his gaze and remembered how much she resembled his own daughter.

When the silence had gone on too long for her comfort, she broke it. "I was really sorry to hear about your daughter." She wanted to take the words back as soon as she'd said them, but it was too late.

Brendan's mouth tightened. "Yes, thank you. You look much like her. I had heard…"

"I wanted to try to meet you to offer my condolences, but I wasn't sure if you would want me there, what with everything that's happened and how I even came to be here. I should have known you'd hear about me, though; this town sure loves to gossip." Brendan's frown deepened even more as she talked. "I'm sorry. I tend to talk when I get nervous. It's not exactly something I have control of a lot of the time, so I'm going to just be quiet again now." Blue pressed her lips together in emphasis.

His expression eased just a bit, and a faint smile crossed his lips before disappearing into overwhelming tiredness once again.

"You are like him, your father. It has been a very long time, but I remember."

"How do you know English?" She wasn't sure why she asked, but it seemed important to know the answer.

He frowned again, but this time it was more puzzled than angry. "He never told you anything about this family, did he?"

"Just that my grandparents on his side were dead and that he didn't have any family for me to meet." Her heart clenched when a new shadow swept over his face. Something about what she had said hurt, and she wanted to make this better. He was family after all. "Considering the situation, he couldn't really have said anything else, could he?" Her voice was gentle.

He took a breath and let it out slowly. "No, I don't suppose he could have."

Silence once again stretched out.

"What do you want?" Blue's whisper echoed loud in her ears. Vivi stirred in her arms and purred low, comforting her.

Brendan's gaze fell to the piquet cub and widened. He stepped back abruptly. "How do you have that?" His voice was higher than it had been.

Blue looked from Brendan to the cub and back. "Vivi? We rescued her. She won't hurt you."

He swallowed and nodded but didn't close the distance he'd put between them. "I would like to ask what you are doing here." He tore his gaze from Vivi and back to her face. "What you are truly doing here?"

"I'm here to find my family. It's just that when we found out that… Well, I decided to put off approaching you. It seemed intrusive." Her voice stayed soft, but the hand on Vivi's back tightened.

"Perhaps." His eyes narrowed, and—for a small moment—a new man looked out at her, one she sensed could be dangerous. She shivered. "It would be wise for you to tell me the truth." His shoulders tensed, but he didn't move, his eyes flicking again to the cub in her arms.

She reassessed. This was not just someone who missed his daughter. This was a man whose name inspired respect and maybe a little fear through an entire city. This was a man who was technically family, but who she had not met until now and who she didn't really know anything about. She took a step back toward the doorway, shifting Vivi to free up an arm.

"I am sorry. I did not mean to... I did not mean to alarm you. I simply need to do something to stop this killer. Please." He reached a hand toward her, and the weary father mourning his daughter was back. It looked real, but Blue couldn't dismiss that other side she'd just seen.

"It's not that I don't want to help, but..."

"Blue, I need you in here. Now." Forrest's voice came through the speaker set just below the screen by the door.

"I have to get back in there." She took a small step back into the doorway.

"Don't—"

"Could you leave us a way to contact you?" Panic of a different kind gripped her. "I would like to get to know my father's family, if nothing else, and maybe... hear about my cousin some time?" She didn't want to lose this new connection to her father.

He dropped his hand. "Of course. I will send my direction to your room." He gave a shallow bow of his head. "Until later, Blue. I do hope to hear from you."

He turned and walked down the hall, disappearing

around the corner. The door opened behind her, and Forrest pulled her back into the room.

"Thank you for rescuing me back there. I'm not sure what I would have—"

"He's waking up, Blue."

She spun and rushed to Levi, kneeling by the bed. Vivi crawled from her arms to her spot at his side and burrowed in, purring again. Blue took Levi's hand in her own and squeezed. Levi groaned, and she saw his eyelids flutter. She let out a breath.

"Come on, wake up. We need you to wake up, okay?" She felt the hand in hers flex and then grip tight. "Yeah, that's it." She heard Forrest talking to someone behind her and assumed he was calling the others, but she couldn't look away from Levi.

His eyelids fluttered again and slowly opened, showing her those golden eyes. A hand slowly came up and swept against her cheek. It came away wet.

"Crying?" His deep voice hit her.

"Well, you were unconscious for a couple of days, and I was worried. I think you shouldn't die, okay? That would really make me mad. Plus, who would save me? Obviously these other bozos aren't really up to the task."

His brows drew together, and he frowned, shaking his head slightly. Blue realized he had spoken in Common but she'd been rambling in English. Again. She shrugged and smiled. "Glad awake," she managed in Common.

Levi's expression eased, and he looked past her. "Yes, glad awake," Forrest echoed. "Felix and Mo'ata here soon." The cubs' purring grew as Levi closed his eyes. A small smile lingered, and he did not let go of her hand.

Chapter 12

BLUE

IT TOOK Mo'ata and Felix an hour to get back. Well, it felt like an hour. Blue wasn't sure how long it actually was; time was just one more thing she needed to figure out here. She knew the hours and months and years didn't correspond to Earth's time, but that was too much to think about right now. She mentally added it to her list, then shoved the distraction aside.

They were all in Levi and Felix's room. The extra mattresses were still there, as no one was quite ready to go back to their own rooms. Levi sat with his back to the wall, propped on pillows borrowed from the others so he could see everyone. Blue and Mo'ata were on one of the sleeping pads from the other room. Forrest was on Felix's bed, while Felix sat at the small desk, his comm out and the map of the city pulled up and hovering in front of him.

Felix spoke to Levi as Mo'ata translated. "Tell us again

what happened. See if you can remember where you were when you first spotted Etu."

They had taken to doing that. Felix would speak for them, and Mo'ata would translate. It was the most efficient method so far. Levi's memory of the incident was spotty, but the longer he was awake, the more he seemed to remember.

Levi studied the map, brows furrowed. He spoke, and a small red dot appeared on the map, close to the warehouse district. It slowly moved down the main street, recreating Levi's route. A sharp word from him and the dot stopped in the area where the apartments and shops transitioned to factories.

He closed his eyes for a moment, then sighed heavily and gestured for Felix's comm, his movements sharp.

Felix handed it over, then rubbed a hand through his hair. "He thinks he remember. Show."

The indicator moved a few blocks farther into the warehouse district. Levi studied the map for a few more minutes, and a new dot appeared. It traveled on a winding path, deeper into the district and then out. It paused near the main corridor. Another marker appeared and traced a path toward the inn, ending in an alley.

Levi handed the device back to Felix.

"That is his path. The first two markers are where he spotted Etu. The last is where he encountered Phillip." A new note of tension entered Mo'ata's voice. He frowned at the Prizzoli but averted his gaze when the other man glanced his way.

Something was up.

Felix, too, had been acting strangely toward Levi. It

was little things, like not meeting his eyes or a slight stiffening when he spoke.

"What's going on?" Blue studied each of them in turn and noticed something new. Shame. From Levi. "Levi?"

He raised his eyes and met hers. The cubs didn't stop purring, but it grew quieter, more subdued. The gold of his irises glowed out of his still ashen face, the dark circles only serving to make them brighter, more beautiful.

"No more secrets, Levi." Mo'ata said in Common, but Blue got the gist.

Levi swallowed, and he leaned his head back against the wall. Pain replaced the shame, and his mouth opened and closed a few times. Finally he nodded, coming to some sort of decision within himself. Mo'ata translated as he spoke, the words and sounds overlapping. "It is not a short explanation. And I would ask that it not go beyond these walls. I... know you have superiors you report to, but the honor and safety of my people rely on our secrets. I kept this from you. Maybe I should not have, but... I still may not tell you all of it."

Felix cut in. "All peoples have their secrets. Sometimes they need to be kept, and sometimes they must be shared." It was an acknowledgment of Levi's words, nothing more, but it struck Blue. She tucked the words away to examine later.

Levi inclined his head. "True." He met her gaze, and though Mo'ata translated, it was as if he spoke directly to her. "I am an agent for my people, as you know, and I was sent to retrieve the crystals. You know some of what they can do."

"Yes," she said.

"I was sent because I have some ability to sense them." Beside her Mo'ata stiffened, but he did not interrupt his translation. In fact, the entire room seemed to still, to hold its breath as Levi continued. "It is actually a prerequisite for becoming an agent or guard of the crystals. We are sought out at a young age and trained for this our entire lives. It is our only purpose, to keep them safe."

Blue's fingers curled into the covers, and she pressed her lips together, suppressing an urge to go to him. From what she'd picked up, it was an honorable task. Who was she to assume he needed or wanted more?

"They are used sparingly and only in the direst of need." A faint note of pleading entered his voice, though his expression never changed. "An only child whom parents depend on. A pregnant mother. A father who will leave behind children with no one else to care for them. And the only time energy is absorbed from others is when they willingly give it. Mostly it is those who are near the end of their lives." Garfield crawled into his lap and stretched up to bat at Levi's cheek with a soft paw. Levi glanced down at the cub and ran a large hand over its fur. "Their secret is kept so tightly," he whispered.

Felix drummed his fingers on the table. "It's out now, though. Even if we stop this, too many people have found out about them or at least what they can do. Zeynar may have eliminated loose ends on his part, but…"

"Yes, and that is more horrible than you can imagine." Levi set aside the cub and scooted to the edge of the mattress, rising unsteadily. Forrest rose to help him and was waved off. "And what Phillip has become is a terrible thing. There are monsters, and then there are... Monsters."

"Levi." She waited until he faced her. "What happened in that alley? What has Phillip become?" Mo'ata translated for her, and a corner of Levi's mouth ticked up in something that was far from a smile.

"The crystals are not just rock and mineral. The more they are used, the more life force they absorb, they more they become... aware." He crossed to where a pitcher of water sat beside Felix and poured. "I know I do not deserve it, but I ask that you trust me. I... will not divulge all the secrets of my people—I cannot—but will share what is needed.

"Sometimes a bond is formed between the crystal and the user that goes beyond the normal. The user becomes... entwined with the crystal and will eventually be able to use it without being in contact. When the bond is complete..." Something close to horror entered his tone and moved through his eyes.

Felix finally spoke. "This is why it took so long for Padilra to accept admittance into the Alliance." He sat unmoving, no expression on his face, no inflection in his tone. "Does your government even know of these crystals?"

"The elders can have much influence."

Not an answer, but an acknowledgment. Of what, she didn't know, but it seemed to satisfy Felix. *Damn political undercurrents.* "Someone want to explain what that means?" She looked at Felix, who just shrugged.

Mo'ata leaned in. "I will try to explain later."

"Try?"

"Universal Politics 101. Wonder if there's a class at the Academy," Forrest said.

Mo'ata peered around her. "Actually, there is something like that."

And now we are totally off topic. Time to reel it in. "So, what does this mean for Phillip?"

Mo'ata straightened and resumed his translations as Levi continued.

"Phillip has not fully bonded to the crystal yet. I saw it. He was able to hold back when I mentioned Blue and you." Levi inclined his head at Forrest, who sat on the other side of Blue.

"How do we get it out of him? This entity?" Forrest's voice was strained, and Blue took his hand in hers, squeezing.

"If we can get him to Padilra, we may be able to draw it out of him. It is a risk. If not managed correctly, he could... contaminate the other crystals. It could spell disaster for my people. Not just *my* people."

"The other option is to kill Phillip and destroy the crystal." Felix's voice was cold, and Blue's stomach shrank. She wanted her playful mercenary back, not this hard man.

Forrest jerked beside her, but remained silent.

Levi cocked his head. "Which is just as difficult. Possibly even more dangerous. Eliminating Phillip may not eliminate the threat. Etu is still out there. And..."

"What else have you not told us?"

Levi looked away. Blue hated seeing this man cowed like this. "If the entity that is the crystal has matured enough, it has long been suspected that it could possess anyone, not just the person it was originally connected to."

"So, there is *no* good choice," Blue said.

Levi looked at her and replied in English. "No."

"But the best one is to get him to your Elders?"

"Yes. We would need to separate him from the crystal, sever the connection somehow while keeping the crystal contained. He has progressed to the point of not needing contact with it, though." Levi sat again on his bed and leaned back. She noted a slight tremble in his limbs.

"How do we do that?" How did the crystals work? How would a being form from excess energy? How did that make *any* sense?

Then again, why not? Anything seemed possible these days.

"I do not know." Levi's eyes fell closed. He needed to get more food in him. As soon as they were done, she'd make sure some was ordered.

Forrest moaned. "So what you are saying is we are screwed."

Levi turned his head to the wall.

She swayed, lightheaded. *Yup, we're screwed. So bad.* Bending over, she put her head between her knees and worked on simply breathing.

Mo'ata stood, crossed to the bed Levi lay in, and spat a string of Common at him. Levi didn't reply. Blue looked up as Felix stood next to Mo'ata, a hand on his shoulder.

Blue leaned into Forrest. "Could you make out any of what that was about?"

Forrest looked down at her, his face pale. "All I caught

was 'debt' and 'split,' or maybe it was 'break.'" His faint tones barely reached her.

Blue looked down to where their hands were still linked.

For a brief moment, she regretted coming back. Was it really better to know than to wonder? Yes, she'd met up with Mo'ata again. Yes, they'd found out what had happened to Phillip. *More than I wanted to.*

She'd started something with Felix and Levi as well. Maybe it was just friendship, but it was something. She honestly couldn't imagine her life without them somewhere in it.

The situation they were in, though, she couldn't see a way out of it. What was worse, the men she had come to rely on, the ones who had kept her safe, didn't know what to do. She'd relied on them for that, counted on them to know the answers. She'd felt safe because of that.

It was a startling realization. She'd been thinking she was so brave to forge ahead and insist on exploring these worlds. To live her own adventures.

What kind of arrogance was that?

Someone spoke her name amidst a continued flurry of Common. Levi, Mo'ata, and Felix all spoke over each other, their voices climbing. The sounds blurred together.

Garfield slowly crawled into her lap, emitting a low purr. She could feel his worry, and buried a hand in his fur, seeking to comfort him and gain some in return. Her thoughts swirled.

"I can't think." Her voice was quiet, but Mo'ata was right there in front of her.

"Shopa."

Blue gazed past him. "I can't think. I thought I had a plan, but I can't think what to do."

He pulled her up and wrapped his arms around her, squishing the cub between them. Garfield let out a small, complaining cry but soon went back to purring.

"I thought I could do this." It hurt something in her to say the words.

Mo'ata tensed. "What are you saying?"

"I don't know." What *was* she saying? That she wanted out? No, though she'd hit her limit. But, damn, there were a lot of undercurrents going on in this room. *I need a fucking break from this.*

"Don't you dare, Blue." Forrest's voice was hard. "Don't you dare do this."

Mo'ata's arms tightened around her, and she pressed into him. A hand fell on her shoulder and tugged, but she was wrapped firmly in the clansman's arms.

"Blue." Forrest still sounded pissed, but there was something else under it, something she couldn't quite pin down. "Octopus."

She twisted her head and met his eyes. He'd never cried octopus. Not once since they'd made up the code words. It was just enough to shock her out of her spiral of doubt.

Maybe what I need is to woman up.

"What do you need?" she whispered.

"I need you back. I need my pixie back. And this?" He gestured at her huddled against Mo'ata's chest. "She isn't my pixie."

Mo'ata spun them so Forrest was blocked from her sight, and a low rumbling filled the room. It took her a moment, but she realized it was a combination of Mo'ata and Garfield. She picked up on puzzlement, worry, and... protectiveness. All from the cub?

Forrest was right, though. She tried to take a page from Phe and ignore the what-ifs.

She wound an arm around Mo'ata and hugged him, taking just a few more moments to break down. *Breathe in, breathe out. And done.*

She crooked a finger and gestured Forrest closer. Well, she hoped she did. Mo'ata's chest blocked out the rest of the room. When Forrest peeked around Mo'ata's shoulder and met her eyes, she stuck her tongue out. "I reserve the right to cast myself into despair and self-loathing at a later date."

A corner of his mouth crooked up. "Deal."

She tried to step back, but Mo'ata's arms didn't budge. She patted his back and tried again with the same result. Eventually, she sighed. "You're going to have to let go of me eventually."

"No, I will not. We will make do like this." His tone was grim, but could he really be serious?

Felix laughed behind her. "She no like that. Need hugs from others too." A few tugs on the arms around her, and she was able to put a couple of inches between Mo'ata and herself. Garfield, the wimp, used that to make his escape.

Another arm wrapped around her waist, and she was lifted away from the clansman and set in front of Forrest, who now wore a small smile.

"Octopus? Really? This was the word we came up with? It may be a little too appropriate." She poked him in the chest.

He batted her hand aside. "Actually, it was your word. I'm beginning to wonder if you're kinkier than I thought." He glanced around. "Yep, I count eight arms in this room that are not yours."

She slapped his arm even as heat filled her cheeks. "Hush."

Their eyes met and held. "Okay now?" Forrest's voice was low and steady.

Blue took a deep breath and nodded. "Better."

"So," he took a step away from her and looked at the others, including them all in the question. "What's the plan?"

Blue raised her hand, and three snorts reached her ears. She ignored them. "We stop Phillip. I know that's more of a goal, not really a plan, but you know, someplace to start." She looked around the room. She needed something to help her think, plot this out. Maybe her earlier idea could still work, with a few tweaks. "I need my pack."

She ran out of the room before any of the others could stop her and darted across the hall. She had a notebook in there and a pen.

It was time for a new list.

Chapter 13

BLUE

AFTER AT LEAST three more hours and a meal break—she made sure Levi got extra portions—Blue sat cross-legged on the floor next to Forrest. She looked down at the notebook balanced on her knee and the too short list they had started. It contained more questions than actions and wasn't nearly long enough.

Shardon Crystal List:

- Stop Phillip. Duh. – Drug him?
- Find a way to contain the crystal.
- Where is Phillip? Find him.
- Find Etu? Lead to Phillip.
- Use Blue as bait again? Probably…
- How to contain crystal? Block it?

- How does bond form? Need to know to break it.
- Use Fausts to flush out Phillip? Contact Brendan to see what he knows.

Blue had just written this one down and said it out loud. The resounding silence this brought about had her looking at each of the men around her. What had she missed?

"Ummm... Blue, you haven't told anyone about today's visit yet," Forrest gently chided from where he sat next to her, polishing off a second bowl of stew.

Mo'ata, seated next to Levi so he could once again translate, stood and moved in front of her. "No, she did not." He frowned and crossed his arms.

"So, yeah, Brendan Faust visited earlier today when you were out. Levi was still unconscious. I was actually talking to him when Levi woke up. He left us a way to find him; I guess I forgot all about it." She hadn't, not really. It just wasn't as important until now.

"You forgot about your family?" The frown remained, but now there was a raised brow.

Oh good, skeptical disappointment. Way worse than anger. She set aside her notebook, her hand trembling slightly, shaking the pages. "Maybe I didn't forget. But it wasn't as important as Levi waking up." She scooted to the side and stood.

Mo'ata twisted, keeping her in sight. "It is important, though. It is your family and information we should have had for the investigation."

She shrugged. "Yes, you're right. I'll apologize for that. But I don't know them, at all. Plus, I think there's something… off there. He was definitely someone used to being obeyed. He didn't like it when we told him to go away. Politely, of course. I also get the idea there's something people aren't saying about my family."

Mo'ata exchanged a glance with Felix.

"What aren't *you* telling me?" She looked between them. "Never mind. Don't answer that. What aren't you telling me that I should know?"

"The Fausts… We did some asking around." Mo'ata grimaced. "Well, Felix did some asking. It turns out they own Sirisa Shipping. They are not the largest shipping company on Karran, but they do have some… connections."

The silence stretched out. So they had connections. Every business had… "My family does dealings with the mob?" Blue's voice rose till she was in manic squirrel mode.

Forrest laughed, doubled over and red-faced. When he didn't stop, Blue slapped his shoulder. There *may* have been a tinge of hysteria in that outburst.

She looked at the others. Forrest wiped away the tears from his outburst. Mo'ata stood with his face set in a stoic expression, but his eyes crinkled. Levi wore that blank but resigned expression he got when they started talking in English and he couldn't understand. Felix frowned at her and tilted his head.

"Mob?"

The question set Forrest off again. Blue ignored him this time and sat next to her big mercenary. "Basically, mob is a word used when you are talking about a… crime family or a family that has dealings in criminal activities, even when they have legitimate business dealings as well. Actually, the real businesses often disguise the less legal activities."

Felix let out a low humming sound and sat back. "So, Earth has too? Yes, Faust mob. Not bad as Martika Families." He grimaced, but the mention of Martika brought to mind Trevon. That hooligan owed them. He owed them big.

Excitement gripped her and her heart pounded, sending her blood surging. "What if we used that? Also, that falls under 'information to share,' don't you think?" She shot a pointed look at Mo'ata.

Felix stiffened. "Use?"

"Yes, and we should pull in Zeynar." She deliberately left off the first name, but Mo'ata scowled and stiffened further.

"He has connections we don't. He also had the crystals in his possession for months. He may have an idea on how to keep them contained." She crossed her arms and leaned back in her chair.

Felix placed his comm on the table, his movements controlled. "No want here. No good involve Families. He trouble."

"Why?" She probably sounded like a petulant five-year-old.

"Families trouble." A fist clenched, but other than that, he held himself in.

"I'll ask again, why?" Felix wouldn't meet her gaze. "Is this more political stuff I don't understand, or is this particular to Zeynar?"

"Other than the fact that he was responsible for your

kidnapping?" Mo'ata asked.

Forrest jerked and then rose, pacing to the other side of the room and then back. Crap, Derrick. Vivi let out a little whine, but he ignored her. He didn't say anything, but he did shoot a searching glance at Blue before his path forced him to turn or hit a wall.

She almost let it go. Almost. Garfield jumped onto the bed beside Levi and butted his side. As the Prizzoli pet him, something new happened. An image came to her. Bodies—lifeless, eyes blank—lay in the streets. A trail of them led to a man with a faint aura of purple. Phillip.

Was Zeynar really worse than that? Also, what the hell? She gestured at her notebook. "We're stuck. Something needs to get us off-center. I really think Zeynar and my family could help."

"I am not arguing about involving the Fausts. It is a good idea. Zeynar, though. He will find some way to twist this in his favor." Mo'ata's tone was hard.

Was he thinking of the kiss? She darted a look at Forrest. She hadn't told him and now was not the time to bring it up. *And how arrogant is that thought?*

She took in a deep breath. "I won't pretend to understand. I don't really know him. I don't know his past or your pasts. Really, I don't know anything, do I?" The words burst out of her.

Forrest stopped pacing and eyed her warily. Felix shifted beside her, and Mo'ata opened his mouth, but she cut him off with a raised hand.

She wasn't done. "I owe you a penny, don't I? It's actually tucked away in my pack. You can cash it in on this one if you want. Hell, you can cash it in on anything. But dammit, I'm out of ideas."

"It's not all on you, Blue. Actually, it's not on you at all." Forrest took a step toward her.

That forced out a strained laugh. "Of course it is. It's on us because we're here. Well, it's also on Zeynar. I don't care if he paid his debt or whatever that message meant when he let me go. He owes us. Think about that. And. I. Don't. Have. Another. Idea." She stood. "Fuck, none of you do, or you would have said it." She unclenched her fists and stretched out her fingers. *Why am I so damn angry?* "All I said was he might know something we don't, and we should use it. Levi, who's the expert, doesn't have a clue how to contain the crystal."

No one said a damn thing. Felix remained stony-faced. Levi watched her wide-eyed, probably because she looked like a crazy woman. And Forrest and Mo'ata gazed at her with concerned expressions. *Concern.*

"I need to get out of this room for a little while. I need some Beast time." She grabbed her coat and shrugged it on. "It really says something when the thought of being around the demon-mount is more relaxing than dealing with you four." She glared specifically at Mo'ata, the most upset with him for some reason.

His concern smoothed away into his usual calm expression. "Don't go alone."

Had she ever thought that coolness of his reassuring? It wasn't. It was… *patronizing.* And that made her even angrier. She snorted. "I wasn't planning to go alone. I have no interest in being kidnapped again. Not that you seem to believe that. If it were up to you, I'd stay here all bundled in cotton candy and never go anywhere ever again."

He stalked to her, muscles bunched and hands fisted. At least the calm was gone. *Good.* "Is that so bad? That I want you safe? Blue, this situation is so far beyond anything you, or Forrest, are equipped to handle. It's beyond anything *any* of us are prepared to deal with. So tell me, is it that unreasonable for me to insist one of us accompany you?"

She closed her eyes as the heat of her anger drained out of her. Now all she felt was tired. "No," she whispered. "Please, one of you, just come down with me. I really do need to get out of here, just for a few minutes, just to... have a little bit of normal. Or as normal as I can have right now. I just need a break."

A large hand grazed over her shoulder and then cupped her neck. A gentle pressure pulled her in until her forehead rested against a hard chest. Herbs and pine surrounded her. "I will go with you so you may see your Beast."

"Thank you."

"You are welcome." Mo'ata let her go and stepped back. "First, I ask that you put on your boots."

Blue looked down at her sock covered feet and let out a sharp laugh. "Yeah, boots would be good."

She caught sight of Forrest as she hurried to pull them on. He tilted his head and raised his brows slightly. *Are you okay?*

She shrugged a shoulder and crooked up one side of her mouth in a half smile. *I'm fine.*

But it felt like a lie. She wasn't fine. She just didn't

know *why*. There was too much to choose from—which simply made it all worse.

Mo'ata remained silent beside her as they made their way through the halls and rooms of the inn and out to the barn. Night was falling, the soft between-time of twilight giving even this dour city a slightly magical air. That, too, felt like a lie.

She pushed open the door to the barn and silently grabbed a grooming brush before heading straight to Beast's stall. He stuck his head over the door but didn't give her any of his usual attitude. He lipped her hair then backed away, allowing her to open the door and enter. He stood patiently as she brushed him, letting her work down one side of his back, then the other. She lost herself in the work until everything, including Mo'ata, faded into the background.

Beast's rumbling purr started, low at first, then picked up in volume. She leaned into him and rested her cheek on his neck, wrapping one of her arms around his neck as far as it would go. She stayed that way until her arm cramped. Pulling back, she stared at Beast's shining fur until a large hand took the brush from her and resumed the grooming. Beast swung his head around, narrowly avoiding her, and snorted, but he didn't stop his purr.

"I'm sorry," she told Mo'ata. "I'm just…"

"Frustrated," he finished for her.

"Yeah." She watched him groom her demon-mount, the muscles in his arm bunching then relaxing, the rhythm of it lulling her. "It's not just being cooped up. It's… everything. It's meeting some of my remaining family and then discovering my father comes from criminal ties. It's taking care of two little piquet cubs who seem to have some sort of telepathic ability and that everyone seems to think will someday shred them open like one of those fancy knives on TV. It's realizing, every day, that no matter how hard I tried, I am not prepared for these worlds. It's dating two men when I've never had sex." His hand jerked slightly on that, then continued with smooth strokes. "It's having to deal with a potentially world-destroying crystal entity, and not even knowing how time is measured here."

He put the brush down and turned to her, though he remained silent. Blue took in a deep breath, the scent of animals, hay, and Mo'ata mixing together. Gathering her courage, she looked into his face. She didn't think she could bear another look of disappointment.

The whites of his eyes were red, though she didn't see a sign of tears. The contrast brought out the green tones so that they fairly shone, even in the low light. His face had softened, and as she watched, the corners of his lips curled up. He reached up and tucked a strand of hair behind her ear. "Then it is a good thing you are not alone." He placed a light kiss on her lips. "And you were correct earlier. As much as I hate to admit it, Zeynar would be an asset in this. As would your family. They know this city and can get the workers and shop owners to cooperate."

Tears welled in her eyes, and she blinked rapidly, willing them away. He was right—she wasn't alone. "Guess we'd better get back to it then. We have a list to finish and a couple of mobsters to contact."

He smiled, the big beautiful one that rarely came out,

and Blue's heart skipped. He leaned down again, and his lips had almost reached hers when a throat cleared.

Blue glanced over, and there stood Jason, the orange of his robes standing out in the fading light. Light from a lamp above the door cast his features into stark shadows.

"Jason?" Her voice was quiet. She couldn't quite believe he was here. "Jason!" She grinned at him and rushed to the barn door, hugging him tight.

She'd often wondered if they could have left things better before he departed. At the time, though, she'd had no plans to ever come to Karran again and trying to form a real friendship had seemed pointless.

Now, seeing him here just after she'd been overwhelmed by all that was new, all she would have to tackle, she was doubly glad for another familiar face. "What are you doing here? How are you? How long have you been back? Did you know Forrest is here too? And we had some sort of weird time warp when we came through so that here it was like only a couple months and back on Earth it was a year." Her words were muffled against his chest, and she pushed back, peering up at him.

He smiled, but it was small. There were dark rings under his eyes, and now that she was closer, she could make out faint worry lines between his brows. He also hadn't hugged her back.

"Jason?" Mo'ata reached her side and placed a hand on her hip. "What are you doing here?"

Jason's gaze flicked down to where Mo'ata's hand rested, and then to Blue's face, and finally settled on the clansman. "I'm here from the Ministry. They received reports of deaths in the area, suspiciously similar to those that occurred two months ago. I expected to find you and the mercenary and Prizzoli. I know you've been working on tracking Phillip. But I did not think I'd find..." He settled his gaze on Blue, and he swallowed. "I did not expect to find you here, Blue."

She shrugged, taken aback by his aloofness. *Though should I really be surprised?* The enthusiasm she'd felt upon first seeing him died away. "We decided to come back."

"I'm—" He cleared his throat and looked away. "I'm glad to see you again. Is... is Kevin here as well?"

"No." It came out harsh, and Blue reminded herself that this was a shock for him too. She softened her voice. "He stayed behind. With Phe."

Jason looked back at her, something between a smile and a grimace twisting his lips. He scanned her face, looking her over. "You said it's been a year?"

Did she imagine the note of wistfulness? He'd always been so hard for her to read. "Yeah. Phe's going to UT in their theatre program. Kevin was also accepted, architecture."

"Is he still playing football?"

"No." She let the silence stretch out.

His eyes fell closed, and he took a deep breath. When he opened them again and met her eyes, the warmth she sometimes saw was there. "I missed you, Blue."

"You did?"

"Yeah, I did. I've been back for a few weeks. It's strange to think that a whole year has gone by back on Earth."

"I'm still getting used to it too." She couldn't think of anything else to say and looked up at Mo'ata.

"You may as well come up with us. We will need to consult with Levi, but I suppose the Ministry should be involved in this as well." Mo'ata's hand tightened on her hip, and he led her out of the barn, Jason following behind.

Chapter 14

TREVON

TREVON ZEYNAR SLAMMED his hand on the desk next to the report he'd just received. "Fuck." After the debacle that had been his life for the last couple of months, he'd needed a bit of good news.

In a way this was fortunate, he supposed.

She was back, his little star. His Blue.

She wasn't really his, though. She'd been in his care for barely two days. That was it. Two days. Then she'd gone back to her own planet. No, she'd chosen to go back to her own planet.

He'd kept tabs on her after the clansman picked her up two months ago. He'd even followed her on one of their outings, the ones before she returned to Earth. He should have been consolidating his power base and meeting with his father's remaining allies to re-contract agreements, but he'd needed to see with his own eyes that she was okay.

He'd been going to leave it at that. She didn't need to get involved in his life, his world. They were a bloodthirsty, ruthless bunch. *No, we are a bloodthirsty, ruthless bunch.*

Now she was back. And she'd involved herself in his unfinished business.

That made her fair game.

He grinned. Now that he'd had a moment to process this new information, he realized this was quite perfect. Phillip and Etu were loose ends he didn't want left hanging, and he'd had people on the lookout for any signs of them. He'd heard there had been similar deaths in Filiri, and when he'd sent one of his men to check it out, he got much more than he'd expected.

Also turned out that his Blue was a Faust of Sirisa Shipping Fausts. He'd only made the connection after she'd gone home and it was no longer a connection he could use. Now he had a way to get an in with Brendan Faust, finally. He may even be able to get all his business away from the Finnegans.

It had taken him a while, but he'd put together all the pieces after Blue and her merry band had gone home. David Faust's daughter. The offspring of the black sheep of the Faust empire. The son who'd turned his back on the business and joined the Ministry, then turned his back on *that* and gone his own way, cutting all ties. His kind of man. The business had passed to a cousin who took over the reins and had done fairly well.

How did she get back? *Why* was she back? Was it another accident, or had she wanted to come back?

Did she think of him? His heart sped up, and he swallowed. *Stop acting like a schoolboy, Trevon.*

He looked back down at the report, and the grin morphed into a full smile. He didn't see a downside to this situation. He would use the Fausts to help him find Phillip so he could put that part of his life behind him. He would help them find and kill their daughter's murderer, they would owe him, and he would be able to gain more time and attention from Blue. Yes, no downside at all.

He opened his comm. "Get me Brendan Faust on the line," he told his secretary. Well, his second secretary. He had *two* now. The one outside he'd inherited from his father. Some of the things he'd had to change about his life when he took over the family still amused him. It was just one more game, playing at the stoic, steady, head of the Family.

"Sir," came over the line. "You have another call coming in, a Blue Faust. I was going to take a message, but since you asked for the Fausts, shall I put it through?"

He froze. She was calling him. "Yes, please do." He was careful to keep his tone even, almost bored. How did one girl affect him so much? It was really quite ridiculous.

"Hello?" A quiet voice said hesitantly. That wasn't how he remembered her. What had happened?

"Hello, little star. Miss me?" He kept his tone light, conscious that his words echoed the ones he'd said to her over two months ago.

He heard a faint laugh. "How do you always do that?"

"What?" He leaned back in his seat, relaxing.

"Make me laugh at the most inappropriate times."

He lowered his voice. "I can be very inappropriate." He paused as she made a choking sound. "Well, when the time is right."

"So, you can be inappropriate when it's appropriate?"

"Yes." He was enjoying this too much. Time to get back to work. "To what do I owe the pleasure of your call?"

"I have a feeling you already know." Her tone was chiding.

Oh, I like this girl. "Maybe. Why don't you tell me? We don't want any miscommunications, now do we?"

"Ummm… I'm not sure how much I'm supposed to say over the comm." He detected a slight tremble in her voice. "We—" Another muffled sound and low voices in the background. "We found Phillip, or where we think he is. And Etu. But we haven't been able to track them down precisely, and there are other… factors."

"What do you need from me?" He would, of course, give it, but he wanted to draw out the game a little longer.

"I—We were wondering if you could exert some influence. The locals aren't that cooperative. Also, you have some experience with the crystals. Did you ever—"

She broke off again, interrupted by a man's deep voice. Its harsh tone stirred anger in him, and he clenched a fist.

Then she interrupted the speaker, her own voice, though muffled, tougher than he'd yet heard. "You agreed to this. Think of it as him repaying a debt." More deep rumblings. Whoever this guy was, he was an ass. "Do you have a better idea? No? Then we are sticking with this one."

Trevon smiled. Oh, to be a fly on the wall. Though why anyone would want to be one of those insects, he didn't know. English was a strange language, but evocative all the same. *Also, why bother wishing?*

"I'll be there in two days." His blood rushed in anticipation.

"Wait! How do you know where we are? Never mind, stupid question. Of course you already know where we are. Okay, yes, please come down, but can you also bring any research or studies or... any information you have on the crystals? Felix—"

A new voice came on the line speaking in Common. "Zeynar. I know you and your father would not have resisted studying the crystals while they were in your possession. We need whatever you have."

"Hello, mercenary. Brought down any empires lately? Killed anyone for profit?" Trevon had no problem with Felix, or the Order, but he couldn't resist the little dig. They were so much fun to play with. It was an open secret that most mercenaries out of Cularna were also part of the Order. Personally, he thought the whole thing a wonderful scheme. Who wouldn't want to try to take over the worlds in the guise of maintaining freedom and peace for everyone?

No, he had no problem with them. As long as they stayed away from what was his.

A low growl and small grunt, then Blue was back. "Sorry. They agreed to let me do the talking, but the sneaky one managed to get the comm away from me."

He laughed out loud at her disgruntlement. "Your mercenary is correct. My father did do studies, seeking to replicate the healing effect. I will bring what I have. Any hints as to why you need it?"

"I'm not supposed to say till you get here. Just bring it all."

Silence fell, and he wondered if she'd cut the line, though his comm indicted it was still open. "Little star?"

"I'm going to ask someday why you call me that."

"And I'll tell you. Now, is there something else?"

"Yeah." The word was a sigh threaded with steel, and he imagined her as she'd looked the last time he'd seen her—weary and wary but with a stubborn determination and humor coming through in everything she did. "So, turns out my family has some dealing in the black market, or whatever it's called here. Sirisa Shipping. Their daughter was one of the people Phillip… killed. I'm going to bring her father in on this too. He already visited once, but it wasn't a good time to— Anyway, we're going to ask him too. Just wanted you to know."

This was perfect. "Oh, no, let me call him. It would be my pleasure. I have additional things to discuss with Brendan anyway."

"Mob things?" Her tone was suspicious, and he could practically see her pink lips frowning.

"Mob things?" he echoed. "Yes, I like that. I will discuss 'mob things' with your cousin."

"Oh. Okay. We'll see you in two days, then."

"Two days. I look forward to it."

"And, thank you. Thank you."

Was that a slight hitch to her last words? "You are very welcome, little star."

He waited until the comm indicated the other line had been cut, then pushed through to his secretary again. "Get me Brendan Faust. Now. And get transport arranged to Firik and a team—use Prin. We leave in three hours. Also, you traced where that last call was from?"

"As usual."

"Get me the address."

"Yes, sir."

He cut the line and snorted. *Sir*. But it was something he had to put up with now that he was head of the family. He looked down at the suit he wore, then at the wood and leather, the expensive cut-crystal and *fogan*-silk rugs that dotted the office. His father's office.

For a brief moment he regretted his father's death. Well, the necessity of it. In the same circumstances, he would do it again. Gladly. But it had forced him into a position and a responsibility that he had never wanted, had hoped to put off for many years.

Now he was back in the game, out of this office, out of the meetings and the tedium. There was way too much paperwork involved in running a... *mob* family.

The grin stayed with him as he waited for Brendan Faust to come on the line. No, there was no downside to this situation that he could see.

BLUE

Blue disconnected the comm and let out a breath of relief. Trevon was going to help them. She'd hoped, but she hadn't been sure he would. While charming, he'd seemed so… changeable.

Blue stared down at the comm she still held in her palm. "He said he'll be here in two days."

"Are you sure this was a good idea? The last time he became involved…" Forrest's voice was tight. He clutched Vivi, and she squeaked.

… *Derrick died*, she finished silently. "I think it's our only option. Or the only one with a chance. We've gone over this." She dropped her comm on the bed and leaned into his shoulder. The muscles bunched under her. She didn't know what to say to make this better. Maybe there wasn't anything.

The other men were ranged around the room, silent and waiting. The tension rose another notch as Jason shifted and pulled away from the wall. "This is a mistake, involving Zeynar."

Mo'ata, seated beside Levi at the only table, pushed his chair back, though he stayed seated. His hands clenched rhythmically, and the silence built. He took a deep breath and let it out through clenched teeth. "We have talked about this, over and over. We are done talking."

Blue relaxed. She didn't want to argue about this again, and Jason's protests could have set everyone else off as well. But it looked like Mo'ata was supporting her views now after their… talk.

"He's also going to contact Brendan Faust for us."

Felix, leaning against the far wall, snorted. "He take—" He broke off and switched to Common. Mo'ata finished for him. "He is taking advantage of the situation. The Fausts usually deal with the Finnegan Family."

"I honestly don't care."

"Not ready to deal with them?" Forrest asked.

"Nope." She didn't need to tackle everything all at once. And family was a big thing to tackle. Once Phillip and the crystal were dealt with, maybe. Until then, she was more than willing to let someone else handle the Fausts of Sirisa Shipping.

"Well, shouldn't we get out there and scout? There must be people you haven't questioned yet. I can call in more agents..." Jason trailed off at Forrest's glare.

Blue wanted to glare herself. Jason kept asking about things that were already hashed out. Only, he hadn't been there for the discussions. "Don't glare, Forrest. He needs to get caught up."

Levi had taken a chance, allowing the Ministry agent to be brought in on the crystals. As suspected, the Ministry already knew some of what they were up against, thanks to Jason's own reports and what they'd found out from Cravin. They hadn't known about the Bonding, though, or that it could take on a personality and life of its own.

Garfield approached the Ministry agent, sniffing at his boots and stretching up to bat at his robes. He looked back at Blue and then up at Jason's face, then back to Blue. A sense of curiosity and caution came to her. No, she didn't want to tell Jason about the piquet, not yet. That was not her decision, not really. She'd leave it to Mo'ata. Jason bent to pet the cub, and Garfield scuttled back out of reach, bounding over to the clansman, who scooped him up to his shoulder.

"He is correct. We do need to continue the patrols. No more people, though." Mo'ata spoke with Levi, who was already looking much better after a few more meals. "It's been a long day. Levi needs to rest. I will bring Jason up to date fully and then patrol. Felix, I think it is a good idea to begin lessons." He inclined his head to Blue and Forrest. "A short one tonight. We'll continue them for a time each day. They do not need to be… wrapped in candy."

"Cotton candy." Blue couldn't resist the correction.

"Cotton candy."

Forrest leaned in close. "Damn, we should have brought in Jason sooner. How much of that about-face do you think was from our big redhead wanting to one-up him?"

She thinned her lips, suppressing a smile. "Or he now fears my wrath."

Forrest pretended to think. "Nah."

Jason's eyes narrowed. "Looks like there's a lot I need to catch up on."

Felix straightened. "Yes. Much." He strode for the door. "Come. Go to stable," he said as he passed Blue and Forrest. "Bring knife." Vivi made a running leap just as the mercenary reached the doorway, latching onto his armor. He continued on, a cat clinging to his back.

"Damn. They grow up so fast." Forrest followed after them.

Blue went last, rushing to get her new dagger from her room and catch up with the other two on the stairs. They headed for the barn. Light from the streets filtered to the side area, and the overhead lights gave them enough to see by.

She took a moment to greet Beast for the second time that day. Felix arranged her and Forrest next to each other, then took up a stance in front of them. "Copy."

Blue pulled her knife, but he stopped her. "No yet. Copy." Then he placed himself again, feet a little wider than shoulder-width apart, knees bent, arms a bit out from his sides.

She and Forrest matched his stance, and he adjusted them. "Stay." After a few moments, he indicated for them to pull their knives. Then he stepped into the position again, this time with his own knife held before him, fist wrapped around the hilt. "One."

They matched him, or tried to. Again, he corrected their stances, getting Forrest lower and Blue's feet farther apart. He also moved Blue's thumb so it wrapped around her fingers, like a fist. Forrest's he left with a sharp nod. "One."

He adjusted the grip on his own knife so the blade was held down, flat against his wrist. She'd seen this in movies. "Two."

They copied him, and he corrected.

"One." He spun the blade back to the first position and crouched down.

Blue didn't spin, but she got her grip back to "one" and checked her stance, pushing her foot out a few more inches.

"Two."

They switched.

"Good. New stand." Felix placed his right foot, the one

on the same side as his knife hand, before him, stance still wide. He twisted just slightly. His left hand protected his middle. He also had a new grip, the blade facing up, thumb on top. "Three."

They got in position, and he corrected. They switched between the three as he called them out over and over, adjusting as needed. After about thirty minutes he nodded. "Next." He grabbed Blue's hand, the one with the knife, and brought it up to his throat. "Aim here." He moved it down to his groin. "Here. Most blood."

He stepped back and fell into "three." Then he slashed up and then down. "No stab. Cut."

Beside her Forrest nodded. "Yeah. You have to slash, not stab. The knife could get caught on bone if you stab. Unless it's the right kind of knife."

Felix eyed him then nodded. "Yes. You learn?"

"My father had some… interesting ideas on how a boy should be raised. We humored him. It's come in handy, though."

Felix's lips thinned. "Not assume know all." He frowned and huffed out a breath. "You," he said, pointing with his knife at Forrest. "Learn with Blue. Most good. Fix some."

Forrest's grip on the knife handle tightened. Then he fell into "one" and nodded. "Fair enough."

For the next hour they practiced those three holds over and over, inserting slashing motions. Felix had her concentrate on the leg and groin area because of her height. By the end, her arm was jelly, but she felt semi-confident she wouldn't hurt herself if she picked up her knife. Felix helped her thread the sheath onto her belt.

She pulled the knife and went into "three." *Definitely on the way to badass.* She tried to sheath the blade and missed. It skimmed along her upper thigh, and she narrowly avoided slicing herself open. *Okay, one foot on the path to badass.*

Chapter 15

BLUE

TWO DAYS LATER...

Blue was just leaving the barn, Felix behind her, when a transport pulled up in front of the inn. A cool breeze blew as two men climbed out, dressed in bodysuits that looked familiar. *They look like...*

"He's here," she said, her breath a small white cloud in the cold of the morning. Felix stood close behind her, blocking some of the breeze.

One of the men hurried into the inn while the other opened the rear door of the transport. A man stepped out, his dark hair tousled, silver studs glinting in his right ear. He looked different. The scruff of beard was gone, leaving him clean-shaven, and he was paler than she remembered. He was also wearing... jeans?

The first man came striding out of the inn and said a few words to Trevon. He looked abruptly toward the barn, and his gaze landed on her. A smile appeared, and he nodded at her. He said a few words to his men, who grabbed bags from the transport and entered the inn.

Trevon didn't move right away, just kept looking at her, that smile firmly in place. Blue shifted restlessly. Why wasn't he coming over? Was she supposed to go to him? And how ridiculous was this? She'd had two encounters with the guy. Two. That was it. They were memorable, yes, but she'd spent *maybe* an hour in this man's company.

It was Felix who broke the stare-off. He placed a hand on her shoulder and pulled her back into his chest until their bodies were flush. Trevon's eyes narrowed, and he nodded toward the inn door. A moment later he went inside.

Blue stared at the transport. "Well, that was interesting."

"He… sneaky man. No trust." Felix guided her to a side entrance.

Felix was calling Trevon sneaky? *The irony*.

They hurried up the stairs, passing one of Trevon's men, who now carried different bags, three men hurrying after him. What the…?

Trevon stood in the doorway of the room beside hers, the one that wasn't Mo'ata's, looking it over with thinned lips. She drew even with him and paused. "I thought the inn was full?"

He shrugged. "I had two days to arrange things. Although I expected the innkeeper to have them gone."

"So you just kicked them out?"

"Well, I could have had them killed, but I decided moving them to another inn in a nicer area and paying for their new rooms would be less messy." He peered back into the room as the other of his men approached.

Felix rolled his eyes. An actual, whites-showing, full-on eye-roll. Blue continued on to her room while Trevon conferred with his man.

"Blue," Trevon said.

She paused at her door.

"It is good to see you again." When she nodded, he turned to Felix. "Maybe we should begin while my men see to the room?"

Felix crossed his arms.

"Felix," Blue said. "I'm going to wash up. Can you check in with Mo'ata? He'll want to know Zeynar is here."

Felix nodded, and Trevon smirked. "So formal. I'll be right here. Oh, and I spoke to your cousin. He'll be sending any information he finds directly to me. I hope that is all right?" His gaze roved over her face. "I can have him funnel it through you if you prefer?"

Did she? "No, he can send it to you. That will be faster." She turned back to her room but didn't step in.

"I can arrange for you to meet with him anytime you like. Anytime you are ready." His voice was closer.

She looked over to find him only a few feet from her. "Thank you. And... I will take you up on that. When this is over." When she had a brain cell to spare for it. A thought struck her. "Does everyone involved in mob things speak English? I would honestly think Spanish or Chinese would be more likely. I read somewhere that more people speak those than English."

"*Hablo esos tambien, pequena estrella.*" He propped a shoulder on the wall. "Do you know what the main...

exports are from Earth? Chocolate, tobacco, ginger, and…
cranberries."

Felix cleared his throat, and Trevon straightened.
"Blue, wash. Trevon come me."

She hurried through her washup and then across the
hall to Levi's room. Everyone else was already there,
arranged on mattresses and chairs. Trevon sat on the floor
near the far wall, legs stretched in front of him. Blue sat
next to Levi this time, listening as Mo'ata filled Trevon in
on the crystals and Phillip. When they were done, Trevon
leaned back, eyes closed, his fingers laced.

A few moments later he opened his eyes and fixed
them on Blue. "This is more than I bargained for."

She couldn't read him, and all traces of playfulness
were wiped from him. She held his gaze. "I didn't know
we were bargaining."

"Everything is a bargain, little star. Everything." He
stood. "I'll still help, but I'll need something in return."

Blue picked up Garfield and held him in front of her
like a shield. The cub tensed and fixed his eyes on Trevon,
though he didn't growl.

Trevon moved closer and stopped just feet away. "I
want another kiss."

The reactions were immediate. Forrest spun to stare at
her, eyes wide. Mo'ata stiffened. Felix and Jason cursed.
Levi's was the most interesting. He grinned.

"You kissed him?" Forrest's tone was guarded, and she
could see the hurt in his eyes.

"Technically, I kissed her. But yes, we kissed." Trevon
crossed his arms, one brow raised. It reminded her too
much of Phillip.

"You are an ass," she hissed, then turned to Forrest. "It was last year. He'd just let me go, and we were in the scent shop. He gave me the crystals and that perfume, and then he kissed me. It wasn't really anything, didn't mean anything. He was just being... a hooligan." She spat the last in Trevon's direction.

"Then why didn't you say anything about it? Why hide it?" Forrest asked. Vivi crept across the floor to him, making small pleading sounds. He looked down at her but didn't pick her up. His eyes when they met Blue's were dull. *What was he thinking?* "And what perfume?"

Her heart stopped. Why hadn't she told him anything about what had happened with Trevon? They'd promised to be honest with each other. Why had she held back? The answer came to her, and she told him, holding nothing back this time. "Because it didn't matter. And because it would have hurt you. I never expected to see him again. The kiss was nothing. It was passably pleasurable, but it was a shock and not particularly welcome at the time."

Trevon smirked, and it definitely wasn't charming this time. "I don't know. You were breathing pretty hard by the end of it."

Felix slapped his hand over Trevon's mouth and squeezed his cheeks. "No talk you."

Trevon grabbed Felix's wrist and dug his fingers into the tendons. Felix's lips thinned, but he didn't let go. Blue held her breath. She should do something, but she felt frozen.

Garfield dug his claws into her arm through her sweater and undershirt. Worry came through their link and an image of Forrest crying. *What? How...?* Another mystery to add to the pile.

"Stop!" The word burst out of her. She stormed over to Trevon and kicked him in the shin. "You stop. You're supposed to be here to help. I don't know what you're trying to do right now, but it's not helping." She glared up at Felix. "Thank you for making him shut up, but this is going too far."

She spun, glaring at all of them, even Forrest. So he was upset she hadn't told him every little thing about herself. Yes, they'd said they'd be honest, but did that mean she could have no thoughts of her own, no memories that she could pull out and look at in the dead of night? No hopes or parts of herself that were just for herself?

"You want to know where the perfume is? It's in my bag. I've never used it. I'll pull it out sometimes and look at it. Want to know what I think when I see it? I think that somewhere out there is a man who is spontaneous and charming, and, yes, he kissed me. It reminds me of my time here. It reminds me of the good and the bad, just like Mo'ata's scarf did." She walked to Forrest and stopped just out of arm's reach. "I never used it because that's all it was. A passing moment. No, I didn't tell you because it was *my* moment. At the time, it didn't have anything to do with you, Forrest. I know that sounds harsh, but it's true."

He met her gaze, his eyes cold, face blank. "You should have told me. Especially when we agreed to come back here. If he was in the running, I should have known."

Her heart skipped a beat. Here it was. Part of her had expected this much sooner. She'd never truly believed that

Forrest could be so accepting of other men being with her, dating her. He'd just thrown himself in. But so had she.

"Maybe so." Her shoulders slumped, and she looked away. "Maybe so."

"It's not that you kept the perfume or that he kissed you. It's that you didn't tell me. It's like... you don't trust me."

What could she say to that? *He's right.*

When she didn't say anything, he rubbed a hand over his face. "Fuck me. Fuck a duck. Fuck. I can't do this right now." He spun around and went to the door, yanking it open. He paused for one brief moment, then slammed it behind him.

Forrest left. He... just left. Blue shivered, suddenly cold to her bones. Forrest had taken all the warmth with him.

A large chest appeared in front of her, then a face. Mo'ata, leaning over until they were face to face. "I will go talk to him. But, shopa, if this is to work, there needs to be trust and truth. Even if the truth is that it is none of our business." He placed a soft kiss on her forehead and went after Forrest.

"See, sneaky." Felix glared at Trevon, who no longer smiled.

"You owe me," she said, voice cold, just like she was. "You already owed Forrest for Derrick. So no deal. No kiss. You will help us find Phillip and neutralize the crystal. You'll help us get it back to Levi's people. And you'll make sure that no one tries to use these again. I don't care how you have to do it. Your father did this. I don't understand the honor system of the Families, or you, but you will do these things. Because. You. Already.

Owe. Us." She was breathing heavily by the end of this, the cold bursting into a burning anger. "You will fix this, and then you will leave us alone."

He closed his eyes and breathed in, holding it. He let it out and slumped. Meeting her eyes again, he nodded. "You are correct, little star." His hand rose as if he reached for her, then fell back to his side. "I will fix this. But I cannot agree to that last. I will not leave you alone. But I will fix this. All of It. I promise." The softest note of pleading crept into his voice.

Blue held her silence. If she opened her mouth, she feared she would either scream or burst into sobs, neither of which she wanted to do in front of this... *hooligan*.

He sighed. "I will see what I can find in my father's research. If we cannot find a way to safely transport and contain the crystal, then nothing else we plan will amount to much." He moved to the door.

Jason intercepted him. "You crossed a line, Zeynar."

Blue tensed. She couldn't handle any more confrontation.

Trevon glanced back at her. "You are correct, *Ministry*. I did cross a line. Don't make it worse. In fact, why don't you come with me and help go through the research data. Two sets of eyes are better than one."

Jason looked at Blue, a stubborn expression on his face.

Children. They're all fucking children. What, does he want me to protest? "I can't read minds. And I am not in the mood to babysit anything or anyone. Just go fucking help him, Jason."

Trevon grabbed his arm and dragged him out of the

room. Blue collapsed onto Levi's bed, holding Garfield to her. *This was* not *how my adventure was supposed to go.*

Later that night, Blue lay in bed, unable to sleep. Forrest had yet to speak to her. Dinner had been full of tense silence and furtive glances. The plates of meat and roasted vegetables had been steaming, the bread fresh, but she'd had to force down every bite she took. Trevon and Jason had eaten in their own rooms. Felix, who had relayed the message, said they wanted to stay on the research. Blue suspected it was Trevon's doing, that he was trying to keep his promise to fix things, to give her some time.

She turned and faced the wall, curling into herself under the covers. She didn't know how he could fix things, not really. And what was between her and Forrest wasn't for him to fix. He hadn't broken it. She had.

Her chest grew tight, and a tear escaped the corner of her eye to roll into the hair at her temple.

A faint creak from the direction of the doorway that connected her room to theirs had her heart pounding, dread and anticipation filling her. A moment later a warm body slid under the covers beside her, and an arm wrapped around her waist.

"Hey pixie." Forrest's soft voice filled her ears, and Blue let out a gasping sob.

She turned and burrowed into him, arms wrapping around his waist. She clung to him like... "Octopus," she said. "Octopus, octopus, octopus."

233

His hand clenched on her back. "Shhhh. I'm here, I'm here."

She sobbed. And it wasn't pretty crying like some girls could do. No, this was ugly crying with snot and drool and puffy eyes. He held her through it. When it finally tapered off, she sniffed, then sniffed again.

"I need a tissue," she mumbled. "Also, I'm a ninny."

Forrest's shoulders shook. After a moment, short gasping laughs escaped him. "I don't have any tissues," he finally said. "I think you'll need to use your sleeve."

"Gross. No." She struggled up and climbed over him, rushing for the bathroom. She picked up a hand towel and quickly wiped her face and looked in the mirror. *I look ghastly*. She took a deep breath. *Time to do this. Time to fix this, Blue.*

She slowly walked back to the bed where Forrest lay watching her. He was shirtless, and the muscles of his chest and arms flexed as he shifted over, making room for her on the outer edge of the mattress. She sat on the edge, one leg dangling over the end, and studied his face.

He gazed back at her calmly, one corner of his mouth crooked up. She opened her mouth, but no words came out. His eyes crinkled. "I guess I'll start." He held out his arm. "Come here. I don't want you quite so far away for this."

She pulled back the covers and snuggled into his side.

"Did I ever tell you about the pennies?" Her question was soft.

"The apology pennies?"

She nodded, her cheek rubbing along his chest.

"Yeah. We've never used them, have we?"

"Never needed to."

"I feel like I should apologize, but I'm not going to." His tone was stern, but there was an underlying warmth she needed to hear. "Mo'ata and I talked. It was… interesting. And I needed some time to think things over." The arm not wrapped around her shoulders came up, and he smoothed a finger over her cheek. "I lied. I do need to apologize. I've been too cavalier about this whole relationship. You asked me once if I was sure, if this was what I wanted. I laughed it off with a joke about ducks. Not very mature, huh?"

She stroked a hand down his chest, watching as the muscles twitched. "What I did wasn't any better. I should have told you about Trevon, what happened. Everything I said earlier was true—about why I kept the perfume, why I didn't tell you about the kiss. It really wasn't anything, not really. But a tiny part of me can't let it go. And you were right—I didn't trust you, not on this. I mean, it can't be that easy for you. I think that's what's always bothered me. You always seemed so accepting, even encouraging, of this… this idea of me being with more than one person. Part of me can't believe you aren't secretly resentful."

"Why?"

"Because… because it can't be that easy. You can't just look up one day and say, 'Oh, the girl I like likes some other guys too? Cool.' That doesn't just happen."

"Says who?"

"Says… I have no idea." She gave a small laugh.

"Comes back to that trust thing, doesn't it?"

"Yeah."

"But I never gave you a reason to trust me, not on this," he said, his voice rough.

"You never gave me a reason not to."

"Then the first time something happens, really happens, that would test this experiment we've got going, I walk out and leave you hanging."

"You had a reason."

He laughed. "I think we've got the roles confused here. I said I wasn't going to apologize, and all I've been trying to do is just that. But you won't let me."

"I'm saying you don't need to because there is nothing to apologize for."

"And I say there is. Let me have this one, Blue." He turned to his side and shifted until they were face to face. "Trust takes time to build. I didn't let that happen. I said I wasn't going to apologize because I'm glad this came up. It's something we both needed to look at, to examine. And I realized something. I didn't trust you either. Part of me was just waiting for you to look at me and figure out that... I'm lacking, that I'm not as good." He closed his eyes, and a pained look crossed his face. "Shit, Blue, some of these guys... I mean, Mo'ata himself, if I were into guys, I'd be all over that. Fucker's perfect. Trevon is a powerful guy, Levi is like a fighting god, and Felix, well, let's just say I would not want to meet him in a dark alley. Who am I? I'm some kid from Earth who got tangled up in an adventure and has nothing to offer." He swallowed, hard.

She waited, sensing he wasn't done. He had to get this all out.

His eyes, those bright blue eyes, opened, and their

gazes locked. "Even Jason can give you more than I can; he has those connections to the Ministry. And they all care for you, to some degree or another. I can see it. So no, I didn't trust you. But it's more like I didn't trust that this would work, even though I *want* it to. I want you any way I can have you, and I want you happy. More than anything, I want you happy." His forehead met hers, and he breathed heavily.

What did she say to that? What could she say? *Try the truth.* "I wouldn't be here if it wasn't for you." He stiffened, and she hurried to continue. "I would still be on Earth, preparing for college. Well, haring off into some third world country, then going to college. I'd be writing, probably, and maybe working on my list. It would be *hell*. Because I'd always wonder what if. I'd always wonder, Forrest. You're the one who gave me the courage to try. You're the one who... crap, I don't know how to say this." Blue closed her eyes, seeking the right words. "You're home. You feel like home. You're my safe place, where I can go when I need to rest or recover. You're my stable place." She put a few inches between them, wanting to see his expression. "I couldn't do this, any of this, without you."

He smiled, and it was a little sad. "I think you could. I don't know how I feel about being the safe one, though."

"Oh, it's a good thing. I probably won't ever kick you. Or want to knife you. Well, maybe, but probably not." She searched his face. "I kicked Trevon earlier."

"Yeah, I saw."

"It was a hard hit too. I totally told him off. Then after you left, Jason tried to start something, and hooligan-boy practically dragged him out of the room. If I hadn't been so… angry-sad, it would have been funny." She took a breath and dove in. "I was scared, too. As I said, how could you possibly be okay with this? It just seemed too easy. I was waiting for the other shoe to drop, and when Zeynar started being an ass and the whole perfume thing came up, it looked like it had. I thought, 'and here it is, I ruined it.' It's like we've both just been waiting for it to blow up in our faces."

"That's part of what I was thinking about. You know those annoying books, the ones where the characters never talk to each other and just assume stuff? That's what we've been doing."

"Yeah, I usually end up yelling at them, 'Just talk to each other!' I feel like a fool." She sniffed theatrically. "Never again. We will tell each other all the things. Like we said we would."

"Well, I don't know about all the things. But, yeah, we've got to talk to each other about the doubts and stuff. Because I really don't see a reason this can't work, unless someone starts acting like an idiot and storms around in a huff. Not me, of course, some other idiot."

"Right." She paused. "Do you really not like being the safe one? God, that does sound bad."

His laugh shook the bed. "How about this? I'll be the one you land on when you need to come down."

"And maybe the one who does wild and crazy stuff with me, like running off to a strange world without knowing what's going to happen."

"And maybe that as well."

Their lips met, and she fell into the kiss. He really did

feel like home. It went on, and she pressed into him, his muscles firm. A hard length pressed against her thigh. Instead of pulling back like she did before, she moved against it, against him. Desire stirred, tightening in her belly and lower.

She broke away from him and tipped her head back. His lips moved to her jaw, pressing small kisses along its edge. It felt so damn good to be close to him. Her hand clutched at his shoulder, nails digging in, and he pressed into her harder, a muffled groan vibrating against the skin of her neck.

Smoothing her hand over the skin she'd just scratched, she once more found his mouth with hers. Her blood rushed, and her skin tingled, sensitive. Forrest's hand kneaded at her side then smoothed up until it rested just below her breast. He hesitated for a moment then slid it up, cupping her breast, squeezing lightly.

Blue gasped against him and arched her back.

"Dammit. Tell me why you're wearing a onesie?" Forrest's mouth found the muscle just under her ear and bit down, lightly.

"Because." She swallowed, her throat dry. "I'm a ninny." She kissed him again. When she pulled back this time, sweat lined his brow and his face was hard. "I have condoms."

He froze. A choked laugh escaped him. Twisting them both until she partially lay beneath him, he cradled her face in his hands. "You sure about this?"

She smirked up at him. "Wouldn't have told you about the stash otherwise." Brushing a finger over one of his brows and wiping away a bead of sweat, she softened her tone. "I'm sure." Her fingers skimmed over his cheek, and she stared, simply enjoying the fact that she could touch him like this. She *should* touch him. She sat up, pressing her lips to his chin. "I'm sure, Fo."

"Thank God." He rolled off her and dove toward her pack. He paused briefly when he found the perfume, then tossed it aside. Then he was there, the box of condoms in his hand and a grin on his face. "Strip."

"Excuse me?" Was he trying to kill the mood? "You first."

"Yeah, I don't think so. I take these pants off and I'll last for like, two minutes."

She sat up and pouted at him. "Aren't you supposed to seduce me or something?"

"Next time. Well, maybe not. Cripes, Blue, I've only done this twice. It's not like I'm a master at it." His eyes widened, and he groaned. "I just fucked this up, didn't I?"

A little imp whispered on her shoulder. "Well, not yet, but if you stop being an ass, you might still be able to… fuck." Heat rushed into her cheeks. "Ignore me. I'm a dork. We'll be awkward dorks together, and it will be horribly painful. Crap. Get over here and kiss me. The kissing was good. We'll skip the talking." She reached up and found the fastenings for the long johns. They were cleverly disguised, running down either side of the front.

Forrest watched her, his gaze following her fingers as they worked. When the last one was undone, she held the panel of fabric in place and raised her brows at him. He shuddered and took a step toward her. "Right. Kissing. Damn, who knew long johns were sexy?" He closed the distance between them, and she moved to her back, letting her legs part to either side of him.

They kissed, and soon she forgot all about clothes and awkward words. Her legs parted further, and he settled between them. The height difference put his lower belly right at her core. Her hands were everywhere, diving into his hair, skimming over his back, gripping his shoulders.

The front panel of her clothes was brushed aside and Forrest's hand found her bare breast, kneading it. A light pinch on her nipple had her gasping against his mouth.

"Like that?" He pinched again, a little harder.

"Ow." She slapped his shoulder. "No kinky shit." His thumb brushed over her nipple again, lighter, and she squirmed. Another pinch. Okay, maybe that wasn't so bad.

"Don't worry. We'll take it easy. Save the 'kinky shit,' as you put it. Also, you still have on too many clothes." His voice was light, but when he sat back, sweat dotted his brow and shoulders and his lungs worked hard.

Her gazed locked on the outline of his... *Come on Blue, you know this word.* "Penis."

Blood rushed to his face, and this time it wasn't desire causing it, but pure mortification. Still, she couldn't look away from that part of him, even if his shoulders were shaking with laughter. It wasn't even bare. She wanted to see it.

"Come on, we have to get these clothes off. We'll work on 'sexy' later." She tugged at her sleeves and pulled until her entire top was bare. Forrest watched, eyes glued to her chest, but she refused to stop. If she stopped because of embarrassment, this would never happen.

She shoved the cloth down and over her hips, lifting

up just enough to clear her butt and down her legs. *Shit, I didn't shave. Well, not like this could get worse.* Bunching up the cloth, she tossed it away. Leaning back on her elbows, she tossed her hair. "Your turn. Strip."

Forrest became a flurry of motion. Tearing open the box of condoms, he snatched one up, shoved his pajama pants down, and settled over her. She barely got to see a thing.

But then he was kissing her again, and they were truly skin-to-skin. Next time. Next time was okay.

Then he did a new thing. He moved down her chest, and his mouth closed over a nipple. He licked her, sending new sensations through her down to her core. Oh, she liked this much better than the pinching. Her nails dug into flesh, and he groaned, sending vibrations against her.

He broke away and fumbled with the condom. "I'm not lasting much longer, Blue. Hell, it's a miracle I've lasted this long." He settled against her, pushing her legs wider apart. Propping himself up with an elbow on one side of her head, his other hand moved down and found her entrance.

She stiffened but didn't pull away. His fingers didn't feel bad, just… new. He skimmed over one spot, and sensation shot through her. Biting her lip, she held back a groan. Her hips pressed up, seeking that touch again, or more pressure, or more… something.

Another brush of fingers, and a moan escaped. Her hips lifted, and she stopped thinking about embarrassing words and what was unfamiliar and new and just… felt. Her eyes slid closed, and her legs fell open further. Her back arched, and she ached to get closer, to erase any distance, any space left between them.

"Please." The word came out on a breath, barely there.

Something hard and thicker than his fingers probed at her. The tip slipped between her folds, stretching her. Forrest's hips rocked against her, working that length farther inside. She tensed as the stretching became uncomfortable. He paused, his breathing harsh, puffing over her face. A drop of sweat hit her cheek, and her eyes snapped open.

He was hunched over her, his back curved, and he stared at her. Their eyes met, and his mouth fell to hers, but he didn't devour. He kissed her lightly, sweetly. "I fucking love you, Blue."

She pressed her lips to his then bit down gently on his lower lip. "Love you too." When he still didn't move, just looked at her, she relaxed. The moment grew, filled with emotion and, well, him. He surrounded her. This was her karaoke buddy, her adventure minion, her artist. She traced her fingers over the branches of trees that wrapped around his arm and melted into the mattress.

His muscles locked, and he shivered. The tremble moved through him and into her.

She clenched.

That was new. She liked that. She tried it again.

"Fuck, pixie."

"You keep promising that." She grew restless. She needed to move, and with the position he was in, there was too much space between them. What was he waiting for anyway? Hadn't he said he wouldn't be able to last that long?

She shifted her hips, angling them, trying to take more of him.

His jaw flexed. "Ready?" He moved, forcing a bit more of his length into her. The stretching was back, the pressure, part pain, part pleasure, all sensation.

"Seriously?" She growled out the word and dug her nails into his shoulder again. She hadn't missed the reaction that had gotten earlier.

He surged forward, and she sucked in a breath as pain shot through her. A sharp tearing followed by a deep throb. She clenched again, but this time she wasn't sure if her body was seeking to reject the intrusion or take more of it.

Forrest pulled back and thrust again. He leaned into her, his upper chest bumping her nose. She turned her head to the side, suppressing a giggle. He moved again, and she tried to angle her hips and meet him halfway, to do her part, but it pulled her farther down, and the side of her face met his chest again.

Maybe it was a sign. The inner imp was back, and she decided to roll with it. The next time Forrest thrust, she darted out her tongue and licked at his nipple. It became a game. Thrust, lick. Thrust, lick. And it was fun. He liked it too, if his gasps were any indication.

The pain had eased as well. She felt full, and the heat that had never left built. Slick skin against her own, small grunts, bright blue eyes locked on hers. One of her hands dove into that short, gold hair, the other clutched at his shoulder.

Her nails dug in.

He stiffened and thrust into her again, deep. His

mouth partially open, face strained, muscles bunched, he let out a low moan.

Had he just…?

He gave a few sharp jerks then pulled out of her, away, leaving her feeling empty.

"Crap. I'm sorry. I should have…" He fell back and groaned again, this one filled with embarrassment instead of pleasure.

She curled into his side. "It's okay."

"No, it's not."

"Well, no, but it is. I think. All the things I've read say it's really common for a girl not to orgasm the first time. Of course, in all the romance books I've read, she usually does," she said, deliberately injecting a musing tone into her voice, teasing him.

"I should have let Mo'ata go first. I mean, he's probably got a lot more ex—"

She slapped his chest. "Don't you dare ruin this. It was my decision. I'm the one who gets to make it and then regret it. Not you. Not that I do. Regret it, I mean. This was perfect for us." She propped herself up on one elbow, conscious of her bare chest but refusing to cover it. This was her Forrest. "Besides, we'll practice." *Maybe Mo'ata will join us and give pointers*, the imp chimed in.

He studied her, brows pulled in, serious. "This isn't you just being nice is it?"

She stretched up and kissed his chin. "Nope. Maybe the stars could have aligned and we could have had the most perfectly simultaneous orgasms ever experienced. But *this* was perfect for me, for this moment."

"I could…" His hand went to her side and slid lower, over her hip then down between her thighs.

Blue grabbed his wrist. Did she want him to finish what he'd started? "No. I'm still sore. And messy." She grinned at him, and his eyes narrowed. "Want to make it up to me? You can wash me." *Yup, the imp was back*. Or maybe it was just her.

Chapter 16

FELIX

FELIX SAT BACK from the screen and rubbed his eyes. The words were blurring in front of him. He needed a break.

They had been searching the reports and data Zeynar had brought for a day and half now, seeking something, anything, that would allow them to contain the crystal's powers.

So far, they had nothing.

Brendan Faust had also come through. He had sent men out to question the workers, the shopkeepers, and those who lived in the apartments at the edge of the warehouse district. He hadn't come to the inn again, had yet to speak to Blue, but Zeynar's influence had opened those doors, and the information was pouring in. Now they just had to put all the pieces together.

"Eye cramp, mercenary?" The mocking tone had Felix grinding his teeth.

Speak of the devil. *That was the phrase, yes?* "You are supposed to be 'fixing this,' are you not?" Felix pushed away from the table and stood, stretching.

Trevon set down a tray of food on a small side table they'd set up in the extra room for just that purpose. "Eat. I'll take over for a while." He looked over to Levi, who sat another small table and had his head buried in printed-out schematics and calculations on the crystal. The Prizzoli had barely come up for air since Zeynar had handed the folder to him. "You too."

Felix grunted and grabbed a sandwich. Zeynar crossed to Levi and nudged his leg with a foot. It wasn't quite a kick.

Felix chewed and swallowed. "You are an *ikpul*."

"Yes, I am a… bastard," he said, switching to English, and the last word was unfamiliar. Trevon looked from Felix to Levi and back. "I could help you with English. I know all the bad words, all the insults." The last was said in a teasing, coaxing tone.

Felix almost laughed. Almost, but he held it in. He would not give in to the charm of this man.

Levi, though, looked like he was thinking about the offer. Slowly he nodded. "I would appreciate that." He rose and crossed to the food. "Thank you for this."

Zeynar shrugged and took Levi's seat, fingering through the papers. He wasn't studying them, not really. He pulled out a few of the schematics and charts on wavelength, looked them over, then tossed them back on the table.

"I am afraid all this is useless. Yes, my father conducted tests, but he never figured out how to replicate the effect. And without a crystal to actively test, we're not going to be able to know for sure if anything works." He slapped a palm over another pile. "I don't like making moves without all the information."

Felix couldn't resist. "Isn't that what you did earlier? With Blue and Forrest? Didn't seem to work out like you wanted."

Zeynar lifted a brow. "And how do you know what I wanted?"

"It was clever." Levi finished off one sandwich and picked up another. This one was lighter meat. "Or not clever, depending on the goal. But he did effectively push them closer together. Were you just testing?" He shot an inquiring look at Zeynar.

He laughed. "Yes, I was mostly testing. The boy came back with her. But he's young, and people that age often don't know what they really want."

"And how old are you?" Felix raised a brow of his own.

"Old enough to know what I want when it's right in front of me. And to do something about it."

Felix stiffened. "Do not... screw with me." Portia's face flashed before him, a hurt so old it had mostly healed over. He'd thought her perfect, and he'd not recognized the façade until it was almost too late. That relationship had messed with him too badly, twisted something in him so that it nearly had broken. Just the idea of opening himself up again sent a bolt of panic through him. *What if Blue...*

Trevon held up his hands. "Wouldn't dream of it. One more question, though. Why learn English? Mo'ata could have translated. And you are very proficient already, much more than our Prizzoli over here. Have a gift for languages?"

Felix didn't answer, just went back to eating. The answer to that question was not so simple, and he refused to examine it. He was being a coward, and he knew it. He swallowed the last bite and took a quick drink of foka. While there was not much alcohol in there, it still burned slightly going down, refreshing him. "Let's get back to work. Like you said, If we can not contain the crystal, then all of this is useless and we have bigger problems than fighting over one little girl."

Zeynar snorted but said no more, just went back to reviewing the data spread before him. After a few minutes he pulled out one report with a small note scribbled in a corner of the top sheet. "If we can't contain the crystal, can we contain Phillip? Drug him, as Blue put on her list? Tell me how this works, the bond."

"There hasn't been a true bond in ages. I don't know any more about how it works than what I've already told everyone. Drugging him... no, I wouldn't. Maybe as a last resort, but we don't know if the bond would break. If it did, like it would if we simply killed Phillip, and if the crystal sought out a new host..." Weariness crept into Levi's voice. "If the crystal seeks out a new host, then we lose any advantages we have."

The advantage he referred to was Blue, and Phillip's fixation. Felix carefully set down the remaining few bites of his sandwich, keeping a rein on his temper. More and more he was coming to hate the necessity of *using* her. It didn't sit well with him.

Zeynar continued, either ignoring the undercurrents in

the room or unaware of them. "Then tell me more about those who can use the crystals. Why did the bonding start with Phillip? Why not Etu, who had been using it longer? Is it the person, how the crystal is handled, or something else? How do you detect who will be able to use the crystals? Is it just a trial and error? Do the Elders go around with a case of them and see who responds? Do they have to use it before anyone can tell? Explain it to me." He studied the paper as he spoke, then picked up a pen and circled a few lines.

"It is like... a selection," Levi said. "All children who reach the age of five are brought to them. Those who can sense the crystals are taken and trained. Some, like me, become guards—agents for the Elders—or enforcers. Protectors. Some, those who are able to direct and control the crystals, are taken in by the Elders and groomed. Etu was one such, but his ability was just passable, if the rumors are true."

"And you could sense these crystals but not use them?"

"It is true. I could sense them, track them, but I failed the test of use." Levi looked away.

"I would call that passing, personally. These crystals are like the worst of drugs, addictive and soul destroying. You'd have to be a *saint* to use them well and wisely."

"Saint?"

"Sorry, Earth term. Basically, you'd have to be beyond reproach, possessing only virtues, all that bullshit," Zeynar said.

"Bull-shit?"

Zeynar laughed, and even Felix grinned. He'd learned

that one already from Forrest. "Deceptive or misleading talk. It is a vulgar slang term," Felix said.

"See? You are learning all the useful English terms already," Zeynar said to Levi with a grin. Then he sobered. "Explain again how the crystals are contained on your planet. How are the potential users kept away from them or given a rest from their influence?"

Levi didn't answer right away, staring into nothing, eyes narrowed. "The Initiates are not blocked, but they are kept away from the crystals. Distance helped. Training was in one camp and quarters were in another. Guards rotate frequently. Distance is the only thing we use." His eyes widened. "Distance. We need to put distance between Phillip and the crystal." His face fell. "I fear it is too late for that. He can already use its power without being in direct contact."

"Right, the connection Phillip has extends beyond a physical one. But any kind of bond or sense is always there without actual contact, or none of you would be able to sense the crystals without touching them. So how do we disrupt *that* connection?" Trevon mused absently as he stared at the report he still held.

Felix's thoughts stilled. That was it. "Levi, at any point while on Karran or your own world, did you feel... muffled? Not just your awareness of the crystal, but in general? Blunted, like you couldn't see something you should or you no longer heard something that you always had?"

Rumors had always abounded about Turamm—a particularly isolated world of the Alliance—that a portion of the population could sense thoughts and emotions.

Though it was an open world, the people didn't travel much, and when they did, they always wore jewelry made of Turammin. Turammin, a metal of high strength and conductance. Turammin, that when a current of a precise voltage was passed through it, it formed a shield most surveillance couldn't penetrate. The reception area of the Turamm branch of the Ministry was coated in it.

And then there was the man he'd once met, drunk in a bar just off the eastern shopping district of Tremmir. He wore chains of the metal around his neck, and cuffs of it adorned his wrists. He'd mumbled of his discontent at being given a job-run that forced him to leave his home. And he'd grumbled that he'd felt "blind," like his head was wrapped in a haze. A little thing. Not much, but…

"Fuck. I am an idiot. A dolt, an imbecile." Zeynar spat out unfamiliar words as he jumped up, waving that paper he'd been staring at. "It says it right here. Right. Here." He spun and focused on Levi. "Did you ever go into the tunnels? I know you were in the shop, the scent shop, but how far into the smuggling tunnels did you go? How deep?"

Levi's eyes widened. "Not far. Just enough to confirm the trackers I'd planted worked. I made it about a mile, then I started to feel disoriented. Like—"

"Like something was messing with your sense of direction," Zeynar finished, satisfaction radiating from him. He thrust the paper in Felix's face. "The draining chamber. They moved it. Had to move it out of the main tunnels. At first they were right under the main house, easy access."

Felix snatched the report and read the scrawled note.

"Interference of waves; no turammin." He and Zeynar were thinking along the same lines. "Too easy."

"Maybe. We lined all but the outermost tunnels in it years ago. We need to test this." He snatched up his comm and was almost out the door when he must have realized neither of the other two were following. "Let's go. We need to see if this will work. Get your asses in gear!"

He smiled despite himself. *Ass… in gear?* It must be another one of Earth's idioms. Blue and Forrest used them frequently as well, and they were nonsense more often than not. He wasn't sure this particular one was translating correctly into Common. No one's ass had gears.

He followed Zeynar out of the room, Levi close behind him. He couldn't wait to tell little Blue what they had discovered. They still needed to confirm it, but it looked like there may just be a way to come out of this.

He wanted to see her smile. As he strode down the corridor, he refused to think of what that meant.

BLUE

Blue squinted her eyes at the footage, then blinked a few times. Everything was blurry. Reaching out, she paused the surveillance feed and leaned back. "I need a break."

Jason paused his own. "I think we all do."

She, Jason, and one of Zeynar's men had all been assigned the task of going through the additional footage sent over by Sora. Meanwhile Forrest and Mo'ata compiled what they found with the information from Brendan Faust and tried to spot a pattern. Things were coming together, but it was slow. Levi, Felix, and Trevon were working on how to block the crystal. They'd gone charging down the hall a few minutes ago but had refused to say more than that they had an idea.

Reaching out, Jason pulled her to her feet. "Come on. Let's get some food. When did you last eat?"

She blushed. Mo'ata had woken her and Forrest with a tray of food and an admonishment to not laze around all day. It had been sweet and slightly awkward. She had been vaguely embarrassed for Mo'ata to see her like that, snuggled in bed with Forrest. Until then, she'd kept her time with the two of them separate, no overlaps. And she hadn't really gotten a chance to talk to Mo'ata about what had happened between her and Forrest. She figured he knew, what with the sly grins she'd caught him giving them. This morning had been... cozy. Intimate, even if it was just for a moment.

I'll have to get used to things like that.

"Blue?" Jason pulled her back to the present. "Food?"

"Oh, yeah. Ummm, I had breakfast."

"It's past lunch. I think food is a good idea." He took her hand and led her to the hall. "We'll bring the other guy back something."

"Killian."

"Hmmm?"

They were nearly to the bottom of the stairs, and the smell of roasting meat and fresh bread had her stomach rumbling. "His name is Killian. He came with Trevon."

His hand tightened on hers. "Right." He stopped at a small table in the corner. "This looks like a good spot."

A larger table close to the front windows was also empty. "What about that one? We could get the guys down here as well. They probably haven't eaten either."

His face closed. "Of course."

When they were seated, he asked a server to check on the various rooms assigned to them and to deliver the message. A few minutes later she returned. "I did not get any answers."

Right, the Terrible Trio had left a little while ago. Something about the three of them together screamed *Trouble!* at her, like either they'd all beat each other senseless or start a brawl somewhere. She wondered briefly where Mo'ata and Forrest were, but wasn't too concerned. They had the other of Trevon's men with them, Jonas, for backup. Things were a bit scattered right now; maybe they were just at the stables.

They put in their order, Blue asking for stew, and waited. The food arrived shortly after, and she dug in. Warmth exploded in her belly and spread through her. "Thank you for dragging me away. I really did need this." She tore off a chunk of bread and dipped it in the gravy.

He shrugged. "It's nothing. Plus, I would have thought one of the men hovering around you would have come to check on you to make sure you're taken care of."

She paused, another bite of bread halfway to her mouth, and raised her brows. Maybe Trevon could help her figure out how to do the one-eyebrow trick. *I'll ask when I'm not mad at him.* "I wasn't aware I needed someone to feed me."

His back went ramrod straight. "I didn't mean…" His cheeks colored, and he closed his eyes. "Sorry. I'm still getting used to the idea that you're here. Really here. I didn't think I'd see you again, see any of you." There was a faint glimmer in his eyes before he blinked it away.

"I get it. But"—she jabbed the bread at him for emphasis—"I've fielded this line of talk so many times already. Between you, the Dynamic Duo, and the Terrible Trio, I'd be stuck rolled up in, I don't know, a fluffy cloud-blanket of bunny fur and locked away in a closet for the rest of my life. Well, maybe not by the Terrible Trio. Or Forrest. Okay, Mo'ata is the worst culprit, but still."

He snorted out a laugh. "Terrible Trio?"

"I just get the feeling if left alone, they'd get in trouble. Or make it. Big time."

"I think you may be right." He relaxed back in his seat. "What are your plans after this?"

"After we avert the end of the worlds as we know them?"

He nodded.

"I go to school." If there was a slight whine to her voice, she was going to ignore it.

"I could try to help out there, talk to the Dean, see if we can smooth the transition some," Jason offered, earnest. "I think that would be great. I haven't gotten a new off-world assignment yet. We could spend some time together, really catch up. I could help show you around."

"That would be nice. I know Forrest will appreciate it as well. He's planning to try to get into the art program at the university."

He nodded, smile still in place, though it looked a little forced now. "I'll see what I can do there as well."

"Blue." Forrest appeared beside the table. "You need to get out to the barn. Beast is acting weird." He grabbed her hand, and she rushed out the side door after him, Jason following right behind. "We can't get him to calm down. We're afraid he's going to hurt himself trying to get out of the stall."

Blue yanked her hand from Forrest's and rushed to the rear of the barn where Beast was housed. Loud, squealing neighs and the sound of hooves and horns crashing into the stall walls set her heart pounding. What could have set him off?

A sense of worry, fear, and anger reached her. It was vague—she almost didn't notice it—but as soon as Beast caught sight of her, he calmed down and so did the worry.

She halted just outside of the door, and Beast stuck his head over the top, sniffing at her. He snorted once, then grabbed the edge of her collar in his teeth, tugging gently. She hurried to open the stall door and slipped in. Beast crowded her into the far corner and stood in front of her, giving off his growl of protection.

"What. The. Hell?" Forrest stared at them with his mouth open.

Mo'ata had his back to her, gaze locked on the doorway to the barn. Jason looked around, a slightly bewildered look on his face.

"What just happened here?" Blue placed her hand on Beast's side, trying to soothe him and push him out of the way at the same time. He didn't budge.

Moments later the cubs came tumbling through the

barn door and raced to Beast's stall. They climbed up the stall walls and perched on top, crouching, hair raised. Images of Beast blocking her, keeping her in the corner crowded her mind along with a sense of satisfaction.

"Something's coming. They can tell." Mo'ata's low voice just reached her over Beast's growls. The cubs soon joined in, sending out high-pitched cries of warning.

We were going to have a talk about these animals when this was over. *And how the hell did they get out of the room?*

Beast pressed into her harder just as Jason cursed. "Shit. Someone grab him. Get him down on the floor."

A blur of orange robes and red hair flashed by, heading to the front of the barn. Beast blocked everything but a small glimpse of a now empty corridor. The back of Forrest's head came into view.

"What is going on up there?" she hissed.

Forrest's shoulders hunched, but he didn't turn around. "I think that's Etu. At least it looks like the guy Levi found on the surveillance. He's speaking in Common, and I can't make out much more than Phillip's name. Fuck."

Blue pulled out her comm and started to call Levi, then thought better of it. She hit the contact for Felix.

"Blue?"

"Get Levi out to the barn. Etu just showed up. I can't tell what's going on, but it's not good."

The line disconnected, and a bare two minutes later, the sound of pounding boots reached her. She really needed to see what was going on. She pushed at Beast, growing frantic at not being able to see. *What if this was a trap?*

"Blue, calm down. They're fine." Forrest squeezed in next to her, and she stilled.

I really have to get a handle on this panic thing. She took a breath, then another. A third one finally had her heart slowing down. "Tell me what's happening."

"They're taking Etu to the inn; he's in pretty bad shape. I'm going to stay with you until Beast and the babies calm down. Trevon and one of his men are up at the front of the barn on watch. Mo'ata thinks the animals were able to sense something wrong coming, and that's why they freaked. Hopefully it was just Etu arriving, but he wants you here in case it's more than that."

In case Phillip was also around. He didn't say it aloud, but she knew.

Chapter 17

BLUE

AN HOUR PASSED. At least. Beast relaxed enough to let her out of the corner, but he continued to block her each time she went for the stall door. The cubs also refused to leave their posts on the stall walls.

Trevon was keeping them updated, but so far there wasn't much to know. Etu had been settled in a bed and given food, then he'd fallen asleep.

"I hate waiting." Blue picked up a handful of the straw on the stall floor and tossed it.

"Don't pout." Forrest frowned and crossed his arms.

That's a pout. She almost pointed it out, but she wasn't in the mood for teasing.

Her comm pinged, and she snatched it up from where it lay in front of her. "Yes?"

"Etu is stable, and he has information for us. As soon as Beast allows, head to the rooms. We need to coordinate." Mo'ata's voice was curt, and he didn't wait for a reply.

As if that call was a signal, Beast moved away from the stall door and the cubs jumped down from their perches. She hurried out of there, Forrest right behind her. Trevon glanced back at the creak of the stall door and nodded. He fell in behind her, a little to the right, while Forrest stayed on her left. His man, Killian, was behind him.

As a group they hurried to the inn's side door. She paused and scooped up Garfield, who was weaving in and out of their feet, and Forrest did the same with Vivi. Felix waited for them at the top of the stairs and gestured them into Mo'ata and Forrest's room.

Etu lay there, skin ashen, just like Levi's had been. His eyes were open, though, and Levi helped him sip from a glass of water.

Etu's gaze fixed on her as she sank into a free chair at the low table tucked into a corner. "I couldn't stop him." Trevon moved to her side and quietly translated. A mix of emotions passed over Etu's face, finally settling on fear mixed with regret. His voice lowered. "I tried to get the crystal away, but I fear I was too late. I should have stopped this long ago."

Levi grunted but held his silence. She could only imagine what was going through his mind right now.

"Why are you here?" Mo'ata's cold tones sliced through the room.

Etu's eyes closed. "I need your help to stop him."

When Trevon relayed this, suddenly all Blue wanted to do was slap this man. *How dare he? Us help him?* It should be the other way around. "You're the one who started this in the first place. All we've been trying to do is stop it." Her voice was as cold as Mo'ata's. Garfield, now in her lap, rose to his paws, balancing carefully on her knees, and growled.

Etu's eyes widened at her harsh tone.

"He has no idea what I'm saying, does he?"

Trevon chuckled. "No, but I believe he got the idea."

Blue glared at him. "I'm still mad at you, too."

He held up his hands. "Noted." He tilted his head to the scene unfolding. "Now quiet, and let me translate."

Forrest moved closer to them, his expression closed, but he listened intently to Trevon's murmured translations.

Felix pulled up the maps they'd been working with, the small colored dots of confirmed sightings standing out like a galaxy of stars. Etu indicated an area, and Felix zoomed in. A new dot appeared.

They had confirmation of where Phillip was staying.

"He is not there now." Etu collapsed back on the bed. "He was muttering, talking about making 'them' pay for trying to take what was his. I thought he was coming here."

"How did you know where we were staying?" Felix growled.

Etu rolled his eyes. "It was not hard. You stand out, all of you. And rumors of a new Faust have been going for days." He gestured, and Levi stiffly propped him up and helped with another sip of water. "I've known where you were for a while, but I didn't tell Phillip. The promise of getting his hands on the girl is all that's kept him in check. If he had her, I think nothing would hold him back."

An image of Phillip as she'd last seen him flashed before her. His face gaunt, pale. He'd looked… haunted.

Trevon leaned closer to her, and a slightly musky scent filled her nose and a tickle started in the back of her throat. She sneezed. "Sorry, I think I'm allergic to you. Or whatever it is you're wearing."

His eyes widened then crinkled at the corners. "Also noted." He pulled away a little. "Levi, Felix, and I think we hit upon something that could contain the crystal, or at least block the connection. That is what Levi and Etu are talking over now."

"What is it?" There was an edge to Forrest's voice, and Blue took his hand, squeezing.

Trevon glanced at their hands. "It's an alloy from Turamm. It's used mostly for shielding from surveillance, but there was a note on some of my father's papers and research indicating it may have had an effect on the crystal's powers." His words were easy, almost casual.

Is he really that unaffected by everything that's happened? She studied him, and their gazes locked. "Think it will work?"

A flicker in his eye, a tightening of his lips. *Not emotionless, then.* "I think it's our only chance," he finally said.

He turned his head to Forrest, and blue eyes met blue eyes. *So pretty. Yes, I admit it, I like blue.* She suppressed a smile. Now was not the time to go off on tangents.

Something that may have been remorse softened Trevon's expression. "I will forever regret what befell your cousin. Please know that. I had given strict orders to have all weapons on stun. I do not mean it as an excuse, but know that the man who fired to kill was... taken care of. If there is ever anything I can do for you, you have only to call upon me. Blue was correct, I owe you."

Forrest glanced between the two of them then narrowed his eyes on Trevon. His lips thinned as he clutched Blue's hand harder.

She held her breath, waiting for what he would say.

"Give me a penny."

Her shoulders slumped, and tension drained out of her. Forrest had just called a truce.

"A penny?" A bemused smile crossed over Trevon's face.

A sharp nod from Forrest. "A penny. Blue can explain it some time, but the short version is, for the big stuff, we don't do apologies. We do pennies. I'll cash it in when I'm ready. And believe me, this one will be big."

"A penny, then. All right." He reached into a small pouch hanging from his belt and pulled out an Earth penny. "You're lucky I keep this with me. I will definitely want it back. It has a...significance to me. I will tell you the story when you redeem it."

Forrest took the penny and clenched it in his palm. "Deal."

"And call me Trev, please. Trevon is too formal." He gave a small bow of his head. He sent a grin in Blue's direction. "That offer is for you, too, little star."

Forrest stiffened, and Blue once again tightened her fingers around his hand. *Not now*, she tried to send through that connection. *Not now*. He opened his mouth to reply but was cut off by the shrill sound of four comms going off at once.

Felix looked at the message, and the color drained from his face. "Is Sora. Another murder. Close to inn. I go." He snatched up a coat and was almost through the door when Mo'ata brought him up short, a hand on his forearm.

"Not alone." He looked around at the people gathered and indicated Killian. "If you would?"

After confirmation from Trevon, the two of them left with a promise to check in once they had more details.

In the tense silence that followed, Blue's next question rang louder than she'd thought it would. "So, will this alloy work?"

Levi and Etu exchanged a few more words as Mo'ata's face grew red and Trevon's grew colder. Finally, Levi threw a hand in the air, and Blue was afraid he would strike Etu. Not afraid, really, but they needed the man conscious.

"Levi," she said, a warning in her tone. The big man tensed but lowered his hand. "What's the verdict?"

Trevon growled. "The verdict is that Etu has a death wish, but it is just possible the alloy may block some of the connection or hamper the power in some way."

"So we just need to get some of this and get the crystal contained." She let go of Forrest and crossed the room until she stood in front of the small Prizzoli as he lay prone. "Then we need to get the crystal away from Phillip and Phillip away from people." Her words were slow, musing. A plan, only slightly modified from her earlier version, slowly formed. It was one none of them were going to like. "I have an idea."

"No." Five voices rang out as one, even Levi's.

Well, at least they're all acting in agreement. I guess that's a good thing. "You haven't even heard the idea."

Forrest crossed his arms. "Don't need to. I know that expression. It's the same one you get when you think of a great plot twist and are about to kill someone off in one of your stories."

Trevon nodded. "I don't know about any stories, but that's the look of someone about to get into mischief."

"You are not becoming bait." Mo'ata's statement was much more direct.

Levi didn't say anything, but that man's silence could sometimes be very loud.

Then Jason stepped forward. He looked her over then nodded. "Let's at least hear her out."

Relief filled her. At least someone was willing to listen to her without putting up too much of a fight. She beamed at him, and the others groaned but didn't protest. "So, here's what I was thinking…"

Chapter 18

BLUE

BLUE, seated atop Beast, shivered as a cold wind sliced through the air, finding little openings in her coat to sneak through. She looked over the clearing they had decided to use for the meeting. It was about twenty feet across, not too large, and surrounded not only by trees, but also with thick brush in places—perfect for the men to hide.

It had taken all of her skills at persuasion to convince the others. Once again, Jason had stepped in and pointed out that she was probably the only one who could get Phillip out of the city and to a particular spot. Forrest had wanted to try himself, but eventually even he had to concede that the allure she held for their former friend was greater and had a better chance at success.

When Felix returned and reported in, it only further confirmed Blue's resolve to end this. The latest victim was a taller man with a red beard, similar in height and coloring to Mo'ata. In addition to being drained, he'd also been... hurt. Felix refused to go into details, but the haunted look in his eyes told her it was not mild.

Phillip was beyond control. Which they already knew; this just made it more... real.

Something rustled in the branches of a tree across from her, and her hands tightened on the reins. Soon.

She'd had a rough idea when she spoke up yesterday, but it was the cubs who'd solidified it. She'd been trying to think of a place away from people, a place to ambush Phillip. Warehouses, the frozen fields, an empty house, all of these had been suggested. And all of them vetoed for one reason or another. Then an image had popped into her mind: a piquet, grown, crouching on a tree limb as its prey passed by underneath. Then one of Beast running through trees and toward a mountain.

"Smart babies," she said now. She couldn't wait to see what they'd become, fully-grown. The old jokes about cats really being gods in disguise and ruling the world secretly didn't seem so far-fetched right now. She'd jokingly said as much to Mo'ata at one point when the others were out of the room. He'd gone silent. Then slowly, cautiously warned her against talking about things like that around the others. Was there more to the piquet? More than D'rama had told her? *Probably*. She'd tried to ask him more, but he'd just said they would talk about it later, after Phillip was taken care of.

So she'd started a new list, titled "The List of Things Someone Doesn't Want to Talk About." The title was too long, so she'd shortened it to "The Secret List."

More movement, this time in the shadows of the trail

leading to the clearing. Two figures approached, one short and slight, the other taller and thinner than she liked.

They emerged into the low light that filtered through the cloud layer, and Blue's breath caught. No matter what he had done, she couldn't stop thinking of Phillip as a friend. Or at least as someone who could have been a friend. *There I go, thinking of what-ifs.*

He looked worse than the brief glimpse she'd gotten outside the shop or the images they'd found on the surveillance footage. His face was pale, almost gray, like the crystal was sucking out not only the lives of others, but his as well. The dark scarf wrapped around his head and neck looked like a cowl, and with the bruised-looking hollows at his cheeks and temples, he looked like Death.

Damn.

Her eyes traveled past him and to Etu, who shook his head slightly. He hadn't been able to get the crystal yet. She took a breath. Okay, Plan B.

Adrenaline surged through her, and her vision sharpened, her thoughts stilled. Her stomach tightened, but the sensation was distant, muffled. All her attention was focused on Phillip and what they had to do next.

"Phillip!" Their gazes locked. As he drew closer, she could see a faint purple glow dancing in his eyes. So this wasn't Phillip right now, not really. She dismounted and moved in front of Beast, keeping a firm hand on the reins. She expected the *quorin* to growl, protest, or kick up a fuss, but he held still, as if he knew his stillness was vital to the success of the next few minutes. Maybe he did.

Phillip stopped a few feet from her, just out of reach.

Etu arranged himself just behind and to the right of the taller man.

She took a breath and dived in. "I'm here."

"You are." Tones and sounds that didn't belong to Phillip echoed in that voice. It was so *wrong*.

"You've been looking for me." Only through pure will did she keep the tremble from her words.

He closed his eyes and drew in a deep breath, his head falling back. When their eyes next met, the purple glowed brighter, overwhelming any hint of the chocolate brown that might have lingered. "I have." He held out a hand. "Come closer, little Blue, come closer."

She unclenched her hand from Beast's reins and let them fall. She took a small step forward, keeping herself just out of his reach. "Let me see it. The crystal, let me see it."

His eyes narrowed, and his lips twisted. "I thought you understood. I am. It does not matter where. I am."

"What are you?"

"I am death, and I am life. I am pain, and I am peace."

"You asked me once if I believed in God."

His face twisted, fury chasing bewilderment before settling into a blankness that was more terrifying than anything. "And you answered that you didn't know."

"And you wondered about becoming one." She softened her voice. "Let me see the crystal, Phillip. Prove to me what you have become."

He arched a brow. It broke her heart, just a little. Images of Kevin and Phe flashed before her. Forrest. All the people who loved this boy. Maybe, just maybe, there was still a small bit of him buried in there.

"How would that prove anything?"

"How could a crystal possibly be a god?" Appeal to his vanity, Forrest had said. Call into question his superiority. Challenge his dominance.

"You think I don't know they're there?" A small tendril of purple, its glow beautiful in the low light, snaked from a slightly raised finger and wound through a stand of bushes on the left. A muffled curse was soon followed by a low thump.

Her heart skipped. *Who had it been?*

She didn't let her gaze waver. "That still proves nothing." She put all the disgust she felt into those words, hoping for a reaction.

She got one.

His hand snaked into his coat, and he pulled out a softly glowing purple stone. He glanced between it, her, and Etu, then he tossed the crystal at the small Prizzoli as he lunged at her. She ducked, twisting to the side. The move had been instinctive. She didn't want him touching her.

Beast reared, his hooves striking out at Phillip, who jumped back. Though they didn't connect, it gave her time to put some distance between them. Beast came down and temporarily blocked her view of the scene.

Etu cried out, and Blue bolted around her mount. They needed that crystal. Phillip blocked her, and she spun away from him. She caught movement from the corner of her eye, and the goal shifted from getting to the crystal to keeping Phillip's attention on her. She held out her hands, still careful not to touch him.

Levi crept closer to Etu, a clutching a small box.

273

Movement to her right showed her Trev, holding a circlet of the same alloy. Phillip started to turn in their direction, and she panicked. She needed his attention on her.

She grabbed his hand.

That purple light inched over her fingers and up her wrist. It didn't hurt. It felt almost warm. A lassitude swept through her body, and her shoulders sagged. She met chocolate brown eyes overlaid by a soft, purple glow.

"Phillip. Please don't." She could barely get the words out.

Purple faded until it was the barest sheen, and some of her stolen energy rushed back into her. Could she reach him? The boy she'd first met? The one who had flaws but who joked and teased with his friends? Was there any of him left?

She clenched her fingers around his. "Hey. You still in there?" Her voice was growing weaker. Forrest edged closer on her left, while Trev, on the right, was mere feet away. Levi struggled to get the crystal from a now convulsing Etu.

Phillip's head started to turn. "Phillip. Hey. Keep your eyes on me."

Forrest edged closer to her. "Blue." At his harsh whisper, Phillip's head twisted sharply, and the purple glow grew brighter again.

"Hush." She tried to block out everything but Phillip. "Phillip. Hey, look at me."

His head swung back to her. "Blue."

"That's right, it's me."

He pulled on her hand, and she stumbled. "Come closer. Closer, closer. Come closer, little Blue."

She swallowed. The purple was back. He didn't drain her this time, though, just kept her hand in an iron grip. All of this counted on Phi's fixation of her.

Forrest reached her side and grabbed her forearm, trying to pull her away. Blue froze. *Stupid, stupid boy.*

"Ah, ah, ah." Phillip's voice, overlaid with that deeper sound, was chiding. "You know better than that, Fo. She's mine." Purple light swirled from him, placing a glancing touch on Forrest's head. "But for old time's sake, I'll let you live. You just need to"—Forrest slowly sank to the ground, and his grip slackened—"let her go. There."

She couldn't see Forrest's chest moving. *What if…?*

"He's fine." Phillip tugged on her hand again, his other hand reaching for her face. "Now, come here." His voice became coaxing, soft.

She let him pull her in. She just needed to buy time for Levi to get the crystal locked away. What was taking so long? Maybe he'd already done it and it hadn't worked? Maybe the bond had been completed and the crystal truly didn't matter anymore.

Time slowed. Just as Phillip's fingers brushed her cheek, a new voice rang out.

"Fuck this shit." A large body, piercings flashing, slammed into Phi, tearing him away from her. Trev.

Purple shot from Phillip just as Trev closed the circlet around his neck. The cubs shot out of the underbrush, Felix and Mo'ata charging after them.

Garfield slashed at Phillip's head as Vivi crouched in front of Forrest, growling that high-pitched baby growl. Felix yanked Trev's now limp body from Phillip and flipped him onto his back. Jason appeared next to Levi, grabbed the box from him, and bent over it, his fingers moving in short jerky movements as he played with the controls for the electric current.

Vivi darted forward and latched onto Phillip's ear just as something clicked in the box and a low hum filled the clearing. Phillip went limp.

Blue stood in shock, surveying the aftermath. Slowly, she knelt beside Vivi and pried her off her new chew toy. Not because she cared if Phillip had a mangled ear, but because if Forrest really was still alive, he needed the cub right now.

She awkwardly crawled to his side and placed the cub on his chest. She felt for a pulse and breathed a sigh of relief when she felt it, slow and faint, but there. A low purr reached her, and she saw Mo'ata doing the same with Trev, Garfield on the hooligan's chest. Their eyes met, and Mo'ata nodded.

Trev was still alive. Forrest was alive. Mo'ata, Felix, Levi, and Jason surrounded them. Etu lay still outside their circle. And there must be one more in the bushes.

She cleared her throat. "Who was it? Earlier?"

Felix glanced at the stand of bushes. "Killian. Zeynar's man."

"And Etu?"

Felix shook his head.

The traitor was dead. She couldn't muster up any remorse, even if he had helped them in the end. Closing her eyes, she took a breath. *Okay, next steps. Get everyone off this semi-mountain and to a healer.*

"Blue?" A small voice, bewildered and lost. She looked over to see Phillip struggling to sit up. "What happened?

What—" He swallowed, his gaze sliding to Forrest. "Will he be okay?"

"Yes."

"Okay." His face took on a tinge of green. "I don't feel so good." Then he rolled over and puked, heaving until nothing but bile came up.

She held her hand out to Mo'ata. "Get us off this mountain."

"Yes, shopa," he said and pulled her to her feet.

Chapter 19

MO'ATA

MO'ATA FLUNG his comm at the wall. It hit with a satisfying thud that still did nothing to alleviate his frustration.

"I take it your contact had no better luck?" Zeynar said from where he sat at the low table tucked in a corner of the room, his voice tight and the constant smug assurance wiped away.

A low snarl was Mo'ata's reply. From one of the beds, Garfield let out an answering growl. It had been four days since they'd captured Phillip, and Mo'ata had been this way for the last two, ever since the talks with the Padilra deteriorated.

They were insisting on three things:

That the crystal be returned to them. Fine.

That Phillip be given over to the Elders of the Prizzoli for the remainder of his life, even after he and the crystal were cleansed. This one went against Mo'ata's own instincts. The boy was getting off too lightly for the crimes he'd committed, but Mo'ata understood the reasoning.

The third was the one that had him calling on every contact he had. He'd put pressure on his mother, as the Mamanna and a member of Karran's Council, as well as his contacts in the guards and the Order. Felix, Trevon, and even Jason had done the same with their own not inconsiderable connections. Levi… well, Levi was another matter. He was holding back information still, and it had to do with the third item. Number three—Blue had to go the Prizzoli as well. And *stay*.

There was no reasoning given. No negotiation, no leniency. If those three things were not delivered, Padilra would withdraw from the Alliance. Refusing to hand over "the girl" would be seen as an act of aggression, and Padilra was willing to start a damned war over it.

Every single person he'd spoken to said the same thing: "Give them the girl." Even Demil, his mentor in the Order. It was as if they didn't care.

They don't.

The door swung in, and Felix entered, Vivi on his shoulder, followed closely by Levi.

The tension rose another notch, and Vivi's growl joined Garfield's. The cubs were becoming more and more on edge the longer they stayed away from Blue and Forrest. Unfortunately, they also did not react well to Phillip's presence, and the safest thing had been to keep them separated as much as possible. Now, they were feeding on the emotions flying about in the confined space with no outlet.

None of them had a damned outlet.

Mo'ata took a breath and got himself under control. He felt like a piquet guarding its territory, ready to tear into anything that threatened. Except in this instance it was the entire Alliance that threatened, and not a particular person he could slash.

There's always Levi.

He pushed the thought away. With the recovery of the crystal, his life debt was technically paid. He did not owe Levi one single thing, but the man had become his friend. Plus, Mo'ata understood torn loyalties and secrets needing to be kept.

But these secrets threatened his shopa, and enough was enough.

He pinned Levi with a glare. "You will tell us the whole of this. Now. Why do your people insist that Blue stay there even after Phillip is under control?"

Levi, still standing just behind Felix, dropped his gaze, and his shoulders hunched in. Vivi snarled louder and swiped at the Prizzoli from her stance on Felix's shoulder, though she didn't connect. Garfield growled again as well, but he seemed almost... protective of the Prizzoli.

Whether anyone else realized it, the cubs' reactions were a very clear indicator not only of the room's emotions, but Blue's and Forrest's as well. It was something to ponder, but later.

Felix stepped away from the Prizzoli and joined Mo'ata in confronting the other man. The mercenary crossed his arms and waited. They all waited.

"We can't deal with this unless we know what's really going on." Zeynar's low voice sliced through the room.

"Your government and your Elders are asking for something they have no right to, and they are willing to risk a lot for one woman. Well, *I* am willing to risk a lot for her as well. So. Start. Talking."

A twinge of resentment, like a small worm, worked its way through Mo'ata. Trevon spoke as if none of the others in this room cared about Blue when *he* was the interloper. He and Jason, late to the game and whose motives were unknown. Mo'ata had begun to think of their small group, the original five, as a family, though nothing formal had been spoken. The bonds, while weak, were there.

Except they weren't a family, a real prida, and Levi's silence reinforced that. The only person in the room he was sure would ultimately put Blue first was himself. He could count on Forrest, but the boy was with Blue and Phillip doing what he could to ensure her safety.

He stepped forward and grabbed Levi's arm, pulling the man to a seat beside Trevon. "My debt to you is paid. You now have a choice. You will speak and tell us what you know, or you will leave and return to your people. They can send someone else to liaise." It was harsh, but he did not care.

Levi's eyes slid closed, and he nodded. He stayed silent for one moment more, then nodded again. He rolled his shoulders back, sitting up straight, and fixed his golden gaze on Mo'ata. "It is not a short explanation. Nor is it straightforward. I need you to know that I never expected them to make this demand. Because of Phillip's fixation, we knew she would need to accompany him there, but afterward... no, it still is no excuse."

Mo'ata did not reply, but he moved away, finding a

spot against the wall near Jason, and waited. The Prizzoli was going to talk, and for now he would listen.

"And you were mad at *me* for withholding information," Jason mumbled.

Mo'ata clenched his arms to his sides, curbing his impulse to hit the other man. *It will not help Blue; it will not help Blue.*

Felix, it seemed, had no such compunction. As he settled into place on the other side of Jason, his hand shot out, catching the Ministry agent's shoulder. "Shut up and listen."

Levi, who had remained stiff in his seat through all of this, studied each man in turn. Finally, he took a breath and started. "As I said, it is long and it is convoluted. I… I will start with a story of my people."

Blue would probably love to hear this story.

"It is a legend of my people. The Prizzoli have always been nomadic. We make our homes on the plains of Padilra. To the north of us is a mountain range, and in the middle is a peak that towers over the rest. For ages it was a place forbidden by the elders. One young man decided he would flaunt their will, and he entered the mountains and explored that peak. When he returned, he brought with him a large violet crystal. He took it to the Council of Elders, claiming it had healed him when he became injured and fell into a cave.

"The elders were wary but intrigued. The young man demonstrated the power of the crystal, curing a boy who had become ill and was almost dead. He healed all who wished it, but soon the crystal would not work, failing again and again. The last time he sought to heal someone, an elder, the crystal reversed its powers, and instead of healing, it absorbed the life of the elder, or what was left of it.

"Thus they discovered the secret of the crystal. It can only give what it has, and when it runs out, it must take."

Levi's words took on a cadence, one used by storytellers and showmen, and Mo'ata could imagine this place he described. But it still did not tell him what he needed to know. Biting back the impatience, he listened as Levi continued.

"The young man changed after that day. He went back into the mountains and returned with more crystals. Instead of using them to heal, though, he sought out the sick and elderly so the crystals could absorb their life, their energy, and in return, the young man used it to heal and energize those who came to him, who supported his actions."

"Like Phillip did, and my father before him," Trevon murmured.

Levi paused, nodding, and continued. "The young man's name was Shardon. He built a following until almost all the elders were either overthrown or cowed in fear that he would absorb their own lives as well.

"Soon, his followers noticed another change. He started spending more and more time alone with the stone. His eyes and voice altered, and though he still went by Shardon, he was not the same man. His decision and emotions became erratic, and he grew ever more ruthless.

"One elder refused to back down or give up and sought a way to defeat Shardon. He stole one of the crystals that had been collected. He studied it and discovered that the crystals would absorb energy naturally, small amounts from surrounding animals and trees. He also noticed that the more he held it, the more tired he felt. The crystal was gradually taking from him as well, though nothing like the horrors he'd seen Shardon commit. The more time he spent with the crystal, the more... aware of it he became, and then he understood. The properties of the crystals were influenced by what surrounded them. Shardon's crystal had become a thing twisted and greedy. The one the elder held was at peace, almost benign, but it still took. In order to use it, to reverse the flow of energy, you had to be attuned to the crystal.

"After a while, the Elder noticed something else. The stone was beginning to answer him, his thoughts. He would wonder something, and the stone would send him a reply. The answers weren't in words, but ideas. This crystal was now *alive*."

Mo'ata shifted, growing impatient. They knew all of this already. Oh, not the backstory, but they knew the crystals were alive. The others showed signs of restlessness as well: Trevon's fingers drummed on the table, Felix fingered the knife at his belt, and Jason tapped his foot quietly.

Levi ignored it all. It was as if once the man had made his decision to share what he knew, he was going to share it *all*. "This crystal was gentle, its thoughts of peace and rest. It only ever took as much as it needed at the moment and was always willing to share what it had. The elder couldn't conceive how a being with such generosity would willingly take the lives of others.

"All this time, Shardon grew ever more powerful.

Soon, he didn't need to be holding the crystal to take life; he could do it at will. He had bonded with the original crystal, just as the elder had bonded with his, but in a completely different way."

"The crystals took in the properties of those who used them," Trevon said.

"Yes, but not just that. They exaggerated the traits of what they were used for. Shardon started out wanting to help his fellow Prizzoli, but ended up killing thousands. How? He was *ambitious*. The crystal picked up on that and soon had his ambition twined with greed and a ruthlessness that drowned out the young man's desire to help his fellows."

"Ambition, stripped of compassion, a monster does make." Trevon's words were mocking, and a wry smile twisted his lips.

Felix let out a small grunt but otherwise didn't comment.

"Tell us the rest. How the hell does Blue even factor into this?" Mo'ata asked, getting things back to what mattered.

Levi raised a brow as if to say "when you are done interrupting" and continued his story. "The elder confronted Shardon and insisted that the man give up the crystal. The elder had brought his own—kinder—crystal, and for a moment, the young man's mind cleared. He handed his over and turned himself into what was left of the elder council. However, as soon as the influence of the benign crystal wore off, the young man reverted to what he had been. But now he was *more*. He had… absorbed the crystal, or it had absorbed him. The being, the consciousness that had formed from all that energy, was now in him. And he was able to kill or give life with just a thought."

"Phillip is not there yet," Jason said.

"No, Phillip is not quite there yet, and that is the only reason we are even alive at all." Levi drew in a breath and leaned forward, bracing his elbows on his knees. "Shardon escaped and massacred the elders and over half the Prizzoli. In his own words, he'd become a god, for what else would you call something that has the power to grant or take life?"

"Not a god," murmured Mo'ata. "He couldn't create, could he?"

A corner of Levi's mouth ticked up. "Good point. No, he could not create. And he seldom gave, only took. These were very dark times for my people. And because he could absorb and use for himself the powers of the crystal..."

"He never aged."

"He did not."

"How—" Mo'ata swallowed. "How was he stopped?"

Levi looked away. "And here we come to why the elders want Blue. It was a woman who stopped him. Shardon had grown lonely." Levi let out a huffing laugh devoid of humor. Vivi growled, but it seemed to be more of a reaction to the emotion of the room than to Levi. Felix reached up and patted her, and she settled a little.

"Her name was Brika. She'd grown up in a tribe farther removed and to the south, where they had not been quite as devastated by the rule of this demi-god of destruction. She was sent in tribute one year, and instead of killing her, Shardon kept her alive and kept her for himself. He married her and raised her to the status of queen. According to legend, she convinced him to give her a crystal so they would be together forever."

"Why wouldn't he just heal her over and over?" Jason asked.

Good question.

"I do not know. These are the stories we're brought up with. They may not even be true." Levi shrugged. "Shardon gave her a crystal, but instead of using it to kill others, she sent herself—her... consciousness—into it somehow. It became known as Brika's Sacrifice."

If the Prizzoli plan to sacrifice Blue, then there will *be a war.* Mo'ata sucked in a breath and let it out slowly, forcing his heart to slow. *Not yet, not yet.*

"In his despair, Shardon neglected security. A group of resistors was able to obtain his crystal and destroy it. This, however, was even worse. The entity fully transferred into Shardon. It had gained enough strength and awareness that when its own home was destroyed, it found a new one."

Levi stopped, his gaze unfocused. A grimace pulled the edges of his mouth down, and he clasped his hands, squeezing until the knuckles turned white.

He had made his decision, but it was obviously not easy for him. "How was Shardon stopped?" Mo'ata asked, his voice low, almost gentle.

"It all came back to Brika. The stone that was now her. She had turned herself into a prison. Shardon was never defeated, not really. In a moment of weakness, or maybe clarity, he allowed himself to be trapped in Brika's crystal, maybe to be with her?" Levi shrugged. "As I said, these are the stories we're taught. Who knows exactly what happened?"

"Huh," Jason said. "So, there's a crystal out there with two… consciousnesses in it?"

Levi's eyes slid closed. "Yes. We, the Prizzoli, guard Brika's Sacrifice, still. It—" He swallowed. "It is what should cleanse Phillip."

"Should?" Mo'ata asked. He needed more information than this if he was to figure out how to save Blue.

Levi nodded. "If we can get Phillip to Brika's Sacrifice, I hope that its influence will calm him, mitigate what the crystal has turned him into. It has been done before. The additional crystals, the ones Shardon had brought in from the mountains, had been tainted as well. After they were housed with Brika's crystal for many years, they gradually resumed their more neutral attributes, and none were near taking on personalities of their own. If Phillip's crystal gets loose among my people before the taint can be drawn out, it could spell disaster. It will contaminate the others, and I do not know if Brika's crystal is strong enough to contain *that*."

Mo'ata's anger surged, and no amount of breathing slowed it. He pushed away from the wall. "They want to use Blue to contain Phillip. They want to *sacrifice* her."

Garfield jumped off the bed and stalked across the room, yowling. When he passed Levi, he swiped at him, much as Vivi had done, but didn't connect.

Levi's head bowed. "I don't know what they are planning to do. Maybe they simply need her there as insurance until Brika's crystal can do its work."

"Which could take years, you said." Mo'ata took a step toward him, fists clenched.

"I didn't think they would do this. I really didn't."

"But you knew it was a possibility. Each time you said it was a good idea to use Blue as bait, encouraged it, and each time we allowed it, you *knew* this was a possibility." Mo'ata took another step, stalking toward the man.

Levi surged to his feet. "It was always a cursed possibility, whether Blue was involved in the hunt or not!"

They stood facing each other, close enough that if Mo'ata decided to attack, the Prizzoli was in easy reach. None of the others moved to intervene. The only thing that held Mo'ata back was the knowledge that hitting Levi wouldn't do one thing to help Blue. "Explain."

"The kidnapping," Trevon said with a groan, his head falling back.

Levi didn't take his gaze from Mo'ata as he answered. "Yes, the kidnapping. It was in all of our reports, even *yours*, Mo'ata. If Phillip was so focused on her even then, so obsessed as to insist she be brought to him when he had just started using the crystal, then this course of events was already set. The variable was whether or not the Elders would insist on her presence. And they did. Even if she'd still been on her own world, it would have been a condition."

"So we're fucked," Trevon said.

"No." The denial burst from Mo'ata. "No, we are not 'fucked,' as you say. She is my shopa, whether there has been a formal proposal or not. I will go with her, and I will protect her. I will figure out a way to get her out of this."

Levi's eyes widened as Mo'ata spoke. Then he held out

a hand. "I have made my decision." Something close to sorrow echoed in his voice. "Please allow me to assist. It is… the least I can do."

Mo'ata eyed his hand but did not take it. Finally, he nodded.

"I think you are forgetting something," Zeynar said from his seat.

"And what is that, *ikpul*?" Felix asked from where he still leaned against the wall.

"You're forgetting the little star herself. She's the ultimate wild card." Zeynar leaned back in his seat, smug grin back in place.

That was all it took to push Mo'ata over the edge. This bastard dared to use an endearment and mock her at the same time? "You don't have the right to call her that." Then he lunged, catching the other man off guard and sending them both to the floor. He got in two good hits before the combined strength of Felix and Jason pulled him off the other man.

Zeynar remained on the floor, breathing hard, and wiped blood from his lip. He met Mo'ata's gaze. "I'm in this, clansman, and you are going to need me. Best get used to it."

Mo'ata shrugged off the hands still holding him and crossed to Zeynar. Hesitating for only a moment, he held out a hand to the other man and helped him to his feet. When he was standing, Mo'ata pulled him close and whispered, "I don't trust you. If you do anything that causes her harm, I will figure out a way to end you."

"Gloves off, huh?"

Mo'ata glared. He didn't know what the phrase meant,

but he wanted Zeynar to get the message. Finally, the other man nodded, and Mo'ata released him.

"We will comply, for now. But I will not be leaving her there. When we leave, she comes with us." Mo'ata wanted to make that very clear to everyone, no matter what the council proclaimed. Now for the part he was dreading the most. "We need to tell them."

Forrest and Blue had been kept in the dark about all the political maneuverings. Mostly because they had their hands full keeping Phillip calm, but also because, in this, there really was nothing they could do to help and telling them would only increase the stress they were under. It was time, though, to fill them in.

"I recommend keeping it to the basics for now. If Phillip thought we were trying to keep her from him…" Levi said, trailing off at the end. He stood and moved to his bed. Sitting heavily, he rested against the wall, propping himself up. His recovery from the attack was progressing, but he still tired easily and had to rest frequently. Despite his anger, Mo'ata was concerned. *Damned family. Yes, the Prizzoli was family.* Garfield crawled up next to Levi and leaned against his leg.

"Fuck." Mo'ata borrowed the word. He swallowed. "Fine. We'll keep it simple for now, but we'll need to figure out a way to tell her the whole of it. She can't be kept in the dark. Neither of them can."

"Agreed," Felix said. "We'll figure it out." There was steel in the man's voice.

Mo'ata picked up his comm and sent a message to Forrest.

BLUE

Blue sighed as she sat next to Phillip in the inn's dining hall. It was dangerous for him to be down here, but they both needed to get away from the confines of the room above. Forrest, the only one besides her who didn't set off Phillip's darker side, took a place across from them. A server hurried over with three steaming bowls of stew, and Blue gave her a smile. They'd learned what she liked.

Four days. It had been four days since they'd captured Phillip and confined the crystal. As long as he stayed calm and Blue was near, they had no trouble. There had been one incident when Mo'ata had kissed her goodnight and Phillip had seen and the something that was the crystal had broken through. Mo'ata's quick retreat and soft words from Blue had averted the potential disaster, but it had been too damn close.

He took a bite of the stew and swallowed, light glinting off the collar he wore. Her stomach twisted, and she put down the spoonful of stew she'd raised to her mouth.

Trevon diving at Phi. Forrest crumpled on the ground. The images haunted her. She thought if she could just... reassure herself they were truly okay, she could get past it. But she couldn't even hold Forrest's hand with Phi around. Forget about Trev. Not that she wanted to hold his hand, but she'd only seen him in passing since he'd regained consciousness. She'd not even been able to thank him.

"Everything okay?" Forrest, still a little pale, kept his gaze on the food in front of him.

She peeked at Phillip, only to see him staring at Forrest, sorrow and a dark satisfaction lingering in his expression. It was an eerie combination. He twisted his head to stare at her next, revealing his bandage-covered ear. He smiled, and she shivered.

A commotion at the door drew her attention. Bodies cleared out of the way, and her eyes met those of Brendan Faust. A petite woman, a touch of gray flowing in her dark hair, stood beside him.

Well, crap on a stick.

He approached with measured strides, and she stood. The woman followed him, moving gracefully, everything from her pale skin to her tailored dress shouting her wealth.

Brendan nodded in greeting, sandy blond hair just going to gray falling across his forehead. "Cousin." He held out a leather glove–covered hand to her. When she hesitated, he pulled it back. "I thought I would extend a common Earth courtesy to you." His voice was stiff as his gaze drifted past her and to Phillip. She resisted the urge to look behind her.

"I apologize. I had not expected to see you here." She licked her lips, and her gaze darted to the woman. "Would you like to join us?" She could have kicked herself. Why would he want to sit with his daughter's killer? *Did he know?*

He focused on her, then flicked his eyes back to Phillip. His upper lip curled in a sneer. *He knew.*

"No, thank you." He cast a look on Forrest, his

expression returning to blank. "I understand you preferred to use the Zeynars as a... go-between for the other matter, but this is strictly family business."

It wasn't that she *preferred* to use them. Trevon had offered, and she hadn't had the energy to protest. She held back the explanation. Now was probably not the time. "All right," she said.

He flicked another look at Forrest, then Phillip.

"Forrest is family, and Phillip... needs me here," she said.

He inclined his head, formal. How could her father have been related to this man? "As you will. I have come to formally and officially request that you relinquish any claim to Sirisa Shipping."

Shock held her immobile. How was she supposed to react to that? To even think about something like this while still dealing with Phillip?

The woman, silent up to this point, raised a hand and, with a motion faster than Blue could easily follow, slapped Brendan Faust, the mobster, on the arm. "You are an imbecile." The woman turned to Blue. "I am Dorani and married to this very stupid man." She held out a hand, just as her husband had, and Blue took it.

Dorani's skin was cool and smooth, her grip firm. When Blue pulled back, Dorani held on to her. "You look very much like my Gabriella," she said. Her voice remained smooth. Other than the brief irritation of a moment ago, this woman showed nothing of who she was, no clue to what she was feeling.

And then she smiled. It was filled with all the warmth Brendan lacked. "What Brendan means to say is that we wish to help provide for you while you are getting established here. I understand that when this… situation is dealt with, you will follow in your father's footsteps and attend the Ministry's Academy?"

Blue gave them a slow nod.

Dorani glanced at the people surrounding them, then jerked her shoulder up in a small shrug. "We simply ask for the other to avoid confusion about who is making decisions. With you being new here and not understanding all the… ramifications of decisions that must be made."

In other words, they don't want me mucking about in their business. Which was fine. Blue still had extremely mixed feelings about the "mob" thing.

"On a more personal note," Dorani continued, "I would very much enjoy it if you would st—"

"Dori," Brendan said in a warning tone.

Her eyes pinched at the corners, and her lips thinned slightly. It was subtle; Blue almost didn't catch the change before Dorani once again wore the perfect mask. "I would very much enjoy it if you stayed with us for a time." Her lips softened, and the warmth of her earlier smile peeked through. "When your business is done, of course." She squeezed Blue's hand and let go, stepping back.

Blue sensed movement behind her, and the couple's gazes locked on something just over her shoulder. Phillip.

"I will send over the exact terms. I am confident that you can find someone to help you sort through it." Brendan turned on his heel and strode out, Dorani once more following behind, leaving silence and averted gazes behind them.

Blue fell back into her seat. What did someone do with that? Did you laugh? Cry? Shrug it all off? What?

A pale hand appeared next to hers. It was too pale, and trembled. The nails were ragged but clean. Phillip placed his fingers over hers and squeezed. "I can take care of him for you if you want."

She jerked her gaze to his. No purple, just chocolate brown. She had to remember that even without the crystal, Phillip had... a competitive side. "No. I'm not sure what I want to do. I don't think I'd really want part of a shady shipping empire." The mention of an allowance had given her pause. What were she and Forrest going to do for money? "But thank you, Phillip, for the offer." She slid her hand out from under his and forced herself to take a bite of the stew.

Whatever else it did, Phillip's presence forced her to cultivate a calm facade, fake as it may be. The other two resumed their meals.

"Any news on our trip?" That was what they were calling it. Phillip still needed to get to Padilra. This wouldn't be over until the connection had truly been severed.

Forrest shrugged. "Still negotiating the arrangements." So the others were still playing politics. Jason, for once, had not gone running to his superiors. The last she had heard, that hadn't stopped them from demanding Phillip be turned over to them for sentencing. The Padilrian government had also demanded he be released to them, while the Prizzoli were listing demands of their own. She didn't know the whole of it yet—negotiations were still ongoing—but the sooner this was done, the better. Blue was surprised the Fausts hadn't also demanded a piece of him. Probably Trevon's doing.

Forrest's comm beeped. He glanced at it. Felix had programmed them with some basic messages in English. You'd think with an advanced society like this there would be automatic translators, but it wasn't a priority for a closed-world language. And if you were part of the Alliance, you spoke Common to one degree or another and it just wasn't necessary.

A bit arrogant and insular, if you asked her.

She looked at Forrest questioningly.

"Mo'ata needs to see us."

Blue took a breath and grabbed Phillip's hand. She dredged up some exasperation, not that hard to do, and put it all into her next words. "Come on. Let's go see what he wants."

"Yeah, he's annoying." Phillip followed after her, sounding like a petulant nine-year-old. Blue rolled her eyes, knowing he couldn't see her.

They went to Levi's room and crowded in with everyone else. And she meant everyone. They looked exhausted. Levi though, he looked… defeated. He sat on the edge of his bed, head in his hands, shoulders rounded. Garfield sat on the floor next to his leg, leaning into it. Vivi was perched on Felix's shoulder, her usual spot if she wasn't with Forrest. No one would meet Blue's gaze.

"What's the news?" Forrest's hand bumped against her thigh, and she grabbed it, not caring if Phillip noticed.

Mo'ata stepped forward. "The Prizzoli have agreed to… host Phillip." He swallowed. "They have a few demands. One, the crystal must be returned to them."

Blue nodded. They'd expected that.

"Two, Phillip must remain with them for the duration of his life."

That one was new, but it was probably smart. If anyone would be able to deal with him and handle his connection to the crystal, it was the Prizzoli. They obviously didn't want him out in the worlds talking about it either. Considering all he'd done, the people he'd killed, he was getting off lightly. It was basically a life sentence instead of the death penalty.

"Three—" Mo'ata swallowed. "Three is something they will not budge on. There was talk of Padilra leaving the Alliance if it was not complied with. Blue, I'm sorry, we've been trying to work with them on this, but—" His eyes fell closed.

When he didn't continue, she sought out each person in the room. The only one who would meet her gaze was Trevon. His lower lip was slightly swollen. He gave her a tight smile, though he didn't speak.

Forrest inched closer to her, and Phillip's hand tightened around hers to the point of pain. "What's the third?" she asked.

"You have to go, too." Mo'ata's voice was dull.

How is that bad? The plan had always been for her to make sure Phillip got to the Prizzoli.

"You have to *stay*," Jason spat out.

"We could always go back to the option where we start a war," Trevon said, his tone musing though his expression was hard.

Felix shrugged one shoulder, the movement almost too deliberate. "I ask again. They say no. *Again.*"

Trevon snorted. "The Order is a bunch of pansies."

At this banter Levi, usually so calm, jumped up and punched Trevon, sending the other man into the wall. Mo'ata stepped between the two. Trevon straightened, rubbing his jaw and rotating his shoulder, but he didn't retaliate.

There were undercurrents here she didn't understand.

Phillip, still beside her, clutched her hand tighter and yanked her closer to him. "Why is this a bad thing? Blue and I were meant to be together. It sounds to me as if the Elders realize this." That deep note had crept into his voice, and everyone in the room froze.

Undercurrents she couldn't ask about at the moment. Time for her to step in. *I feel like a damn babysitter*. Except this baby would go on a murderous rampage instead of hitting the floor. "You're right, Phi. Nothing at all wrong with this. I look forward to it. Forrest can come too, do some exploring. I hear there are really nice mountains in the area that he'd like." She held still as Phillip put an arm around her, and her stomach twisted. For a moment she feared the stew would come back up. "He c—he could maybe do some drawings of the area." She remembered her tree drawing, still back at the Dramil camp. Levi turned to her, fists clenched, but he made no move at anyone else.

"Would you like that, Forrest? Coming with Blue and me?" The deep note was gone, replaced by smug satisfaction.

Phillip had won. And he knew it.

"Yeah, that would be good," Forrest said.

She risked a glance at him. His chin was set, his gaze direct. He wasn't leaving her.

"Make the arrangements," she said to Mo'ata.

He looked to her, then Forrest, and nodded. He took one step toward her. "Of course, shopa."

She smiled. He wasn't leaving her either.

"We will ensure you have the best protection for the journey." Trevon left off her nickname, but she heard it anyway. *Little star.*

Felix nodded. "I on job. You safe."

Levi gave her a short bow and finally met her gaze. The gold in his eyes glowed, and his jaw firmed. She'd always been able to read him, but now she couldn't.

Then his expression softened, just as it had the first time she'd seen him, in an alley off of the shopping district of Tremmir. His accent was thick, but the English was perfect. "I will protect you."

Phillip's arm tightened around her, and her fingers threaded with Forrest's. *Just one more adventure, Blue, just one more adventure.*

Glossary

WORLDS

Cularna – An open world of the Alliance. Also has space travel capabilities, traveling to Martika separately from portal travel. It is the homeworld of the Order of Terril and is where their headquarters are maintained, though this is known only to a few. Most think the Order is stationed on Karran, and it is to a certain extent—at the least the overt agents are. Cularna has a philosophical and ethical overlap with the peoples of Martika. Cularna is known as a world of mercenaries, and they have a very strict code of honor. Like any society, they have different classes of citizens: farmers, artists, lawyers, and healers. All are afforded their own respect and honor for the roles they play in the society and what they contribute. Though mercenaries and soldiers are the world's main "export," all are respected.

Earth – Currently considered a closed world—limited travel, restricted to agencies only for the purpose of monitoring.

Falass – A closed world. Known for its exotic plants and scents.

Karran – Main world, where all portals lead to and from. Capitol: Tremmir. Governed by a Council of representatives from each region: Tremmir, Filiri, Seradnes, Semina, and the Clan Territories. The head of the Council is appointed on a ten-year rotation and is selected from each region in turn. Karran serves as the hub of trade for the Alliance; the Ministry holds a tight monopoly on trade between the worlds, and though not technically part of the government, has much influence.

Martika – An open world governed by the Families, many of whom dabble in smuggling. The Families are structured like large clans, with smaller clans pledging allegiance to larger ones. Although the Families' version of morality isn't what most people would consider "moral," they still have a strong sense of honor. Generally, the Families are left to their own devices unless their activities spill into other worlds. Additionally, Martika has space travel, and through this is able to trade directly with Cularna, another open world of the Alliance. Because of this, there is a cultural and philosophical overlap that doesn't exist with other worlds.

Padilra – An open world, but only in the last 100 years or so. Padilra is generally governed by an elected president, who serves a 7-year term, and a council, whose terms are for life. One of their main populations are the Prizzoli [see below for further information.]

Sturi – A closed world.

Turamm – Another open world; member of the Alliance. Little is known of them, as they keep mostly to themselves. There are rumors a small population possess mental abilities, such as telepathy. Their main exports are metals and alloys used in some of the higher technologies.

CULTURES

Clans of Karran – Live in western Karran. They have a matriarchal and polyandrous society and seek to minimize technological use in day-to-day life, only allowing advanced healing and bathing facilities, recognizing these as important for the health of their society. Much of their culture still revolves around training for and practicing the art of war, though most clans now live in peace in their own territories under the central government of Karran. Most clansmen stay within their own clan, though some marry into another, and rarely does a clansman leave. When one does, they are usually accepted readily into any of the enforcement branches for their weapons and protection skills.

Prizzoli – Ethnic and cultural group on Padilra. They are governed by a council of Elders and are strongly religious. Though they will defer to the government of Padilra, they consider themselves separate. Generally nomadic, they control a large portion of the land on Padilra. They are the guardians of the Crystals of Shardon. The Council of Elders consists of those who have achieved a high level of skill in the use of the crystals and have proven a resistance to the corrupting influence of the power. The woman are considered the "saviors" of the Prizzoli, and the men the protectors. However, unlike the clans of Karran, the women are not in positions of power or authority.

Mercenary Guild – A highly respected group on Cularna. Many of their members are also part of the Order of Terril. They have control of much of the military technology of Cularna, giving them a distinct advantage over other worlds. Though they are separate, they are considered to be the military branch of their government on a permanent retainer.

TERMS

The Academy – A sister organization to the Ministry, where those with potential in portals, as well as those who desire to become agents of the Ministry, are trained and educated. Different from the university.

The Alliance of Cormant – An alliance of worlds connected by portals, made up of all those who have been opened to trade. Also includes some worlds not connected by portals but with close ties via space travel to those that do.

Bota – the vote conducted by a prida to accept new members.

Chuka – An insult in clan dialect. Means someone who is not to be trusted, with a side meaning of asshole.

Closed World – Used to designate a world that has been discovered or has naturally occurring portals, but that has not yet been brought into the Alliance. These are usually worlds that are too primitive to understand the ramifications or who have been shown to be too warlike to play nice with others. Earth is considered both. The tipping point for inclusion in the Alliance is usually when a cohesive world government has evolved.

Corin – In Alliance currency, equivalent to about $100 Earth U.S. dollars.

Crystals of Shardon – A rare, naturally occurring crystal on Padilra that, when properly prepared, are able to store life-healing energies. Used exclusively in religious ceremonies or by those who are members of the Prizzoli, they are really a last resort because, in order to charge the crystal, someone must give up a portion of their life force. Traditionally, the life force is given by the elders once they have decided to leave this life. The years remaining to them are then stored in the crystals, where it remains until used. Similar to the Portals on Karran, the ability to manipulate the crystals requires an affinity for their energy that not all Prizzoli have.

Culan's Bones – an exclamation used on Cularna. Ties in with legends up Culan, the original founder of the Mercenary Guild.

Draga – Title for the war chief of a clan of Karran.

Druada – Means "blue" in the clan dialect.

Fogan silk – A silk only available from Falass. Highly sought after from collectors though it is from a closed world and therefore illegal.

Foka – an alcoholic drink on Karran, similar to beer.

Ikpul – Cularnian slang for bastard. Basically, asshole.

Life-Debt – Used among the clansmen of Karran. If a clansman owes a life-debt to another, this means that he must take on the burdens of the one to whom his debt is owed until such time as the debt is discharged. The one owed determines when this is. It is not something given or stated lightly. Usually, a life-debt only occurs when the Heart of the prida is protected or defended by someone not of her prida, as it is a point of shame when the priden fail at her protection, no matter the circumstances.

Mamanna – The title for the matriarch of a clan of Karran.

The Ministry – An organization appointed by the Karran government to train those who operate the portals, as well as monitor and regulate their use. Those who have a natural aptitude can be trained to recognize and manipulate the energies needed. The Ministry has their own agency to handle issues with portal abuse.

The Order of Terril – An enforcement agency for the Alliance. It is an elite organization of enforcers. Each world and territory has their own police, those who handle the day to day monitoring of the laws. The Order of Terril is an interplanetary enforcement agency, only called in when the crimes have spread beyond one planet. In addition to their stated purpose, there is a branch made up of sleeper agents, those placed in various positions throughout the worlds and activated when necessary. The stated purpose of this branch is to monitor and maintain the freedom of individuals on the alliance worlds, no matter what. This is actually the true purpose of the order, and the more apparent enforcement agents are merely a cover.

Piquet – a large feline, similar to a cross between and tiger and a lion, striped but with a small mane. They tend to run in packs and have a very set social structure. Extremely territorial. Usually will leave you alone unless they feel you have trespassed in one of their breeding grounds.

Portals – A naturally occurring phenomenon on Karran where "thin spaces" create a kind of shortcut between areas, similar to wormholes. These portals form when the specific energy signature of an area on Karran matches that of an area on another world, or even another area of Karran. Most occur naturally around Karran, and form to the same or similar areas each time. Some people on Karran are born with an ability to manipulate these thin spaces, attuning the energies to create – and open and close – portals at will. Occasionally, especially if a person with untrained potential is in the vicinity, a natural portal will be activated.

Prida – Among the clansmen of Karran, the term is used to denote the family unit, one woman and multiple men. The prida is made up of the Heart and her priden. All members are selected by the Heart and the First Priden, and all those in the prida must agree when a new member is proposed and selected.

Quorin – A type of mount similar to a horse with horns. They choose their own riders and sometimes will form a deeper bond with them.

Ransyi – a term used by the clans to mean the balance of trust and equality for each member of a prida. It emphasizes the idea that each person has their duties and responsibilities equal to the others, and that each person's thoughts, wishes, and wants are sought to be accommodated.

Shopa – Means "heart" in the clan language. The heart is the center of the pride and is also used as a term of endearment from a priden to his Heart.

Tiri – Small pack-animals, like a cross between a cow and a deer.

Toka – short blade used by the clans of Karran.

Trial period – A term specific to Cularna. Very similar to a hand-fasting, this is the practice of specifying a period of time for a couple to live as a married unit before making the union official. Could also be thought of as an engagement, but with the legal benefits of an official union for the designated time. If at the end of this trial the couple decides they will not suit, the union is severed with no legal repercussions.

Trilki Root – The root of a plant known to grow in the Filiri region of Karran. When pressed and processed the correct way, it produces a non-addictive drug that causes sleep. Usually used in low doses to assist those with chronic insomnia; in higher concentrations, it can keep someone under for hours, unable to be woken. If the dose is strong enough, it can cause a coma.

Tripi – The equivalent of a penny in the clans' monetary system.

Turammin – metal from Turamm used for shielding

About the Author

Cecilia Randell was born in Austin, Texas and grew up in a home with her very own Cheerful Bulldozer. After some brief adventures in various places such as California and Florida, she returned to her hometown and took up a career in drafting.

A lifetime lover of words and stories, the transition to writing was two-fold: a comment from a relative and a short line from another author, saying to write what you want to read.

And thus the new adventure was born.

Now she can be found most days curled up in a comfy chair and creating new tales to share with others.

Website:
https://ceciliarandell.com

Sign up for the Newsletter:
http://eepurl.com/divLmj

Give her a visit on Facebook:
Author Page

Or join her group here:
Facebook Group

91788179R00195

Made in the USA
Columbia, SC
22 March 2018